Dark Power Unleashed

THE CHILDREN OF THE GODS
BOOK FIFTY-ONE

I. T. LUCAS

Dark Power Unleashed is a work of fiction! Names, characters, places and incidents are products of the author's imagination or are used fictitiously and are not to be construed as real. Any similarity to actual persons, organizations and/or events is purely coincidental.

Copyright © 2021 by I. T. Lucas

All rights reserved.

No part of this book may be reproduced in any form or by any electronic or mechanical means, including information storage and retrieval systems, without written permission from the author, except for the use of brief quotations in a book review.

Published by Evening Star Press

Contents

1. Kian — 1
2. Cassandra — 7
3. Margaret — 13
4. Syssi — 19
5. Kian — 24
6. Annani — 29
7. Kian — 35
8. Onegus — 39
9. Bowen — 43
10. Margaret — 48
11. Cassandra — 53
12. Margaret — 59
13. Eleanor — 64
14. Emmett — 69
15. Eleanor — 73
16. Emmett — 79
17. Eleanor — 85
18. Onegus — 90
19. Cassandra — 94
20. Onegus — 101
21. Margaret — 106
22. Bowen — 113
23. Margaret — 118
24. Bowen — 122
25. Margaret — 126
26. Cassandra — 130
27. Kian — 135
28. Margaret — 142
29. Onegus — 147

30. Margaret	152
31. Cassandra	157
32. Onegus	162
33. Bowen	168
34. Margaret	173
35. Bowen	178
36. Eleanor	183
37. Margaret	188
38. Annani	195
39. Kian	200
40. Syssi	206
41. Margaret	210
42. Onegus	216
43. Kian	220
44. Cassandra	226
45. Onegus	234
46. Eleanor	239
47. Cassandra	244
48. Kian	252
49. Cassandra	256
50. Margaret	261
51. Cassandra	266
52. Margaret	272
53. Onegus	277
54. Emmett	282
55. Eleanor	287
56. Emmett	293
57. Cassandra	298
58. Eleanor	302
59. Cassandra	306
60. Onegus	313
61. Cassandra	318
62. Onegus	323
63. Cassandra	327

64. Onegus	332
65. Cassandra	338
66. Onegus	344
67. Cassandra	349
68. Onegus	354
69. Cassandra	360
70. Onegus	366
71. Cassandra	370
72. Onegus	374
73. Cassandra	379
74. Onegus	384
75. Cassandra	390
76. Onegus	394
77. Cassandra	398
Excerpt: Dark Power Convergence	403
The Children of the Gods	429
The Perfect Match Series	441
Note	447
FOR EXCLUSIVE PEEKS	449

Kian

Six o'clock in the morning was too early for a smoke, but since Kian hadn't actually slept, it could be argued that it wasn't really morning for him. Syssi was in the shower, and while he waited for her to get ready for breakfast, he could sneak outside for a few minutes and get his fix.

As usual, too much was going on all at once, and his mind was spinning in circles trying to make sense of it.

What were the damn Fates up to this time?

"Good morning, master." Okidu bowed. "Would you like a fresh cup of coffee? It has just finished brewing."

"Yes, please."

A steamy mug of coffee in hand, Kian opened the living room sliding doors and walked out into the backyard. Sitting down on his favorite lounger, he put the mug on the side table and picked up his box of cigarillos.

Lighting up, he took a grateful puff and leaned back.

The Fates had played another of their games, bringing yet another Dormant into the clan's fold, and not just any Dormant, but Wendy's long-lost mother.

The text message from Bowen had arrived a couple of hours ago.

The Guardian probably hadn't expected Kian to read it right away, so he hadn't elaborated beyond the basic facts. But Kian could piece it together from what he already knew.

The irony wasn't lost on him.

Margaret had been under their noses for nearly two weeks, but Bowen had figured it out on the same day Vlad and Richard had traveled out of town to have a talk with Wendy's asshole of a father and find out what he'd done with the mother.

If Bowen had figured it out a day earlier, he would have saved them the trouble.

Had Wendy's bastard of a father been left to sully the earth with his presence for another day?

If Vlad had managed not to kill him, the kid had much better self-control than Kian. If he were in Vlad's shoes, Kian would have torn the jerk's throat out, and no one would have been able to stop him. It wouldn't even have mattered if Wendy's father had killed her mother or not. He deserved to die for the abuse he'd inflicted on his family. But Vlad was a gentle soul, and he'd made a promise to Wendy not to kill her father, so maybe the scum was still alive.

In any case, Kian wasn't going to ask or even hint that he knew about Richard and Vlad's trip.

Plausible deniability and all that.

Then there was Onegus and his unconventional request to bring a date to Sari and David's wedding. The chief had met the lady at the annual charity ball, and it seemed like he was seriously smitten, which was uncharacteristic of him. Onegus was a player who never hooked up with the same woman more than twice, which was how it was supposed to be for immortals engaging with humans.

As Kian heard the sliding door open, he turned and smiled at his wife. "That was quick." He extinguished his cigarillo.

"Isn't it too early for a smoke?" She lowered herself onto his lap with effort, her pregnant belly nestling against his. "What's troubling you?"

"Nothing major. Just many little things." He wrapped his arms around her to keep her warm. "Isn't it too cold for you out here?"

Syssi leaned her head on his shoulder. "Not when I'm lying on top of you. You are like a furnace." She lifted her eyes to him. "Are you nervous about Sari and David's arrival?"

Their flight was scheduled to land at LAX at twelve-thirty in the afternoon, and instead of them taking a taxi to the newly renovated building across from the keep, Syssi had insisted on picking them up at the airport.

"I'm nervous about most of the clan being here for their wedding. It's a logistical nightmare to keep everyone's arrival unnoticed. But that's just one in a long list of things keeping me awake at night."

"What else? The Kra-ell?"

"Yeah. That too. I want to get a move on it, but I have to wait until after the festivities. On top of that, Onegus has invited a human date to the wedding, and I was so shocked by the request that I said okay before thinking it through."

Smiling, Syssi cupped his cheek. "It was nice of you to allow it, and it's not a big deal. Gerard's human crew is serving at the wedding, and their minds will need to get wiped at the end of the night. One more human will not make a difference."

"True. But that's another annoyance. There will be too many humans working in the bowels of the keep to prepare and service this wedding, and later, having their memories wiped. Then there are the Chinese crews building our village, who will have to be wiped as well."

"You had every one of them checked for responsiveness to thralling, so it's not like some might be immune. You're fretting for no good reason." She lifted her head and kissed his cheek. "Relax, enjoy. These are happy times for us and for the clan."

Kian shook his head. "I feel like I've become complacent, and I'm taking too many risks." He ran his hand over her back. "The Kra-ell are wise to keep their communities small. They can pick up and go with ease."

"Perhaps they are nomadic in nature." Syssi put a hand on her belly. "I like staying in one place, and despite being an introvert, I love having a big community of people to interact with when I'm in the mood for it. I think I would have gone nuts with just a couple dozen people to talk to. For some reason, that seems more intimate and more intrusive." She rubbed her belly again.

"Is Allegra kicking?" Kian put his hand over hers.

"She's sleeping. I just like touching her. It's so cool that I can feel the contours of her little body through my belly." Syssi shifted, finding a more comfortable position. "Onegus's date must be special if he invited her to the wedding."

"He claims that he can sense some sort of strange energy from her that intensifies when she gets angry or excited. He says that her mother emits similar energy, but not as strong."

"Fascinating." Syssi sat up and put her hands on the small of her back. "I'm going to ask Lisa to sniff Onegus's date out at the wedding. After all, she was right about Anastasia being a Dormant."

Kian moved Syssi's hands aside and started massaging her back. "She was, and I regret not sending her to sniff out Anastasia's friend as well."

It was a gentle way to break the news to Syssi. He didn't want her getting overly excited in her condition.

"Why? Is she a Dormant too?"

"Confirmed."

Syssi turned wide eyes to him. "Did she transition and no one told me?"

There was no way to soften the delivery of what he had to tell her, so he attempted a softer tone. "Margaret is Wendy's mother."

Syssi gasped. "Impossible. How?"

"Apparently, she escaped her abusive husband when Wendy was a baby and has been hiding in Safe Haven ever since. Bowen somehow connected the dots, mother and daughter had an emotional reunion last night, and Bowen is bringing Margaret to the village today."

Syssi tried to push out of his arms. "We have to prepare lodging for them."

He tightened his arms around her. "There is no rush. Ingrid is too busy to deal with that right now, and if we let someone else do it for her, she'll throw a tantrum. Bowen and Margaret can stay with Vlad and Wendy for a week or two. I'm sure Wendy and her mother have a lot of catching up to do."

Cassandra

Cassandra glanced up at the rearview mirror to check her makeup. She'd been in a rush this morning and it showed. There wasn't much she could do about it while driving, though, except perhaps fixing her lipstick. Reaching over the central console for her purse, she was rummaging for the tube when her phone rang.

The familiar number popping up on her car's display brought a smile to her face. "Did you forget something?"

"Are you driving?" Onegus sounded like a stern schoolteacher, displeased with her supposedly reckless behavior.

"Yes, but don't worry. I'm not holding the phone, my hands are on the wheel, and I'm looking at the road."

Given that she'd had her hand in her purse and was about to apply lipstick while driving, Cassandra had been guilty of intent but not of actual infraction. So technically, she hadn't lied.

He chuckled. "How did you know that I was worried?"

"Your tone. You sounded like a policeman or a schoolteacher about to give me a lecture."

"If it turns you on, I can get into either of those roles with ease." His tone was teasing, but his voice had dropped by half an octave, stirring interest in her lady parts.

"I bet." She shifted in her seat.

On the face of things, Onegus appeared charming and easygoing, but she could sense the steel he was hiding under all those panty-melting smiles of his. He had a dominant streak, which would normally put him on her do-not-call list, but he wasn't overbearing and seemed more concerned with her pleasure than his own, so she didn't mind.

In fact, it was a big part of the attraction.

He was the kind of guy a woman could lean on, rely on, and he certainly wasn't a man who would fold under the slightest pressure.

Besides, he could handle her and wasn't intimidated by her, which was no small feat.

"Did you tell your mother about the wedding?" he asked.

"I didn't see her this morning, so no, I didn't tell her yet."

"Don't tell her or anyone else about it. It's crucial that the event stays confidential."

"Are you worried about paparazzi?"

He sighed. "I wish that was the extent of my worries. Our family has enemies, old feuds that go generations back. They would love to find out that nearly the entire clan is gathering in one location."

What the hell was he talking about?

Mafia wars came to mind. "You are kidding, right?"

"I wish I was, and before you jump to the wrong conclusion, it's not a mafia turf war. It really goes back many generations in time."

Onegus had a very slight Scottish accent, but Cassandra wasn't aware of any active feuds between Scottish clans. Then again, she wasn't a history buff, and what she did know came from her mother's Highlander romance novels. Not the most reliable source of information.

"Should I be worried?"

"Not with me by your side. I'll keep you safe."

She chuckled. "A warrior billionaire. It sounds like the title of a bodice-ripper."

"What's a bodice-ripper? It sounds intriguing."

"It's a sexually explicit romantic story that takes place in a historical setting. Highlanders are very popular in that genre."

"Is that so?" He let his Scottish accent come out full force. "I'm up for ripping your bodice anytime and in any setting."

She laughed. "I'll keep that in mind when shopping for a dress to wear to the wedding. No bodice."

"That sounds even more intriguing and fashion forward. But then I'd have to kill all of my male family members for looking at your breasts, and that would ruin everyone's fun."

"We don't want that." She chuckled. "A dress can cover up everything without having a bodice. How formal is the event?"

"As formal as they get. But you don't have to get a new dress. You can wear the same one you wore for the gala. You looked stunning in it. I'll be the envy of all my bachelor cousins."

She couldn't help the grin splitting her face. "Just the bachelors?"

"Yes." His tone changed from teasing to gruff. "We are a very traditional and loyal bunch, and mated males don't stray, not even with their eyes. Once we commit, it's for life."

"That's commendable, but I doubt it's factual. Forty percent of marriages end in divorce."

"Not in our community."

Cassandra had no idea what the official religion of Scotland was, but she was pretty sure it wasn't Catholicism.

"Are you Catholic?"

"It has nothing to do with religion."

"A code of honor then?"

"It's just the way it is. You will have to make do with just the bachelors' admiration."

He sounded cold, and Cassandra didn't like it. She liked the smile in his voice, his light-hearted banter. Had she put her foot in it again?

Perhaps Onegus had a history with an unfaithful girlfriend, and it was a sore point for him.

"I was just teasing. I hate players and cheaters with a passion, which was why I got so mad when I thought that you didn't want to be seen with me. That's the number one sign that a guy is dating several women at the same time. They don't want to get caught, so they find excuses for not going out."

"Has it ever happened to you?" His tone had warmed up a little, but he still sounded serious.

"Yeah, there is no avoiding it. It's not like guys have it written on their foreheads or in their dating app profiles. But as soon as I noticed the signs, I booted the two-timers out so fast that they didn't know what hit them."

"Good for you."

"What about you? Did you ever have a two-timing girlfriend?"

"I've never had a girlfriend."

She rolled her eyes. "Fine, a lady friend then, a woman you've dated. I don't care what you call them."

"I've never been with the same woman more than once, so the only terms that apply are one-night stands and hookups."

Great. So, he wasn't a two-timer, just a serial player. It was almost as bad.

"Fear of commitment much?"

"I just haven't met the right woman before."

Oh, he was smooth. "And I am her?"

"You are the first one I'm willing to explore the possibility with. When I commit, it's forever, Cassandra. I need to make absolutely sure that I'm committing to the right woman. My one and only."

Margaret

Margaret stayed in bed long after waking up, afraid to go out of the room and face the others.

What if it had all been a dream? Or a drug-induced fantasy?

Except, she was clean. She hadn't touched opioids in over a week. Margaret also wasn't creative enough to dream up what she'd learned the day before. Somehow, Wendy had been turned immortal, and so had Bowen, Leon, and Anastasia, but Margaret didn't know how it had been done. Last night, she'd been too overwhelmed to ask.

Supposedly, they all had special genes that could be activated.

Anastasia had been turned with ease, so the activation process couldn't be too bad, and Wendy hadn't mentioned anything terrible either. Maybe it was as easy as getting some miracle elixir intravenously. Ana had joked about the doctor putting a miracle drug in her IV, and maybe that was what had been done to activate her dormant immortal genes.

If that was all it took, Margaret was willing to give it a try.

But did she really want to live forever?

Life was hard. Why would she want to drag it out indefinitely? Didn't the immortals get tired of living?

She wanted time to get to know her daughter, and maybe to explore a relationship with Bowen, who was actually much older than her but looked a decade younger.

Her mortal lifespan was long enough to do both.

If she became immortal, would the process reverse her aging and turn her young and beautiful again?

Could she start anew?

Margaret chuckled softly. The transition might shave ten years off her appearance, but unless Bowen thralled her to forget her ugly past, there was no getting rid of the memories she'd accumulated, and not many of them were good.

She'd learned not to feel too much, not to think about what she'd lost or about how meaningless it all was. She didn't want eternity to ponder the depressing reality of existence.

Margaret had learned to live in the moment, to keep so busy that she didn't have time to think. Idle moments were her enemy, as were the moments before falling asleep.

That was why she'd worked so hard, why she'd kept reading and researching material until her eyes burned from exhaustion and she knew that she would fall asleep as soon as she closed them. Anything less than that meant staying awake for hours and agonizing. To spend eternity like that would be hell.

When a soft knock sounded on her door, she wiped the few tears she'd shed with a corner of the duvet. "Yes?"

"Can I come in?" Ana asked.

"Sure."

Her friend walked in with a cup of coffee in hand. "Bowen is worried about you. He sent me to check on you." She sat on the bed and handed Margaret the cup. "How are you feeling this morning?"

"Strange. Did last night really happen, or did I dream it all up?"

"It happened." Ana smiled. "Your beautiful daughter came. She wasn't angry at you, she hugged you and kissed you, and she called you Mom. It doesn't get any better than that."

"It doesn't." Margaret took a sip from the coffee.

"So why were you crying?"

She shrugged. "I'm not sure that I want to live forever. I mean, I want time with Wendy, but I'm not old. I still have many years left to make up for those I lost."

Ana regarded her with puzzlement in her eyes. "Why wouldn't you want to live forever?"

"Because life is hard, and it's sad. Why drag out the misery?"

"It doesn't have to be miserable. You can learn to be happy." She leaned closer and whispered, "You have an amazing guy who wants to spend that eternity with you. What can be better than that?"

"Does he? When Wendy called him my mate, he told her that we were not there yet."

Anastasia rolled her eyes. "That's because you haven't had sex yet. It's like marriage. It needs to be consummated to be official. Bowen is in love with you, and you are in love with him. It's time you let yourself feel it."

Margaret opened her mouth to refute Ana's claim, to tell her that she wasn't in love with Bowen, but she closed it when she realized that Ana was right.

She'd fallen in love with Bowen from almost the very first moment. When he'd brought her to that ambulance and stayed with her, she'd felt the pull, the yearning. But she hadn't allowed herself to internalize it, in the same way she hadn't allowed herself to internalize anything else.

She'd been existing, not living.

To open her heart would have opened the gates not only to love, but also to misery, to the self-loathing, and to the horrible memories, and Margaret wouldn't have survived it.

Her capacity for pain had been maxed out a long time ago.

"You need to get up and get dressed." Ana patted her arm. "We can leave as soon as you are ready."

Margaret swallowed. "Do you mean the four of us?"

"Of course. There is no reason for us to stay here any longer. We are going to the immortals' village." Ana grinned. "I can't wait to see it. Leon has told me so much about it, and it sounds like a real haven, not the fake one Emmett created." She pursed her lips. "Which reminds me that there is one more piece of information that might shock you."

As panic constricted her throat, Margaret lifted her hand to her neck. "I don't know if I can handle any more shocking news."

"I think this piece will explain a few things, or at least make you see them more clearly. The clan has captured Emmett, and they have him locked up in their dungeon. Apparently, he's also an immortal, just from a different breed, and he used compulsion to make you and the others worship him. The guy who helped you, Kalugal, is not a motivational speaker. He is also a compeller like Emmett, and all he did was override what Emmett has done to you. The leader you admired so much compelled you to get panic attacks every time you thought of contacting Wendy or even just seeking information about her."

Syssi

By the time Okidu parked the limo in the underground garage of the building, Lisa and Ronja had talked up a storm, updating Sari and David on the latest village gossip.

Luckily, mother and daughter weren't aware yet of the one item that would most likely bother Ronja the most once she found out about it.

Syssi wasn't sure what kind of a relationship Ronja and Bowen had, or if it had developed into anything romantic, but even if it hadn't, the news about Bowen's newfound love would probably be upsetting to Ronja. Now that he belonged to another woman, he wouldn't be spending time with her like he used to.

Anandur, Brundar, and Kian had been busy talking about security and didn't pay attention to the prattle, but she'd caught Okidu stealing glances at Ronja through the rearview mirror.

Lately, he'd been acting even stranger than usual. Well, stranger for an Odu, but less strange for a human. Could it be that he was developing real feelings? Was he concerned for Ronja?

The butler knew everything that was going on, heard all the gossip, and stored it in his cybertronic brain.

Syssi shook her head. She was being silly, and it was all in her head. She'd gotten so used to Okidu that he seemed human to her.

"This building needs a name," Lisa said. "I'm tired of calling it the building across the street from the keep."

"What would you suggest?" Anandur asked.

Lisa shrugged. "I don't know. Anything would be better than that. Name it after one of the presidents or something. The Adams building, or Madison, or Monroe. Or the Shangri-La."

Syssi chuckled. "I like Shangri-La, but don't forget that we intend to lease these apartments at some point. I don't think prospective tenants would like their building to be called after a fictional place."

"We can discuss this upstairs." Kian opened the passenger door at the same time Okidu opened the one on the other side. "Mother and Amanda are waiting for us with lunch."

As the eight of them headed toward the elevators, Okidu lifted Sari and David's luggage from the trunk and followed behind them.

"I shall wait for the next elevator, master." He bowed.

"Thank you for getting our luggage." Sari patted his arm. "I left Ojidu home to take care of those who volunteered to stay behind."

The perpetual shroud around the castle meant that those in charge of maintaining it couldn't leave. Usually, that wasn't a problem, but it was a shame that they couldn't take part in the celebrations. It was time to replace the shroud with technology, but, for some reason, Sari was dragging her feet about it.

Perhaps she wanted to move out of there. She had refused Kian's offer to join the village because she liked her independence, but that didn't mean that she couldn't move her people to another location in Scotland. The castle was beautiful, but it was old, and there was only so much that could be done to bring it into the twenty-first century.

"Your apartment is on the top floor." Kian pressed the button to call the elevator. "It's not a penthouse, because the building wasn't designed with residences in mind, but you'll still have a nice view."

Sari cast him an apologetic glance. "You've gone to so much trouble to make this event possible. We could have made the wedding a smaller celebration in the village."

As the elevator arrived and they all crammed in, Kian wrapped his arm around Syssi's shoulders. "The plans to convert the building from offices to apartments were made long before I decided to host the clan here. Your wedding only hastened the construction, so don't feel guilty about it. I just wish that you could stay in the village during your visit."

Sari shook her head. "I need to be near my people, and they are all staying here. But David and I will come visit the village on Sunday. Miranda can't wait to see it."

"When is she arriving?" Syssi asked.

"Later today." David held the elevator door open until all of them spilled out. "The logistics of bringing everyone here without attracting attention were complicated. Only a small group is arriving straight from Scotland, and not all from the same airport. Others are making stopovers at other major cities, in Europe and in the States, before heading here."

Kian nodded. "We are using delivery trucks to pick them up from the various collection centers they will Uber or taxi to."

Sari winced. "Please tell me those trucks have nice interiors. I don't want my people shuttled in like cattle."

"Of course." Syssi put her hand on Sari's arm. "This is a celebration not an evacuation."

As they started down the corridor toward the corner unit, the door opened and Amanda rushed out. "Sari!" She pulled her sister into a hug. "You look amazing." Amanda smiled at David. "Thanks to you, no doubt." She let go of Sari and hugged him too. "I'm so excited about your wedding. Especially since I didn't have to do anything. Gerard took care of all the details, including hiring the decorators and supervising their work."

Sari shook her head. "I don't know how you managed to rope him into organizing our wedding and Kian's birthday. You must teach me your magic spell."

Amanda pursed her lips. "Got guilt? That's my magic."

"I see." Sari turned to Kian. "Your birthday was supposed to be a surprise, but at some point, it was decided to include you in the plans."

Syssi lifted her hand. "That was my doing. Kian doesn't like surprises, but he loves big clan-wide parties. I figured that he would prefer to be included in the planning, especially since security was a major concern."

"You know me so well." He kissed the top of her head. "Let's not keep Mother waiting."

Kian

Kian waited patiently for the emotional reunion between Annani and Sari to be done with and for everyone else to exchange greetings.

When it seemed to be done, he pulled out a dining room chair for his mother. "Oridu is wringing his hands in the kitchen, waiting for us to sit down so he can serve lunch."

Annani smiled up at him. "Oridu is not doing any hand wringing. Are you hungry, my son?"

"Starving."

"Then let us eat." She motioned for the others to join her.

"I thought that Andrew and Nathalie would come and bring Phoenix," Sari said as David pulled out a chair for her. "I can't get enough of that little girl. She just cracks me up with her grown-up talk. She sounds like a seventeen-year-old."

Syssi smoothed a hand over her belly. "Andrew had a big meeting at work he couldn't wiggle out of, and Nathalie didn't want to come without him."

"Why is he still working for the government?" Alena asked.

"He's not willing to give up the connections and the access to classified information that his job provides him with." Kian passed the basket of bread to Syssi. "Frankly, I haven't been encouraging him to leave. He's in the know, and he can alert us to new developments in real time. Right now, he's trying to get into UFO classified information. He might discover something connected with the Kra-ell's arrival. If what Emmett told us is true, then they arrived sometime at the beginning of the nineteenth century. Perhaps there are records of sightings from back then."

Leaning back, David crossed his arms over his chest. "Have any of you heard about the Tunguska event?"

The name sounded familiar, and after digging in his memory banks, all Kian could come up with was that it was something that had happened in Russia more than a century ago. "Was it a meteor?"

David nodded. "In 1908, there was a massive explosion near the Tunguska River in Russia. It flattened trees in an area of about a thousand square miles, maybe a little less. I don't remember the exact number. The theory is that the explosion was caused by a large meteoroid, or rather the airburst it created. It must have disintegrated at an altitude of several miles above the ground because no impact crater has been found. Based on the size and magnitude of the impacted area, the shock wave from the air burst would have been a 5 on the Richter scale. That's enough to destroy a large city. Fortunately, it happened over a remote, sparsely populated area, and only a handful of casualties were reported."

"What are you trying to say?" Annani asked.

David shrugged. "It's the largest impact event in recorded history, and there is no definite explanation for what actually happened. Perhaps it was an alien ship that went down, a large vessel that hadn't been supposed to enter the atmosphere and should have stayed in orbit. From what Sari told me, I understand that Emmett's group is small, and he was led to believe that they were the only survivors. It fits the narrative."

"I don't think they are," Kian said. "I have a feeling that there are many more of them scattered around." He unscrewed the cap from the large Perrier bottle and poured some into Syssi's glass and then his.

"There might have been several escape pods," David suggested.

Sari patted his back. "Is this the scientist talking or the sci-fi author?"

"Can't I be both?"

"Of course, my love. But this sounds like you've let yourself get carried away on the wings of your wonderful imagination."

Kian didn't think so. "Reality is often stranger than fiction, Sari. I'll mention the Tunguska event to William and see what he thinks of it."

"Speaking of William." Amanda shifted in her chair. "Is he making any progress with deciphering the Kra-ell language?"

"He is, but it's a slow process." Kian scooped a large serving of baked fingerling potatoes onto his plate. "William is not a linguist, and although we have many members who speak a lot of languages, no one is an actual philologist. He was able, however, to confirm Emmett's translation of the email he'd sent to his leader."

"The reason I'm asking, is that I had a great idea." Amanda paused for dramatic effect, looked around the table to make sure she had everyone's attention, and then smiled at Kian. "You are going to thank me for coming up with this one." She paused again. "You should send Mey with Arwel and Jin to China. Even if Emmett's people didn't leave any breadcrumbs, they still left echoes of conversations embedded in the walls of their former compound. She can listen to them and perhaps find out where they were planning to move to."

Annani clapped her hands. "That is a brilliant idea, Mindy. You are so clever."

The idea was solid, provided they could decipher the entire language and Mey could learn it in a couple of weeks, which wasn't going to happen.

Anandur chuckled. "You know what this reminds me of? The joke about the solution to the German U-boat problem during WWII. Someone came up with the bright idea that raising the ocean temperature by four degrees Celsius would make the U-boats inoperable. When asked how he proposed to do that, the guy said, 'I offered the solution, someone else will have to figure out the details.' Mey listening to the echoes in the walls will not achieve much if she doesn't understand what she hears. It's not like she can record it and then have Emmett translate it."

Amanda crossed her arms over her chest and jutted her chin out. "Then we should put her in the cell with Emmett and have her learn as much as she can until it's time for the team to leave for China."

Kian shook his head. "The question is whether she would agree, and even if she does, it will still take her a very long time to learn."

"Isn't it ironic?" Syssi sighed. "The two girls that the Kra-ell considered worthless and got rid of might lead to their capture."

"Yeah." Anandur grinned. "Payback is a b…" He cast an apologetic glance at Annani. "I mean, the Kra-ell will get what's coming to them."

Annani

"Perhaps that is why the Fates brought Mey and Jin to us." Annani turned to Kian. "How do you plan to use Jin's talent?"

"I'm not sure how her talent will be utilized, but given the circumstances, Jin and Mey could be our only hope of finding Emmett's group."

"I wish I had a cool talent like that," Lisa said.

"Yours is even cooler." Amanda patted her arm. "You were right about Anastasia. She was a Dormant, and now she's an immortal. I only regret that I didn't send you to sniff out her friend."

Lisa perked up. "I can still do that if you want me to."

Amanda waved a dismissive hand. "It's too late. We know that she's a Dormant for sure because she's Wendy's mom."

No one had mentioned Bowen's involvement yet, and Annani wondered whether it was intentional since Ronja was there. She liked David's mother even more than she had expected to and regretted that the news might pain her. Amanda suspected that Bowen and Ronja had been more than friends. If she was right about that, then Bowen finding a mate would no doubt disappoint Ronja.

"How did you hear about it already?" Kian asked. "I only found out about Margaret being Wendy's mother today, and that was at two o'clock this morning."

Syssi lifted her hand. "From me. I couldn't sit on news like that and not tell anyone, so I called Amanda."

"And I called Mother and Alena." Amanda cast Sari an apologetic glance. "I didn't call you because you don't know Wendy, so the news would have been meaningless to you."

Sari grimaced. "Discovering a new Dormant is never meaningless. I just wish some would find their way to my people." She lifted a pair of love-filled eyes to her mate. "I feel guilty about being the only lucky one so far."

Annani cast a quick glance at Ronja, but it seemed like she had not figured out yet that Margaret and Bowen had become an item.

Perhaps now was not the best time for her to discover that, and a change of subject was in order.

Syssi must have arrived at the same conclusion because she turned to Lisa. "I might have another sniffing mission for you at the wedding. Onegus is bringing a human date who he suspects might be a Dormant."

Lisa's eyes sparkled with excitement. "I'll be more than happy to sniff her. Just point me in her direction."

When a long moment of silence followed the exchange between Syssi and Lisa, and everyone kept sneaking glances at Ronja, Annani turned to Kian. "Has Jin agreed to take part in the expedition?"

Hopefully, her question would shift the conversation back to a neutral subject.

"She has. But to use her talent, she needs to learn Chinese, and according to Arwel, she's linguistically challenged. For an immortal, that is." Kian raked his fingers through his hair. "I wish we had more time for Mey and Jin to learn Mandarin and the Kra-ell languages properly. As it is, I'm afraid that they will have to make do with just rudimentary understanding."

"Fates willing, that will suffice." Annani smiled. "I also heard that Eleanor is becoming a useful asset to the clan."

"She's guarding Emmett," Syssi said. "Regrettably, things didn't work out between her and Greggory."

Annani had heard the news about the breakup. "If it was not meant to be, it is best that it has ended sooner rather than later. This brings me to my next question. Are there any new romances between Kalugal's men and our clan ladies?"

Amanda uttered a frustrated huff. "There are plenty of hookups, that's for sure. They are all acting as if they must sample every flavor available first. I guess having so many cookies in the jar makes it difficult to settle on just one."

Annani arched a brow. "Are you saying that none have formed relationships?"

"Not as far as I know." Amanda sighed. "It also doesn't help that Kalugal keeps his men busy in his downtown offices six days a week. By the time they get back to the village, the café is closed, and for now, that's the only meeting place we have."

Annani was not happy. The infusion of eligible males was supposed to result in many new pairings and hopefully a few pregnancies. What were the Fates thinking?

"Perhaps we should organize mixers. Are Kalugal's men invited to the wedding?"

Amanda shook her head. "Kalugal and Jacki are obviously coming, and so is Rufsur because he's mated to Edna. The rest are not part of the family yet." She glanced at Sari. "I didn't know whether you would want them at your wedding."

"I don't mind," Sari said. "It could be a good opportunity for them to mingle."

Everyone's eyes turned to Kian, who was shaking his head. "I need Kalugal's men to provide added security at the village while nearly all of us are at the keep. If we invite them, we will have to leave several more Guardians behind, which is not desirable on two accounts. The obvious reason is that the more Guardians can attend the wedding, the better. And secondly, we need them to secure the event and this building. They can take part in the celebration and safeguard the clan at the same time."

It was a valid point, but Kian was not using his emotional intelligence and thinking how the exclusion would affect Kalugal's men and their loyalty to the clan.

"If you want Kalugal's men to become an integral part of the clan, you need to treat them as such." Annani lifted her cup for Oridu to refill. "Since they are all trained warriors and therefore can be regarded as an auxiliary force to the Guardians, I suggest a lottery. Decide how many men are needed to maintain security in the village and have the Guardians and Kalugal's men draw lots in proportion to their numbers."

"Isn't it too late for that?" Syssi asked. "The wedding is in two days, and the Guardians have already been assigned their posts. I don't think it's a good idea to cause resentment among them because we want to include Kalugal's men in the celebration. There is enough of it going around already, especially among the males."

"I suggest a compromise," Amanda said. "We leave the wedding arrangements as they are, but we implement the lottery for Kian's birthday."

"It is a reasonable solution." Annani looked at Kian. "It is your birthday, my son. Is it agreeable to you?"

He looked conflicted. "I have nothing against Kalugal's men, but I prefer to have more of our Guardians attend the celebrations. I'll talk it over with Kalugal and see what he thinks. He might have a different take on this. Perhaps a small selection of his men can attend both events."

Kian

As coffee and dessert were served after lunch, Kian texted Kalugal to ask his opinion about inviting some of his men to Sari and David's wedding, and perhaps a larger group to Kian's bimillennial birthday celebration.

If he were a private man, Kian would have preferred to celebrate with his immediate family, but he was a leader, and his people needed as many reasons to celebrate as he could provide them. That's why his personal preferences regarding the attendance of Kalugal's men didn't really matter. If he could promote their integration into the clan by inviting them, then he was all for it.

Kian's end goal was for the offspring created by unions between clan females and Kalugal's men to belong to the clan and fortify its numbers, and for that, he needed the men to feel part of the community.

On the other hand, Syssi's argument was valid as well. Not everyone was happy about them joining the village, and having them attend might increase feelings of resentment rather than promote integration.

As he waited for his cousin's response, Kian observed his mother's interaction with Ronja. They were acting like old friends who hadn't seen each other in a long while, sharing gossip and talking about everything from Lisa's school experience to world politics and Ronja's conspiracy theories.

It was a shame that Ronja was too old to transition. She would have made a wonderful companion for Annani, maybe even freeing Alena to finally pursue her own interests.

His eldest sister had done a lot for the clan, birthing and raising thirteen children, and at the same time keeping Annani out of trouble. She had paid her dues and then some. It was time she started doing things for herself, living her life and finding her passion. Not that motherhood wasn't a worthy goal in itself, but it seemed like Alena's incredible fertility had been exhausted in her younger years and she could conceive no more. She needed something new to fulfill her.

After Kalugal had finally responded, promising to supply two lists of the men he wanted to bring along to each of the events, Kian pushed to his feet. "We should be heading back soon. I still have work to do today."

Annani looked up at him. "Is there an available apartment in this building that Alena and I could use? Our people will start arriving tomorrow, and I decided that we should be here with them."

Kian shook his head. "I don't know if there are any left, but even if Ingrid can rearrange things and free up an apartment for you, I'd prefer that you stay in the village. Otherwise, I'll have to beef up security in this building, and the Guardian force is already stretched thin as it is."

The stubborn tilt of Annani's chin didn't bode well. "I have made up my mind. Please check with Ingrid if she can reshuffle occupancy to make an apartment available for Alena and me."

He pinned her with a hard stare. "Beefing up security here means canceling even more rescue missions. Do you want that on your conscience?"

It was a low blow, but it was true. Besides, he really didn't want her to stay in the building.

Sari winced. "You are making me feel guilty for having the wedding here. I didn't know that you'd canceled missions because of us."

"I also had to cancel missions because of my birthday, so I should share the guilt. But neither of us has to feel guilty. The plan is to compensate for the reduction by doubling up after the celebrations are over and everyone goes home."

"There you go." Annani waved a hand. "This is the solution. Cancel all the missions until next week and then double up on the effort in the following weeks. I am sure the Guardians will appreciate a break for the duration of the festivities. Guarding me is not as taxing as what they usually do, and it is certainly not as depressing. It will also give them an opportunity to spend more time with their visiting relatives."

As the others all nodded in agreement, Kian knew that he'd lost the argument. "I'll speak with Ingrid and Onegus and see what can be done."

Annani didn't even try to hide her triumphant smile. "Thank you."

"Speaking of relatives," Sari said. "What's going on with Carol and Lokan? Are they joining us for the celebrations?"

"It's too dangerous for Lokan, and Carol has decided to stay with him in DC." Kian offered a hand up to Syssi. "They are flying out to China on Monday." He supported her back as she struggled to her feet.

Sari leaned back. "Together?"

Syssi nodded. "Lokan hired Carol as the marketing expert for the fashion label he's about to launch. They are flying out together, and he's reserved a two-bedroom suite for them in the Waldorf Astoria in Beijing."

"Fancy," Ronja said. "Does Lokan need a personal assistant? I would love to see Beijing and stay at the Waldorf."

"Me too." Lisa lifted her hand. "Does he need a teenage model for his fashion label?"

Onegus

Ingrid strode into Onegus's temporary headquarters looking as if someone had pissed on her designer shoes. "Annani wants an apartment in the building, and I don't have any furnished ones left. How am I supposed to reshuffle people as they are coming in?" She plopped down on the couch. "I need a drink."

Onegus walked over to the bar. "What would you like?"

"Whatever you make is fine." She waved a hand in dismissal. "Just not beer. I can't stand that vile stuff you guys drink."

He mixed her a gin and tonic. "You can give this apartment to Annani. I can move operations to my old office in the keep." He handed her the drink.

Ingrid lifted a pair of grateful eyes to him. "Are you sure? You said that you needed a place in the building for the Guardians to rest between shifts."

"They can rest in the keep. It's just across the street. Or we can section off part of the lobby for them. There is already a sitting area, and if you put screens around it and add a snack and drink bar, that should do it."

"I like it. I can make it look as if it's sectioned off for construction. That way, when people walk by, they are not going to wonder what's going on or try to get in to take a look."

As his phone rang, Onegus had a good idea who was calling. "Good afternoon, boss. Are you calling about the Clan Mother's request for lodging in the building?"

"I see that Ingrid beat me to it. Is she still freaking out?"

"We found a solution. Annani can have this apartment, and I'll move to my old office in the keep. We will also section off part of the lobby for the Guardians."

"Double the space you had in mind for that. With Annani in the building, we need to beef up security."

"We are already maxed out. I don't have enough Guardians."

"I know. We need to cancel the rest of the rescue missions until after everyone goes home and things return to normal."

"Did you speak with Bridget?" Onegus walked over to his desk and sat down on the swivel chair he'd brought from the keep just that morning.

"Yeah. She's on it. To compensate, we will double up starting next Monday."

"I don't like it, but I guess we have no choice." Onegus started collecting his notes and piling them up. "What the Clan Mother wants, the Clan Mother gets."

"That was my initial reaction as well, but Annani raised a valid argument. The clan is celebrating, and the Guardians have the same right as the others to take a pause from what they are doing and concentrate on happier things. I hate the thought of the victims suffering through one more week of torment while we are having fun, but we can't save everyone, and there will always be people suffering somewhere no matter what we do and how hard we try."

"Ain't that the sad truth. I assume that Annani wants the place by tomorrow?"

"She wants to be there when her people start arriving."

Onegus heaved out a sigh. "I'll pack my things and move to the keep today. Ingrid will have the place cleaned and ready sometime tomorrow." He glanced at the interior designer. "Do you have anyone other than the Odus to do that?"

The cleaning crews had left long before the guests had started to arrive, and they wouldn't be back until the guests were gone. The Odus were available only for emergency cleanups. Other than that, everyone was responsible for keeping their own place clean.

"As soon as you vacate the place, I'll get the cleaning crew in. They are very discreet, and they know not to ask questions. I can get it ready for Annani and Alena by tomorrow mid-morning." She reached for her purse and pulled out her phone. "I need to call the construction crew chief and get him back here to section off part of the lobby."

"Double the number of Guardians starting tomorrow morning," Kian said.

"Consider it done."

When Kian ended the call, Onegus rubbed a hand over the back of his neck. "I hoped to steal a few moments to see Cassandra, but evidently, it's not going to happen today."

Ingrid lifted a hand to indicate that she was still busy on the phone. When she was done, she dropped it back in her purse and pushed to her feet. "You can go for half an hour. I'll hold the fort for you."

He shook his head. "I need to reorganize the Guardian schedule, and then I have to greet my mother when she arrives tonight."

"You need to eat, right? You can eat with Cassandra. Have her meet you somewhere nearby. I'll cover for you."

"You are the best." He kissed her cheek. "I'll take care of the schedule and then call Cassandra."

"Give me fifteen minutes notice before you leave."

"I'll do that."

Bowen

"It's like taking a ride into the future." Margaret glanced at the car's opaque windows. "I can't get over the car driving itself."

"Autonomous driving is going to be commonplace shortly." Bowen leaned over the center console and took her hand. "The technology is already incorporated into several car models, but the legislators haven't approved it yet."

"What about the windows?" She put her hand on the glass. "Is that a common thing too?"

"No. The technology is not new, but no one is implementing it the way we do. For us, it's a necessary precaution to keep our location safe. If a clan member is caught by our enemies, he or she won't be able to provide the village's exact location because they don't know it. Their cars drive in and out of the village autonomously, and the windows turn opaque so they won't see the entrance to the tunnel."

"We are in a tunnel?" She tilted her head to listen to the echoes.

"We are, and in a moment we will enter an elevator that will take us up to a parking garage."

"Do you know where the entrance is?"

He shook his head. "Only a few members have that information, head Guardians included, but I'm not one of them."

"Does it bother you?"

"Not at all. The clan's security comes first, and the fewer people who know how to get to our village, the better."

"But it's aboveground, right?"

He nodded.

"Then it can be seen from aircraft."

"You are correct, but we have ways to hide it from view by sophisticated camouflage technology."

When the car entered the elevator, the windows began to clear, and Margaret pressed her nose against the glass, looking like a kid on an amusement park ride.

Bowen smiled. "Usually, when a new Dormant or immortal arrives at the village, there is a welcoming committee. But everyone is busy with the upcoming wedding and the arriving guests, so you are not going to get the usual treatment." As the elevator opened at the garage level, Bowen took over the driving. "But I think you'll like yours better." He drove into his parking spot, where Wendy and Vlad were waiting for them.

Leon and Anastasia, who had arrived a couple of minutes earlier, were waiting for them as well.

"Everyone I need is here." Margaret's voice quivered.

Wendy opened the passenger door and offered her mother a hand up. "Welcome to the village, Mom." She chuckled. "Well, you need to get out of the parking garage to actually be in the village, but that's what everyone says."

Bowen walked over to the trunk and pulled out the folding wheelchair. "The walk to Wendy and Vlad's house is long. It would be too difficult for you to traverse with the crutches."

"We brought a golf cart," Wendy said. "But it can be used for the luggage. If you're okay with the wheelchair, I can show you more of the village on the way, and maybe even introduce you to some people."

Margaret paled. "I don't know if I'm ready for that."

Wendy helped her into the wheelchair and then leaned and kissed her cheek. "I just want you to see where I work and to meet Wonder. Are you okay with that?"

"I guess so. But what about the other people in the café?"

"Don't worry about it." Wendy patted her shoulder. "I'll take care of them. You only need to smile and wave."

Cradling the front of her neck, Margaret still looked as if she had a frog stuck in her throat, but she nodded.

As Vlad helped with the luggage, taking some of the load from Leon and Bowen, Anastasia joined Wendy behind Margaret's wheelchair.

"Don't forget that I'm here as well." She put a hand on her friend's slim shoulder. "And people are going to want to say hello to me too. I'll deflect attention from you."

Margaret blew out a breath. "Thank you."

"No problem."

"Before I forget," Wendy said. "Syssi and Amanda apologize for not being here to welcome you both. They are having a family lunch with the bride and groom outside of the village and will try to stop by tomorrow afternoon."

"Who are Syssi and Amanda?" Margaret asked.

"Amanda is the goddess's daughter, and Syssi is married to the goddess's son," Wendy said. "They usually welcome the new Dormants and newly-turned immortals."

When Bowen's phone started buzzing the same time Leon's did, they exchanged worried looks, put the luggage down, and pulled out their devices.

"What's going on?" Vlad asked.

"It's a group message," Leon said. "All rescue missions are canceled until next Monday, and we are to report to the keep tonight at eight-thirty for an orientation."

"Did something happen?" Anastasia asked.

Onegus was doubling security at the newly converted building, but he hadn't elaborated on why. Hopefully, it wasn't because a new cause for alarm had presented itself.

"It's probably about additional security for the wedding," Leon said. "With the entire clan gathering in one place, Kian must be freaking out." He put the phone in his back pocket and lifted the two suitcases. "I, for one, am happy." He glanced at Bowen. "My mother is arriving tomorrow. I'd rather spend time with her than go out on rescue missions."

Bowen groaned. "I completely forgot. I don't even know when my mother's flight is landing." He pulled out his phone and scrolled through his emails. "She's arriving tomorrow morning." He let out a relieved breath.

"What time?" Leon asked.

"Ten-fifteen."

"Then she must be arriving on the same flight as my mother. We can pick them up together."

Bowen shook his head. "We might get assigned a post at the meeting tonight. Besides, Turner has the entire transportation of arriving clan members nailed down. He doesn't want us to collect anyone from the airport."

"Right." Leon's smile wilted. "I guess we will have to wait to see our mothers after they arrive at the building."

Margaret

Margaret felt her throat constricting again, and this time it wasn't Emmett's compulsion that was causing it.

"Your mother is coming to the village?" she croaked.

"She's going to stay in the clan's building downtown, but I'm sure she'll want to visit."

"That's awesome," Wendy said. "Bowen's mother can meet you, and Leon's mother can meet Anastasia." She leaned over Margaret's shoulder. "I never expected to have an extended family. Isn't it wonderful?"

Margaret forced a smile. "Yeah, it is."

It wasn't.

Bowen's mother was going to hate her, and rightfully so. She didn't deserve a guy like him, and if she had a son who was dating a woman like herself, she wouldn't have liked it one bit either.

"By the way." Wendy stopped in front of the elevators and pressed the button. "Vlad's mother and her boyfriend are at the house, waiting to meet you."

Margaret tried to swallow, but her throat was so constricted that she started to cough.

In an instant, Bowen was at her side, crouching in front of her. "Look at me, Margaret."

She tried, but the coughing was getting worse, and she couldn't catch a breath.

"Everything is going to be alright."

His words penetrated the haze of panic like a wave of calm waters, and suddenly, she was able to breathe. Had he thralled her?

"Better?" He cupped her cheek.

She nodded. "Did you thrall me?"

"Just a smidgen. I hope you don't mind."

"Thank you." She covered his hand with hers. "I'm sorry for falling apart like that over nothing. Everything is happening so quickly, and I feel overwhelmed."

"I bet. It's too much." Bowen lifted his eyes to Wendy. "Perhaps it wasn't a good idea to cram everything into one day. Your mother needs time to adjust."

"I can tell Stella and Richard to come some other time."

"It's okay." Margaret turned around to look at her daughter. "I'll be fine." She forced a smile. "I need to adjust to this new reality, and the sooner the better."

As the elevator door opened, Wendy wheeled her inside, and the others followed. It was cramped, but having them there, surrounding her, felt comforting. Everyone she cared for and who cared for her was in that elevator.

"You are going to love Stella," Wendy said. "She's so creative. She designs costumes for theater productions, and now she's also working on a fashion line. Richard is awesome too. I met him in the government program, and he was always nice to me even though I was a drag back then. When we escaped, and I betrayed everyone to the director, he stayed with Vlad and me in the cabin and was still nice to me despite that. Then we moved into the village, and he was our roommate for a while, but then he and Stella fell in love, and he moved out to be with her."

Apparently, Wendy talked up a storm when she was nervous, but Margaret didn't mind it in the least. She loved hearing her daughter's voice, and she was thirsty for every little bit of information about her past. They had so much catching up to do.

As the elevator doors opened, Wendy wheeled her out, and the others followed.

"This is the entry pavilion," Wendy explained. "The artifacts behind the glass belong to Kalugal, who's an archeology buff. I would have taken you on a tour, but Stella and Richard are waiting for us at the house."

"It's beautiful." Ana gasped. "Just look at how green everything is." She followed Vlad out the sliding doors.

"What do you think, Mom?" Wendy pushed the wheelchair out.

"It's paradise." Margaret wasn't referring to the lush greenery. "The place is beautiful, but what makes it special is that it's your home."

"It's your home too, Mom."

When the men were done loading the luggage onto the golf cart, Vlad hopped behind the wheel. "I'm going to drop off Leon and Anastasia's things at Leon's house first." He looked at Bowen. "Where should I take your and Margaret's things?"

"To my place." Bowen pulled out his phone. "I'll just let my roommate know that we are here."

"I thought that you were staying with us," Anastasia said. "What is Margaret going to do all alone in the house when you go to work?"

"Good point," Bowen agreed without argument. "I called Ingrid about getting us a place of our own, but she won't have time to take care of it until after the celebrations."

Anastasia shook her head. "Even when she gets you a place, you can't move in there until Margaret is independent."

Wendy looked conflicted. "I thought that you and Bowen would stay with us, but I'm working at the café, and Vlad is working at the bakery and attending classes in college. So maybe Mom can spend the days with Anastasia but come to our house in the evenings? Your place is in the new phase, right?" she asked Leon.

He nodded. "It's only a few minutes' walk away from yours. Even with the crutches, your mother can handle such a short walk."

Margaret cleared her throat. "Is no one going to ask me what I want?"

"Nope." Ana crouched next to her. "I know you. You'll say that you can manage on your own and argue that you don't want to be a bother. But I don't want to hear it. Leon is going back to work as well, and I don't want to be alone in the house either. You and I will brave this new world together."

Cassandra

Throughout the day, Cassandra's snowflakes had been sneaking curious glances at her. She hadn't chewed anyone out, hadn't criticized their work or lack thereof, and had been giving out more smiles than, well, ever.

They were probably whispering behind her back that she must have gotten laid, which wasn't far from the truth.

But it was much more than that.

Onegus, the most amazing guy she'd ever met, was serious about her. The invitation to his family wedding was the best proof she could have asked for. In fact, it was more than she'd ever expected. Getting invited to his home to meet his roommate or a dinner out with a couple of his friends would have sufficed.

Was she ready to meet his family?

Talk about intimidating.

Onegus seemed like a down-to-earth kind of guy. He wasn't a snob, didn't flaunt his family's wealth, and didn't act like a spoiled rich guy. That didn't mean, though, that his entire family was like him.

They might look down their noses at her, and she would have to smile and pretend not to notice for Onegus's sake. The problem would be reining in her temper. Perhaps she should take one of those relaxants that she'd experimented with a while ago. The problem was that they were probably expired, and it was too late to make an appointment with her doctor to get a new prescription.

Positive thinking would have to do.

She would have to focus on Onegus and how wonderful he was, reaffirm her self-confidence by reminding herself of all that she'd achieved and ignore any snide remarks or disapproving looks, or just not let them get under her skin.

Easier said than done, but not impossible.

When Cassandra's phone buzzed with Onegus's number on the screen, a happy grin spread over her face, and her heart gave a little flutter.

Did he miss her?

In the morning, he'd said that he would be busy until Saturday and wouldn't be able to see her.

"Hello, Onegus. What a nice surprise. I didn't expect another call from you today."

"I hope that I'm not interrupting, but frankly, I don't care. I need to hear your voice. When can you get away from the office?"

"At around seven. Why?"

"We could meet for a cup of coffee or a very quick dinner, and I mean fast-food quick. I can get away for half an hour."

He really missed her.

"I was resigned to not seeing you until the wedding. What changed your mind?"

He chuckled. "Do you want to hear me say that I can't stay away from you and that I need to see you?"

Switching the phone to her other ear, she crossed her legs and leaned back. "Only if it's the truth."

"Every word. I feel like a junkie who has to get his fix."

She arched a brow even though he couldn't see her. "Are we talking about a quickie or a coffee?"

He was silent for a long moment. "I won't lie. If a quickie was on the menu, I would have taken it. But seeing you, smelling you, and hearing your voice, that's all I need to tide me over."

Cassandra wanted to say that she felt the same, and that not seeing him until Saturday would be a torment, but that would reveal too much too soon and give him too much power.

Besides, Onegus was a man, and he would take sex over mushy declarations any day and twice on Sunday. Well, probably twice on any day. The guy had some stamina.

Heck, Cassandra would take sex with him over coffee or dinner anytime as well. She'd never craved a guy with such intensity.

"I can meet you at the apartment we spent the night in."

The groan he emitted sounded pained. "That's the best offer I could have hoped for, but, regrettably, that place is not mine exclusively, and right now there are at least three other people in there. Besides, I have a meeting at eight, and my mother arrives at eleven tonight, and she will expect me to spend time with her."

"Your mother?" Cassandra squeaked.

She'd never squeaked before.

"My mother is coming to the wedding."

"Are you going to introduce us?"

"Of course."

"Isn't it too early for that?"

"Why would you think that? I met your mother. It's only fair that you meet mine."

Oh God. She'd dug that hole for herself and had no way out of it. Could she fake a sudden sickness?

"Why so quiet all of a sudden?" Onegus sounded amused. "No snarky, witty comments?"

"Frankly, I'm speechless. It should have occurred to me that your mother was coming to the wedding, but it didn't, and I don't feel ready to face her. What if she doesn't like me?"

"She's going to love you. And even if she doesn't, which I can promise you is not going to happen, I'm a big boy, and I don't need my mother to approve of my choices."

"You might think so, but we all want our parents' approval. It means a lot to me that my mother likes you. Even though Geraldine has memory problems, she has good instincts about people, and I trust her opinion."

"Well, what's not to like, right? I'm every mother's dream guy for her daughter."

Cassandra laughed. "I'm sure that your modesty is what impresses them the most."

"It's only one among my many other exceptional qualities, but I will be more than happy to list them to you one by one when we meet. Can you get off a little earlier?"

"Six is the earliest I can manage. Does that work for you?"

"Have you eaten lunch already?"

"I never do. I live on coffee and candy until I get home."

"That's not good. Can you take a break and meet me for a late lunch around three o'clock?"

"That would actually work better for me. I can return to the office after we are done and finish what I need to do with no rush."

"If you don't mind, it will have to be somewhere close to where I am."

"No problem. Text me the address."

"I will. Until we meet again, my queen."

Long after ending the call, Cassandra was still grinning like a fool, but then she remembered that Onegus's mother would be at the wedding and her good humor evaporated.

Onegus might be every mother's dream guy for her daughter, but she wasn't every mother's dream for her son.

She would have to be on her best behavior, rein in her snarky comebacks, and definitely avoid making anything explode.

Margaret

"We should go." Bowen put his beer down. "Margaret needs to rest."

"I'm fine." She waved a dismissive hand. "I can stay a little longer."

The truth was that Bowen was right, and she was tired, but Margaret wasn't ready to part with Wendy yet, or with Vlad, whom she was starting to adore, or even his quirky mother and her mate.

Vlad was a sweetheart, and his love for Wendy was evident in every glance, every touch, and every word, and the same was true for Wendy.

Stella was an interesting character. She was the typical creative type, a little flamboyant, a little dramatic, but she'd raised a really good man all on her own, and that spoke volumes about her character.

Richard, who was also a recently transitioned immortal like Wendy, was oddly protective of both Vlad and

Wendy, and he acted fatherly toward them even though he was only thirty-four and hadn't known either of them long.

"We haven't talked about the wedding yet," Stella said. "Now that you are here, I'm sure you would like to take part in the planning."

Margaret shook her head. "I don't want to interfere. Whatever Wendy and Vlad decide is fine with me."

"You will need a nice dress," Wendy said.

"There is plenty of time for that. When is the wedding?"

"In about three months," Vlad said. "Annani is going to preside."

Wendy's eyes widened. "You are so lucky, Mom. Annani is presiding over Sari's wedding, and you'll get to see her even before your transition. That's such a rare treat."

Margaret still felt like she'd been cast into a fantasy novel. All that talk about the gods from mythology being real was difficult to believe, and the prospect of meeting one of the only two remaining goddesses made her nervous.

"Did you get to meet her?" she asked.

Wendy nodded. "Annani is indescribable. Prepare to be awed."

"Is she terrifying?"

"The opposite of that," Richard said. "Annani is powerful, but she uses her power for good, and you can actually feel it. Being in her presence is like being bathed in love."

He chuckled. "But it takes a few minutes to get over the shock. She doesn't look human."

"Do you mean that she's inhumanly beautiful, or are you talking about the glow?" Wendy asked.

"Both. But it's more than that. She's like a force field. You can feel the energy emanating from her."

"True." Wendy nodded. "I thought that what I felt was awe, but you are right. When she enters a room, it feels like the air is sizzling with energy."

"That sounds scary," Margaret admitted. "I hope she'll be too busy to notice me."

"Don't worry about it," Stella said. "Annani will not seek you out. You will only see her from afar when she presides over the mating ceremony. When you transition, she might grant you an audience."

Margaret blew out a breath. "That's a relief. I'm barely ready to meet immortals. I'm not ready for a goddess."

"I want to meet Annani." Anastasia turned to Leon. "Can you introduce me?"

He shook his head. "The Clan Mother chooses who she wants to talk to. I can't initiate it."

"Since you've transitioned already, Annani will want to welcome you to the clan," Stella said. "Newly transitioned females are the key to our future."

Anastasia frowned. "In what way? I mean besides providing a child or two if we are lucky."

Stella turned to Leon. "Didn't you explain?"

"I thought that it was self-explanatory. All Annani's descendants are considered closely related. That's why we need the infusion of new genes, especially female because the heredity is determined by the mothers."

"We need genetic variety, period," Wendy said. "Both males and females can contribute."

Stella shook her head. "I see that my son didn't do any better job of explaining than Leon. Every new female immortal that is not Annani's descendant is a potential originator of a new maternal line. Her descendants can mate with Annani's, and the more lines we have, the better." She looked at Margaret. "You might be blessed with another child, and this time, you can actually enjoy raising it."

Margaret swallowed the lump that had formed in her throat. "I don't think I can have any more children. I've been taking contraceptive shots for years, and I can't even remember the last time I menstruated."

"The transition will fix whatever has gone wrong with your body." Stella chuckled. "You never know. I'm sure Wendy would love to have a little brother or sister."

Wendy wrapped her arm around Margaret's shoulders. "Babysitting will be good practice for Vlad and me."

Richard pushed to his feet. "With the way the Fates like to mess with us, you are both going to have babies at the same time." He offered Stella a hand up. "Let's go home and start working on a baby of our own."

Vlad groaned. "TMI, Richard."

Taking her boyfriend's hand, Stella cast her son a loving smile. "Wouldn't you like a little brother or sister to practice your parenting style on?"

"I would love it, and you know it. I just don't want to hear about you and Richard making it."

Eleanor

"Good afternoon." Eleanor walked into Emmett's cell, holding a tray. "I have a treat for you. Alfie got fresh blood from the butcher."

The silent Guardian walked in behind her, looking appropriately threatening.

Emmett dipped his head. "Many thanks, my friend."

"Enjoy." Alfie turned to Eleanor. "If he gives you any trouble, I'll be here in a heartbeat."

"I know." She cast him a thankful smile.

The truth was that having the Guardians watching the feed from the other suite was far from ideal, and it limited what she could do with Emmett. For now, though, Arwel had agreed to mute the feed, so at least their conversations would be semi-private. But if things got heated between her and Emmett, they would have an audience.

As the door closed and they were left alone in the cell, she put the tray on the coffee table and sat on the small couch next to him. "Eat."

"Thank you for keeping me company." Emmett eyed the tall paper cup filled with blood but didn't reach for it.

"It's okay. Go for it. It's not going to gross me out."

He arched a brow. "Yesterday, you started gagging and had to leave. I don't want to lose your company."

"This time, I'm mentally prepared." She waved at the cup. "If we are to be friends, I need to get used to your culinary preferences."

Emmett's expression was the picture of surprise. "You want to be my friend?"

She shrugged. "It might come as a shock to you, but I don't have many friends, and most clan members still don't trust me. So I sympathize with you. You are all alone in here, and you don't have any friends either."

Lifting the cup, he held it between his palms. "It depends on who you consider a friend. I happen to like Arwel, and I enjoy his company. Does that make him my friend?"

She scoffed. "He's your jailer."

"So are you, my dear."

"True."

He shifted to face her. "Let me ask you a question if you don't mind."

"Ask away."

"If you haven't earned the clan's trust yet, how come Kian made you my Guardian?"

Damn. Way to go giving herself up.

"I'm not a Guardian yet. I'm a Guardian in training, and I'm supervised. But I was assigned to guard you because I'm immune to your compulsion."

"Arwel and the others wear those specialty earplugs that render my compulsion useless. Kian didn't need an immune to guard me. What's your agenda, Eleanor? Or should I ask, what's Kian's agenda?"

The guy was too smart to play games with. She had to give him something, or he would clam up and not tell her anything.

"I asked Kian for the position." She reached for the mixed nuts, which were supposed to be Emmett's dessert.

"Why?" He took a slow sip from the cup, careful not to let even a drop spill on his chin.

It was helpful, but it didn't solve the problem. She could still smell the blood, and her gag reflex kicked in.

Looking away, she popped another nut in her mouth in the hopes that it would drown the smell. When she was done chewing, she cast a quick sidelong glance at Emmett.

He was watching her like a hawk. "I'm still waiting for an answer."

Affecting the expression of a blasé attitude, Eleanor shrugged. "I felt something back in Safe Haven, and I need to figure out what it was."

Emmett's eyes shone with interest, the nearly black of his irises turning a lighter shade of a dark purple. "What did you feel?"

Fascinating.

Eleanor shrugged again. "You know what I felt. I bet your sense of smell is just as good as that of the other immortal males. What I want to know is whether you emitted some kind of potent pheromones that messed with my hormones, or whether I was genuinely attracted to you."

His smile could only be described as wolfish. "How about now? Are you still attracted to me?"

She'd been doing her best to suppress her reaction to him, mainly the horniness, but if his sense of smell was as acute as Greggory's, he'd probably sniffed it already anyway.

"You tell me," she challenged.

Putting the cup on the tray, he leaned toward her and smelled her neck. "Oh, yes. Definitely. The smell of blood masked your feminine scent, but I can smell it now." He shifted closer to her. "What are we going to do about this, my sweet Eleanor?"

Calling her sweet was like calling a badger cuddly.

She lifted a hand to stop his advance. "For now, nothing. I want to get to know you. And I want you to get to know me. I've traveled the road that started in a hookup and turned into a relationship. That hasn't worked well for me in the past, and you know what they say about repeating the same mistakes and hoping for different results."

Getting her meaning, he shifted a few inches away. "It's the definition of insanity."

She lifted her eyes to him. "Have you experienced the same?"

Emmett seemed conflicted. "All I ever wanted from women was sex and a little taste of their blood. Nothing else could have been possible because of the charade I had to maintain, and I definitely didn't want to father children that I would outlive. The friendship you propose is something I've never tried before." He pushed his fingers through his thick hair. "I've never had a real friend, either, let alone a partner, and I'm not sure I have what it takes to form a relationship." He eyed her from under lowered lashes. "That's what you're after, correct?"

Emmett

Eleanor looked unsure, but she nodded. "Yes. Well, I don't know. It depends on whether you are worthy. But since I have a terrible track record of determining who is and who isn't, I don't trust myself, and I don't know what I'm looking for."

Emmett might never have had a relationship, and given the way he'd been raised and the community he'd grown up in, he should know nothing about the special bond between loving partners, but he was an excellent observer, and he was well-read. He'd spent a long time pondering the philosophical topic of the human condition.

Eleanor yearned for love, that much was evident to him, and the question was how he could use that yearning to his advantage.

The clan's culture seemed to be more similar to the humans' rather than the Kra-ell's. They chose mates and formed lasting, exclusive bonds. Furthermore, Eleanor had been a human up until not too long ago, and she no doubt was still a human at heart, with all that implied.

He could use what he'd learned from fiction, psychology, and philosophy to manipulate her. A woman in love might go to extremes for her man, perhaps even betray her people to help free him.

Eleanor was a fighter. She was cunning and, to a degree, devoid of scruples. Also, she'd worked for the government, which meant that she had a lot of experience manipulating people to do her bidding.

Perhaps she'd even possessed some undercover spying skills.

She was a compeller, had been one even as a human, so it hadn't been difficult for her to manipulate her victims. But she couldn't compel immortals, and yet, only three months after getting captured by the clan while trying to entrap them, she'd managed to convince the suspicious Kian to let her go on a mission and then to give her a Guardian position.

Emmett couldn't have asked for a better ally.

The woman could be an incredible asset to him, provided that he could make her fall in love with him. The trick would be to make her believe that he loved her as well, and that wasn't going to be easy. She was jaded, had gotten jilted more than once, and was mistrustful by nature. If he was to convince her that he was worth saving, he would have to put up the best performance of his life.

Since she was wary, his best tactic would be reverse psychology. Instead of insisting that he was worthy, he would do the opposite, presenting himself as a lost cause and giving her a challenge.

Assuming a contemplative expression, he shook his head. "I'm probably an even worse bet than the others who've disappointed you. I come from a society that doesn't believe in love and scoffs at the concept of exclusivity. It's not that I'm enamored with the multi-partner lifestyle and can't see myself giving it up. I would do it in a heartbeat if I knew how to be different, but I don't."

She looked at him with sadness in her eyes. "Have you never been in love?"

The good news was that Eleanor hadn't gotten defensive, which meant that she'd bought his act, and that was the first step toward building trust. The bad news was that she seemed despondent.

He needed to give her hope.

"I've loved many, but I've never been in love with one particular woman."

She straightened her back and looked at him down her nose. "What do you mean by loving many?"

He spread his arms. "I was a shepherd, and I truly loved my flock, each and every one of them. Not equally, mind you, some I loved more than others, but they all had a place in my heart." He put his hand on his chest. "I can't say that they were like children to me because that would make me an incestuous pervert." He laughed. "I had sex with every woman who joined my community except for one, and it was only a matter of time before she too would have graced my bed."

"Are you referring to Anastasia?"

"The one you came to retrieve." Emmett chuckled. "Your mission was unnecessary. I don't know what stories her father told your friend, but Anastasia could have left whenever she wished. She was immune to my compulsion, so I can't be blamed for manipulating her to stay."

If looks could kill, he would be dead now.

Apparently, bringing up Anastasia had been a mistake.

Eleanor glared at him. "There are many forms of manipulation, and a young, vulnerable woman is putty in the hands of someone like you even without the help of compulsion. And once you had sex with her, how would you have made her forget about the biting? Drugs?"

He lifted his hands in surrender. "That's old news, Eleanor. Why are you getting upset over it?"

She blew out a breath. "I don't know. For a moment there, I forgot about the drugs, and your story about bedding every woman in your community reminded me of them."

He leaned closer to her. "I never used drugs or compulsion to manipulate a woman into my bed. I only used drugs to make them forget the details that would have incriminated me as a bloodsucker."

Eleanor

"You also used it to compel people to stay and worship you without question."

Emmett might have been able to pull the wool over the eyes of a more trusting soul, but Eleanor wasn't buying his act. He was well aware that his actions had been self-serving and manipulative.

Still, she wasn't looking for a saint.

Fates knew that she wasn't one.

Assuming an innocent expression, he puffed out his sensual lips. "Anastasia is a perfect example of someone I couldn't manipulate and who still decided to stay. Safe Haven was true to its name. For some, it was a lifeline, and leaving would have been detrimental to their well-being. I acted in their best interest."

"Are you referring to Margaret?"

"Among others." He narrowed his eyes. "What do you know about her?"

As far as Eleanor knew, no one had told Emmett about Anastasia's transition, and he definitely couldn't know about Margaret being a Dormant. The news was so fresh that only a few clan members were in the know.

Was Arwel one of them?

Probably not.

Should she tell Emmett?

Heck, why not. The news flash would wipe that smug expression off his handsome face.

Leaning back against the couch cushions, Eleanor crossed her arms over her chest. "Did you know that Anastasia and Margaret were good friends?"

"Of course. I knew everything that was going on in my community."

"Didn't it strike you as odd?"

"Why would it? Anastasia wanted to become a counselor, and Margaret was an experienced one. She took the younger woman under her wing, so to speak. Also, Anastasia lost her mother at a young age, and Margaret yearned for a daughter. They adopted each other."

Eleanor shook her head. "Nevertheless, despite having very little in common, they were best friends rather than a mentor and an acolyte. There was a thirteen-year age difference between them. Anastasia was a rich heiress while Margaret had nothing, Anastasia attended a prestigious law school while Margaret has never attended college. What on earth did they have to talk about?"

"They both wanted to help people." Emmett drank the rest of the blood and wiped his lips. "Where are you going with this, Eleanor?"

Apparently, Emmett didn't know enough about Dormants and the affinity they had for each other to guess where she'd been leading him.

"Anastasia and Margaret were both Dormants. That's why they were drawn to each other."

His eyes widened. "How? I mean, how did the clan find out that they were Dormants? Peter said that they were extremely hard to find. He also said that Anastasia's father hired you to retrieve her. He didn't say anything about her being a Dormant, and he was under compulsion to answer my questions truthfully."

She'd definitely ruffled his feathers, and it was very satisfying. "Did you ask him whether she was a Dormant?"

He shook his head. "How was I supposed to know to ask that?"

"That's why he didn't tell you. You and I both know that compulsion needs to be phrased precisely to be effective, and thanks to me, Peter was aware of its limitations and how to work around it."

Emmett looked flabbergasted. "I should have suspected something. Margaret wasn't my type. She was a pretty girl when she came to me, but she was too timid, too weak. I prefer more assertive women. The taste of her blood, however, was delicious." He looked at her with hooded eyes. "Not nearly as exquisite as yours, of course, but better than that of other humans."

Eleanor felt stupid for taking his comment as a compliment, but she couldn't help it. Was her blood the most delicious he'd ever tasted?

"What about Anastasia?"

"I never got the chance to taste her blood, but her immunity should have raised my suspicion. In fact, if she weren't so wealthy, I wouldn't have invited her to join the community." He smiled sheepishly. "The taste of her father's money was almost as good as Margaret's blood."

Eleanor chuckled. "I bet you regret never tasting her. She might have been as delicious as I am."

He lifted his hand to her face, and she thought he was about to caress her cheek, but something passed over his eyes, and he dropped it. "I doubt that any woman would ever taste as good to me as you do." He sighed. "I wish you weren't repulsed by my bite."

"I'm not."

His eyes started to glow, and he lifted his hand again, this time making a feather-light contact with her cheek. "Are you sure? I saw you look away when I drank the blood."

When Emmett dropped his hand again, Eleanor fought the urge to lean into him. As annoying and as full of crap as he was, she still found him irresistible.

Maybe his potent Kra-ell pheromones were messing with her, but she was quite sure they weren't solely responsible for her reaction to him.

Emmett's masculine magnetism was about much more than a chemical reaction.

If Greggory was a Corolla—plain and reliable, Emmett was a Ferrari—sexy, sophisticated, powerful, and dangerous.

What was she, though?

Not a Corolla, because she was neither plain nor reliable, but not a Ferrari either, because she was neither sexy nor a great beauty. Perhaps she was a Harley-Davidson? Powerful, edgy, and opinionated?

Usually, she wouldn't have thought herself the type of woman a man like Emmett would go for, but he'd admitted to preferring assertive women.

She also had something even more desirable to him than beauty—delicious blood.

"I might have trouble watching you drink animal blood from a cup, but I'm not grossed out by your bite. Immortal males also bite during sex, and the sensation is so similar that, at first, I didn't even realize you were drinking my blood. It was pleasurable."

"And yet you tried to fight me off."

"I was taken by surprise and scared."

He lifted his eyes to the camera mounted near the ceiling. "What would happen if we tried that again?"

She followed his eyes. "It's probably not a good idea to try while we are being watched."

"Is there a way to solve this conundrum?"

As his fangs elongated, all the blood in Eleanor's body rushed to her core. She didn't feel fear. All she felt was an intense desire to once more experience his bite, but this time, along with everything else that came with it.

To hell with caution and waiting to get to know each other. Emmett was a captive audience. He couldn't leave even if he wanted to.

Emmett

Eleanor was ripe for the taking, but if Emmett made a move, the males of her clan would come rushing in and beat the hell out of him.

Would he have enough time to get a taste before they stopped him?

He was sure that they wouldn't activate his cuffs when he was so close to Eleanor, but there would be retribution. Besides, the immediate gratification wasn't worth the sacrifice of his most valuable playing card.

His only card.

"I wish there was a way," Eleanor whispered. "I asked them to mute the volume so we could talk privately, but they'll never agree to turn the camera off. If only there was something that would convince them it was okay to give me privacy with you."

Eleanor was moving in the right direction, and with proper motivation, she might find a solution. Perhaps she would even think of a way to sabotage the recording. Emmett didn't know much about surveillance, but he'd watched enough movies to know that there were ways to circumvent it.

Pretending to be deflated, he sighed and shifted away from her. "This is a small room, and the only place where the camera can't see us is in the bathroom. I would never dare suggest intimacy there." He smiled sadly. "It's not very romantic, is it?"

Surprisingly, Eleanor didn't agree with him right away and seemed to contemplate the idea. But then she shook her head, dispersing the mist of hope her hesitation had offered. "Even if I was willing to do that, the Guardians will see us going in there. They won't let it happen."

"That's what I thought." He took her hand and lifted it to his lips for a kiss. "I'm afraid that our relationship will have to remain platonic until Kian allows me out of here."

It was a damn shame that he couldn't sample Eleanor's delicious blood again, but if he played his cards right, he could charm her into falling for him even without sex. Emmett didn't know enough about the clan customs, but there was a chance that mating Eleanor would be his ticket to at least partial freedom.

If Kian didn't find any clues as to the Kra-ell's whereabouts, the offer he'd made Emmett would be null and void, but mating Eleanor might grant him the same reward.

He needed to explore the possibility without showing his hand.

Eleanor leaned her chin on her fist. "Do you think he ever will?"

"Not really." Emmett brushed his thumb over her wrist, eliciting a shiver. "The information I gave him was correct, but knowing my people, they didn't leave any clues behind for anyone to track them. And unless Kian finds breadcrumbs to follow, he's not going to let me out of here."

She nodded. "Is there anything else you can think of that would help us find them?" She glanced at the empty cup of blood. "Maybe going from one butcher shop to another and asking who their most frequent customers are?"

"That's not going to help. Blood is used in many Chinese dishes, and it's not unusual for butchers' shops to sell it."

"The quantities would be larger, though."

"Restaurants buy large quantities. Besides, human minds are easily manipulated, and just like your people, mine ensure they are not remembered." He put his other hand on hers and caressed it. "Maybe Kian will learn to trust me like he did with you. How did you pull it off?"

"They needed me for the mission because of my compulsion ability, and Kri vouched for me. It helped a lot having a friend who's a Guardian."

"What about other newcomers to the clan? How do they earn their place in the clan's society?"

She chuckled. "They mate a clan member. The belief is that the bond between true-love mates is so strong that it takes priority over everything else. A mate will never betray her or his bonded partner."

That was both fascinating and useful. Mating Eleanor might indeed be his ticket out of prison. "Is it just a belief? Or is it real?"

"At first, I thought that it was all a load of crap, but I've witnessed enough to no longer shrug it off as a myth. Just think how improbable it was for us to find Anastasia and Margaret in Safe Haven. When Anastasia's father hired Turner, and we agreed to help retrieve her, no one suspected that she was a Dormant." Eleanor paused. "Well, that's not entirely true. Her father told Turner about the voices in her head, and a paranormal ability is one of the strongest indicators of dormancy. But Margaret wasn't on anyone's radar. The Fates, or some other higher power, had something to do with her being there in the first place, and subsequently us finding her."

Emmett wondered if the clan's Fates and the Kra-ell goddess were similar entities. The Mother of All Life was also believed to shape people's destinies. But that was a discussion for another time. Right now, he wanted to find out more about Anastasia and Margaret, how they were discovered, who they had bonded with, and whether the bonds were enough for them to get accepted into the clan.

"Have they both transitioned?"

Eleanor shook her head. "So far, only Anastasia has transitioned. Margaret broke her leg when we staged the fake fire at Safe Haven, so even though she and Bowen seem to be an item, they haven't consummated their connection yet."

"Does she have a paranormal talent?"

He knew the woman well, and she'd never exhibited anything unusual.

"I don't think so."

"So how do you know that she's a Dormant?"

Eleanor's smug smile promised an interesting revelation. "Since her daughter transitioned, there is no doubt that the mother is a Dormant."

Talk about a huge surprise. The daughter Margaret had left behind with her abusive husband somehow ended up an immortal.

"Wendy joined the clan?"

Eleanor nodded. "She's mated to a fine young immortal, and now she and Margaret are reunited."

"I'll be damned." He shook his head. "I'm starting to believe in those Fates as well. How did Wendy end up with the clan?"

"She was in the government program that I recruited paranormal talents for. The clan came to retrieve Jin, who as Mey's sister was a confirmed Dormant, and several of her friends jumped on the escape wagon and joined them. The team brought a compeller along, and he overrode the compulsion I had placed on them to stay loyal to the program. Otherwise, none of them would have been able to escape."

"Was it the same person who overrode mine?"

Eleanor shook her head. "His brother. Lokan is a weaker compeller than Kalugal, but he was good enough to override my compulsion. I doubt he could have done anything about yours. His younger brother is incredibly powerful, but their father is even more so."

The clan's Fates must be smiling upon him because Eleanor was giving him a lot of information that he might find useful in the future. And because she was romantically interested in him, the audio surveillance was turned off, so the Guardians had no idea that she was revealing more than she was supposed to.

"Jin is mated to Arwel, correct?"

With a nod, that knowing smile bloomed on her face again. "And she might be related to you. In fact, she almost certainly is."

Eleanor

"What do you mean?" Emmett asked.

Given his shocked expression, Eleanor had a feeling that she'd said too much.

Why hadn't anyone told him about Jin and Mey? Wasn't Jin curious to meet Emmett?

"As I mentioned before, Mey and Jin were Dormants, and once they went through their transition, the sisters developed traits that were uncommon for immortal females. Also, their paranormal talents are unique and unheard of in the clan. It was suspected that they were descended from a different god or goddess, or that somewhere along the line the immortal genes have mutated. But now that we know about the Kra-ell, it's quite obvious that they were fathered by one of you."

Emmett's eyes blazed with excitement. "If that's the case, it means that our Dormants can be activated."

"I hate to disappoint you, but it's a no. First of all, the Kra-ell males probably can't transmit the immortal genes the same way our males can't. Mey and Jin wouldn't have them because you said only the Kra-ell males hooked up with humans, the females didn't. But even if the Kra-ell males could transmit the gene, they can't activate Dormants. If that was possible, Margaret would have transitioned a long time ago. The only way Mey and Jin could have been born Dormants and been able to transition was if their mother carried the immortal genes."

Leaning back, he smoothed his hand over his chin as if he still had a bushy beard. "What are the chances of one of our male hybrids encountering one of your female Dormants?"

"Probably none. It must have been fated."

He let out a breath. "Again with the Fates. Maybe it's the goddess."

"Annani?"

He waved a dismissive hand. "Annani might call herself that, and she might be very powerful, but she's not a real goddess. The Kra-ell believe in a female deity that is similar in power to the human God." He chuckled. "More similar to the biblical God of wrath the Hebrews believed in than the more modern interpretations of a benevolent deity that is full of love and compassion. Our Mother of All Life is vengeful and demanding like her Kra-ell female embodiments. She rewards fearless warriors who give their life in battle with heavenly mates who will cherish and adore them in a way their Kra-ell mistresses never did or would."

Eleanor tilted her head. "I thought that the Kra-ell didn't believe in love or even understand the concept."

He shrugged. "Believing in love is not practical for a society that has four males for every female, and since it's also very militant and aggressive, tender feelings are frowned upon. But I believe that the Kra-ell are similar enough to humans to have it in them to love. In order for us to be compatible and produce hybrid children, gods, immortals, humans and Kra-ell must have a common ancestry."

"Do you know that for sure? Or is it speculation?"

"It's an educated guess. Regrettably, the purebloods didn't share much with the hybrids, so I don't have the full story. They've never mentioned another species that was similar to them but even longer-lived. Still, I suspect that they knew about the people you call gods and were wary of them."

That was news to her, and probably also to everyone else who had interrogated Emmett. He hadn't said anything about his people suspecting that there were other immortals on earth, and neither had the guy who Stella had hooked up with twenty-something years ago in Singapore.

"What makes you think that?"

"I've often wondered about the need for extreme secrecy and the frequent moving from place to place. It seemed excessive if their only concern was discovery by humans. I thought it was because they knew of other Kra-ell groups and feared them, or just didn't want to be discovered by them. But after what I learned from Peter, I started thinking that maybe the purebloods knew about you."

If Emmett was right about the common ancestry, it was a logical assumption. If the gods and the Kra-ell came from the same planet or solar system, they probably had known about their neighbors' interstellar expeditions.

"It's a shame that your father didn't tell you anything about your origins." Eleanor pushed a strand of hair behind her ear. "I bet we could have learned a lot about ours from that."

A contemplative look passed across his eyes. "Just out of curiosity. What are Jin and Mey's special talents?"

She'd already told him a lot more than she should have, while he'd only disclosed a suspicion that he'd had about the Kra-ell being aware of the gods and their descendants.

"I'm not sure that I'm allowed to tell you that."

His thumb brushed over her wrist. "I'm only asking to see if their unique talents could be attributed to my people."

When she didn't offer him an answer, he continued brushing her pulse point with his thumb. "From what I could observe, the purebloods didn't have any special talents except for what you call thralling. So if Mey and Jin have uncommon talents, it could be that there is a third species of long-lived people on earth. Another explanation could be that those born to a Kra-ell male and a female descendant of gods are a superior breed."

Onegus

The café on Santa Fe Avenue was one of Kian's favorites, but it wouldn't have been Onegus's first or even fifth choice for meeting Cassandra, and the only reason he'd chosen it was its proximity to the keep and its outdoor patio.

Humans emitted too many smells, and whenever possible, Onegus preferred either outdoor dining or places that weren't overly crowded.

Hopefully, Cassandra wouldn't mind the vegan cuisine. It was actually pretty good, but not everyone appreciated the creative substitutes, like cashew macadamia cheddar cheese, or the espresso cashew flan with chocolate olive oil cake.

Onegus was still poring over the menu when he sensed Cassandra walking onto the patio. Something in the air sizzled, and he wasn't the only one who'd noticed. Every head lifted and turned to look at the stunning, statuesque beauty sauntering over to his table.

Dressed in a pair of palazzo white pants, a black blouse, black and white stilettos, and several gold necklaces of different lengths and widths, Cassandra looked classically elegant and every bit the cover model she used to be.

Rising to his feet, he greeted her with a smile and a chaste kiss on her cheek. "Every time I see you, I'm awed anew at your beauty and how well you accentuate it with what you wear." He pulled out a chair for her. "No wonder Kevin pays you so well."

She arched a brow. "Because of how I dress?"

"Because you have impeccable taste, and it translates into everything you create. There is a cohesiveness, a theme, and it's sophisticated and elegant." He waved a hand over her. "You are the most put-together woman I know, and that's saying a lot."

She rewarded him with a tentative smile. "Thank you. It's nice of you to notice."

"It's impossible not to." Onegus sat down and took her hand, just because he had to touch her, and that was the only way he could do so without causing a scene.

"Most guys just see the end result and have no clue what went into achieving it." She smiled. "And usually, I prefer that they don't."

"I'm not most guys." He winked. "And I have very discriminating taste as well." He leaned closer. "That's why I chose you. I love how creative you are, and that you apply it to everything you do."

"You are right about my personal style being an extension of my creativity and reflecting my eye for esthetics. It gives me pleasure to dress well. But some might say that I'm overdressed for today's casual work environment, or that a woman as tall as I am shouldn't wear high heels. Others might say that I'm vain for paying so much attention to my looks, and that I wear heels to intimidate people."

Lifting her hand to his lips, he kissed it. "It doesn't matter what anyone thinks. You should dress in a way that makes you feel good. I've seen you in shorts and sneakers, I've seen you in jeans and a T-shirt, and I've seen you in an evening gown and in a cocktail dress. You looked amazing in all of them. But, for some reason, this power look is my favorite so far." He leaned closer. "It's the sexiest."

That earned him a bright smile. "Sexier than nothing on at all?"

Tricky lady. "It's a hard choice." He leaned forward. "But it doesn't have to be. The sexiest thing would be for me to peel this beautiful outfit off you, one item at a time, until there is nothing left except for those gold necklaces."

As her fingers entwined in the delicate chains, her breathing became shallower, and her feminine scent flared. "They are not real gold." She shook her forearm, jingling the five bracelets on her left wrist. "And neither are these. I hardly ever buy real jewelry."

For some reason, Onegus didn't think it was because she was frugal. Gold jewelry wasn't that expensive, and Cassandra could definitely afford it. Maybe she had something against real gold?

"Why is that?"

She shrugged. "I like variety, and costume jewelry usually has more creative designs." She lifted her hand and wiggled her fingers. "Only the rings are real gold, but as you can see, they are devoid of precious stones. I chose them for the intricate designs."

"Beautiful." He didn't look at the rings. Instead, he gazed into her eyes.

She smiled. "Yes, you are."

The waitress stopping at their table disturbed the intimate moment. "What can I get you, folks?"

Tearing her eyes from his, Cassandra looked up at the girl. "I'm sorry, but I didn't have a chance to look at the menu yet. Could you give us a few more moments?"

"Certainly. In the meantime, can I get you something to drink?"

"I would like your chilled mint tea," Onegus said.

"I'll have the same." Cassandra lifted the menu, hiding her beautiful face from him. "On second thought, I'll have the cucumber juice."

Cassandra

It was a cowardly move to hide behind the menu, but Cassandra wasn't ready to bare her soul to Onegus yet. Maybe she would one day tell him why she didn't buy precious jewelry for herself, but it wasn't going to be today or tomorrow or even a month from now.

Maybe not ever.

She thought of real jewelry as gifts of love, not something a woman bought for herself—an engagement ring, a diamond bracelet for an anniversary, a necklace for her birthday, and so on. If she told him, he might take it the wrong way.

So yeah, a successful, independent woman shouldn't wait for a man to buy those things for her, provided that she really wanted them, but Cassandra didn't crave possessions for their own sake. Unless they were gifts, an expression of love, gemstones were meaningless to her. She could enjoy cubic zirconia just as much as she would a diamond for a fraction of the cost.

Not that she was into that either. Pure metals, gold and silver, or imitations of them were her thing.

But that was beside the point. She couldn't tell Onegus any of it because it would sound as if she expected him to buy her expensive gifts, and she would never do that. If the time came and he proposed, she would love a beautiful engagement ring, but she wouldn't expect anything extravagant. She wasn't after his money. She was after everything else—his heart, his soul, and his body.

Those were much more precious than any gifts he could ever buy her.

"Have you decided what you want to have?" Onegus asked.

She hadn't even read through the selection. "It's difficult to decide." She moved the menu aside to peek at him. "What do you recommend?"

"Pretty much everything once you get over the weird substitutes. For starters, I recommend the warm rosemary butternut squash dip with radicchio, or the winter butter lettuce and endive salad. For an entree, I like the forbidden black rice bowl. The southwestern-style enchiladas are also good."

As she glanced at the menu again, it finally dawned on her that it was a vegan restaurant. "Interesting choices." She looked up at him. "Josie, my boss's wife, is vegetarian. I need to tell her about this place."

"Before you do that, you need to sample the offerings."

"Of course. I'll take the salad and the enchiladas. If I don't like them, you can eat them." She lifted her hand to summon the waitress.

When the waitress arrived, Onegus ordered for her and then added three more appetizers, two main courses, and two juices.

"Are you that hungry?" Cassandra asked when the woman left.

"Vegan food is not very filling."

"Then why did you choose this place? I've seen you demolish a filet mignon the size of a loaf of bread, so I know that you are not vegan."

"I'm not, but my boss is, and this is one of his favorite places. It's also close to the building I currently work in, and it has a nice outdoor patio."

"Who's your boss? An uncle? An older brother?"

"My cousin is the head of the family business in the US. I don't have siblings."

That reminded her of his mother, and that she was about to meet her at the wedding.

"Isn't it difficult for your mother to be so far away from her only child? She must be lonely."

"My mother is never lonely. She's surrounded by extended family, and we talk on the phone quite often."

He winced. "She used to call me every day, but I've negotiated it down to no more than twice a week."

That was bad. Onegus's mother sounded like one of those tiger moms who were possessive of their sons. She wouldn't like sharing Onegus with another woman.

"Did she give you grief over it?"

"I'm a busy man, and I can't drop everything because my mother is bored and wants to chat. We had a long talk, and in the end, she understood that it wasn't because I didn't love her or didn't care about her, but because I held an important position, and I couldn't afford to spend hours on the phone." He folded his napkin and put it aside. "My mother is a strong-headed woman, and she can be unreasonably demanding at times, but she's smart and accomplished, and I have a lot of respect for her."

Fortunately, Onegus's mother lived in Scotland. Cassandra had a feeling that if the woman lived anywhere near her son, she would have been a major pain in her backside.

"Did you tell her about me?"

He shook his head. "I don't share my love life with my mother, and she doesn't share hers with me. Are you going to bite my head off for not telling her about you?"

"No, I get it. We've just started seeing each other. But she's going to see me at the wedding. How are you going to introduce me?"

He smiled, but the look in his eyes was indecipherable. "How would you like me to introduce you? My girlfriend? The lady I'm dating? My significant other?"

Perhaps there was tension between Onegus and his mother? His comment about not wanting to hear about her love life might have been a hint of that.

Not that it was a big surprise. It sounded like the woman wanted to dominate her son's life, but Onegus wasn't the kind who would allow anyone to control him, not even his mother.

Heck, maybe that was how he'd developed his resilience. It probably hadn't been easy for him growing up.

"Any of those will do. You said that your father passed away a long time ago. Has your mother remarried?"

It occurred to her that Onegus's mother might have eased up on the phone calls because she'd found a new man.

He leaned toward her. "I'll let you in on a secret. She was never married, and she doesn't even know who my father was."

That explained it.

"Oh, wow. We have that in common." Cassandra sighed. "I don't think my mother knows who my father was either. That's why she keeps making up stories about him. Or maybe she forgot who he was."

Except, her mother was a sweetheart, and it didn't sound like his mother was. But then Cassandra had always taken care of her mother, while Onegus had moved across the ocean from his. No wonder his mother felt neglected.

"Geraldine is a beautiful woman, and she looks incredibly young. How come she never married?"

Cassandra grimaced. "I don't know. I could understand why she didn't date when I was growing up, but I've been old enough to handle her having a boyfriend for many years, and yet she hasn't brought anyone home even once."

He arched a brow. "Perhaps she's not into men?"

Cassandra laughed. "Oh, she's definitely into men. But unlike me, she's all about casual hookups. She thinks I don't know that she's sexually active, and that I believe her outings are all about book club meetings and hanging out with her girlfriends. I'm just grateful that she's infertile and can't get pregnant again. With her memory issues, she would have forgotten about birth control. I just hope she remembers that pregnancy is not the only issue she needs to be worried about."

Onegus's forehead furrowed. "How do you know that she's infertile? Did she tell you?"

"She didn't have to. We used to live in a tiny apartment with only one bathroom, and until I got my first period, I never saw any of the feminine paraphernalia that's required to handle monthly cycles. My mother no longer gets periods, and she can't get pregnant."

"Maybe she was very discreet about it and kept everything hidden?"

Cassandra shook her head. "I would have known."

Onegus

Goosebumps rose on Onegus's arms. Subconsciously, he'd known there was something odd about Geraldine, but with Cassandra's latest revelation about her mother, the pieces had finally snapped into place.

Geraldine was an immortal.

He felt it in his bones.

Her youthful looks, the story of her driver's license getting lost, and her never applying for a new one, the lack of menstruation, and the gentle currents sizzling underneath the surface, all pointed toward her being an immortal.

Then again, he might be jumping to conclusions because he wanted Cassandra to be a Dormant. Geraldine might have had her uterus or ovaries removed after a complicated birth or for any other number of reasons, her youthful looks might have been the result of good genetics, and her memory problems could explain the lost license and her inability to get a new one.

"What happened?" Cassandra asked. "You look even paler than usual." She chuckled. "I'm dating Casper the friendly ghost."

He was glad that the waitress arrived with their appetizers, and he didn't have to respond. What could he tell Cassandra that wasn't a lie?

"Is there anything else I can get you?" the woman asked.

"If you can bring out the main courses as soon as they are ready, I'd really appreciate it." Onegus cast her one of his charming smiles. "I'm a little pressed for time."

"I'll check with the kitchen."

"Thank you."

Cassandra lifted her fork. "Let's see if this tastes as good as it looks."

He waited for her to take the first bite before attacking one of his three appetizers.

"Not bad." Cassandra took a sip from her cucumber juice. "I might come back."

"I'm glad you like it."

For the next several minutes they ate in silence, but his reprieve didn't last long.

"You haven't answered my question yet." Cassandra pushed her plate away. "Why did hearing about my mother's infertility bother you so much?"

He affected an indifferent expression. "I was just reflecting on how similar our families are. You are an only child to an unwed mother, and so am I. Your mother looks incredibly young, and so does mine."

If he managed to get Cassandra drunk during the wedding, she might not notice the other oddities about his family, but no matter how inebriated she was, she would notice that his mother looked too young to have a son his age.

She nodded. "Were you wondering whether your mother became infertile after having you?"

It seemed that his remark about his mother looking young had gone unnoticed. Cassandra was more interested in the infertility part.

"It has never occurred to me."

"That's because you are a guy, and men don't think about stuff like that. But now that I've brought it up, do you think it's possible that she never married because she couldn't have any more children?"

He knew for a fact that wasn't so. "My mother has a full life. I don't think she's interested in sharing it with a man." That was true in regard to a human male, but he was sure she would be overjoyed to find a true-love immortal mate. In fact, if she found her one and only, she might even give him a little brother or sister.

"That's my mother's excuse too. But sometimes I think that her infertility is my fault, that it happened to her because of my birth. According to Geraldine, I was born a big baby, almost ten pounds. She's a small woman, delicate, fragile, and delivering a huge baby like me might have caused complications that resulted in the removal of her ovaries. Geraldine denies it, but what if she just can't remember it? Or worse, what if the memory problems are the result of the mental trauma of losing her ability to have more children rather than a head injury? I might have singlehandedly ruined her life."

Was that why Cassandra took such good care of her mother? Because she felt guilty?

"Oh, Cassy." He reached for her hand. "That's a lot of what-ifs, and I'm sure none of them are true. Your mother adores you, and she regards you as the best thing that ever happened to her."

She let out a breath. "I know. But it kills me that I don't know for sure. I'm always torn between wanting to find out the truth about her past and respecting her wishes. I bet a private detective could have found out everything in a few days, and it wouldn't even cost me an arm and a leg. But if I hired one, the guilt would be even worse."

"I might be able to help you with that."

She arched a brow. "How?"

Roni could find out everything about Geraldine Beaumont in less than an hour, but telling Cassandra about his in-house hacker was not advisable.

"One of my cousins is married to a guy who works for the government, and he has a pretty high security clearance. I could ask him to run your mother's name through the database and see what comes up."

Letting out a breath, Cassandra closed her eyes. "I don't know about that. It's still snooping into things that my mother prefers to remain private. And it doesn't matter that it is you doing the digging, if you are doing it for me."

Margaret

"That's us." Leon stopped next to a house that was nearly identical to Wendy's.

"It's nice," Ana said without much conviction.

Margaret thought that it was beautiful. It looked brand new, and it had rosebushes in the front yard.

"Ready?" Bowen grabbed one side of her wheelchair, Leon the other, and together they lifted her over the stairs.

Once they set her down on the porch. Leon turned to Bowen. "Can you get the door?" He swung Ana into his arms.

Laughing, she wrapped her arms around his neck. "Carry me over the threshold, my love."

As he did, Bowen cast Margaret a tentative smile, and for a moment, she hoped that he would pick her up and carry her over the threshold as well. Instead, he put his hands on the wheelchair's handles and pushed her through.

Well, it was better than nothing.

Besides, they hadn't pledged their lives to each other like Leon and Ana had done. They weren't even officially a couple yet.

Or were they?

Despite voicing his intentions, most of the time Bowen was reserved with her. They'd gone out on a date and shared a few passionate kisses, but she didn't feel like his, and he didn't feel like hers.

Maybe she just didn't know what to expect. Her marriage had been a disaster, so that wasn't a good example. After that, she'd spent nearly two decades in a 'free love' community, where there had been no couples. Her only examples of what a loving couple was supposed to be like had been observing Leon and Ana, and now also Vlad and Wendy, Stella and Richard.

Her relationship with Bowen wasn't anywhere near that close, that loving, or that passionate.

Perhaps now that they had no more secrets between them, their relationship would flourish.

Emerging from the bedroom a little flushed, Ana waved a hand around the living room area. "This house is almost identical to Wendy and Vlad's. I like it, but it needs some redecorating."

Margaret had never lived in a house that nice. The one she'd shared with Roger had been okay, but she hadn't been allowed to make any decorating choices. Not that she'd been allowed to choose anything else. Roger had ruled over her with an iron fist. She couldn't do anything without getting his permission first, and if she'd dared to disobey, there had been consequences.

Shaking the bad memories away, Margaret shifted her focus to the furniture in the house. If it were up to her, she wouldn't change a thing.

Besides, she and Bowen would be staying with Ana and Leon only temporarily. Once the cast was off, they would move into a house of their own.

But what if things didn't work out between them?

What would become of her?

Perhaps she could get a job in the clan's sanctuary for rescued trafficking victims like they had discussed. If the position came with lodging, that would be a good plan B.

Ana paused her inspection of the living room to glance at her. "What do you think? Should we make it look a little more contemporary? I'm not a fan of all these boring earth tones. It's so nineties."

"I think it's gorgeous as it is. But if you want to decorate, go for it. It's your home."

Leon opened the fridge. "We need to get groceries." He looked at Bowen. "We can get some on our way back from the meeting."

"Right." Bowen cast a worried look at Margaret. "Are you going to be alright?"

She smiled. "Of course. While you are gone, Ana and I will unpack and put things away in the closets."

"I almost forgot." Anastasia slapped a hand over her forehead. "Wendy said that Syssi and Amanda are going to stop by tomorrow. Is there anything in the fridge that we can serve?"

Leon shook his head. "Make a list. Bowen and I will get everything you need on our way back from the meeting."

"It's going to be a long list."

Smiling, Leon pulled Ana into his arms. "It will be my pleasure to provide everything your heart desires."

As he followed with a passionate kiss, Bowen leaned down and pecked Margaret on the cheek. "You've had an exciting day. Try to get some rest."

Her gut squeezing, she nodded. "I need to unpack, but I don't plan on doing much else." They hadn't been apart since day one, and the thought of him leaving made her anxious. She cupped his cheek. "I'm going to miss you."

"Ditto." He smiled, but his facial muscles were tensed, making his jaw look even more prominent than usual.

"I'm going to wait up for you," she called after him.

"Don't. Onegus's meetings tend to be lengthy." He opened the door.

Tearing himself away from Ana, Leon followed his friend out the door.

Anastasia let out a breath. "It's difficult to be apart, but I will have to get used to that. We can't continue our honeymoon indefinitely." She cast Margaret a worried look. "Are you okay?"

"Yeah. I'm glad you convinced me to stay with you. It would have been scary for me to be left alone in a new place."

Wendy had to go back to the café, and Vlad had a school assignment he needed to work on. If she stayed at their place, she would have been all alone, counting the minutes until Bowen's return.

Ana smiled. "I'm glad that you are here as well. Let's check this place out. Do you want me to wheel you around, or do you want your crutches?"

"Definitely crutches. My bottom is feeling numb from sitting down for so long. I need to move."

Ana helped her up. "There are only two bedrooms in this house, but they each have their own bathroom and are about the same size. Leon says that the decor is slightly different, but I've only seen one so far, and we've rumpled the bed a little. I hope you don't mind."

Margaret was still stuck on the 'only two bedrooms' news flash.

She leaned on the crutches. "Am I supposed to share a bed with Bowen?"

Ana's forehead furrowed. "Is that a problem?"

"Of course, it is. We haven't had sex yet. It's going to be incredibly awkward. Perhaps I should stay with Wendy and Vlad after all. At least at night."

Ana shook her head. "What are you, seventeen? You are a grown woman, and Bowen is a grown man, and this is not the nineteenth century."

"I know. But we are not comfortable with each other yet. Bowen says that he wants more, but so far, we've only kissed. We need to date a little, get to know each other better."

"Nonsense." Ana waved a hand. "You've been together twenty-four-seven for almost two weeks. That's like dating three months. I say it's way past time for you to take it to the next level."

"It just doesn't feel right. Not for Bowen and not for me. Neither of us is ready."

Letting out an exasperated breath, Anastasia put her hands on her hips. "What are you going to do? Ask Bowen to sleep on the couch?"

"No. I can sleep at Wendy's place and come here in the morning. It's only a short walk away."

It was empty talk, and she knew that. Her defense mechanism was kicking in, trying to protect her from disappointment because she was afraid of rejection.

Grow a set, Margaret.

Was that what Ana would say?

"Suit yourself." Ana started toward the bedroom. "I'm going to unpack."

Bowen

"I hope they are still awake." Leon hefted a bunch of grocery bags out of the trunk.

Bowen glanced at his watch. "It's past eleven. Anastasia is probably awake, but I doubt Margaret is." He pulled out the rest of the bags and closed the trunk.

It had been a long and exciting day for her, and she'd looked tired when he and Leon had left.

"It's a bummer that we need to return to work tomorrow." Leon broke into a fast walk, no doubt anxious to get back to Anastasia. "But at least we are stationed at the keep, so we can see our mothers when they arrive."

Bowen fell into step with him. "Did you tell Rowan about Anastasia?"

"I've sent her a long text from the cabin, telling her the entire story. She can't wait to meet her. What about you? Did you tell your mother?"

Bowen shook his head. "At first, there was nothing to tell because I didn't know whether Margaret was a Dormant. And then everything happened so fast that I didn't have time to even think about it."

"How about now?"

"I'll tell her tomorrow, but I wish I didn't have to."

"Why?"

Wasn't it obvious?

Everyone was so excited, taking Margaret's transition for granted, but at her age, it was dangerous. The clan hadn't lost a transitioning Dormant yet, but that didn't mean that their luck would hold up forever.

"Margaret is thirty-eight, Leon, not twenty-five, and besides, we are not at that stage yet. Because of her injury, things are moving super slow for us. I would have preferred to tell my mother about Margaret after her successful transition."

"Elise is a strong woman." Leon chuckled. "She had to be to raise a hellion like you. If things get rough, she won't fall apart. She will help you through it."

"I know. But I would rather spare her the anguish if I could." He cast Leon a smile. "After all I put her through growing up, my mother deserves only the best from me."

Leon laughed. "You were such a troublemaker. Who could have foreseen that you would grow up to be not only a Guardian, but the savior of damsels in distress and an all-around standup guy? When did that transformation happen?"

Bowen hadn't told anyone the story because it hadn't been one of his proudest moments. Most of the Guardians were much younger than him and therefore unaware of his past. He'd been an unruly teenager who had run wild, joining a gang of human boys and using his superior immortal strength to become their leader. He'd believed that the mischief they'd done had been mostly harmless, but it could have gotten them in a shitload of trouble. At the time, he'd thought that stealing sheep and chickens was hilarious, and that releasing horses out of the stables and having them run wild was fun. He hadn't considered the damage they had caused.

"My mother, Onegus, and Annani happened. Nowadays, it would have been called an intervention. I was given a choice between hard labor, working on the addition to the castle, or I could join the Guardian training program, which was even harder. The idea was to keep me busy from sunrise to sunset, so I would be too exhausted to even think about causing trouble. I chose the Guardian force because that suited my overinflated self-image better."

Leon nodded. "Now I get it. I couldn't understand why they let you join the force at such a young age. You said it was because they recognized your potential early on. But you lied. It was a punishment."

"I didn't lie. Onegus said that I was a born fighter and that the force was my destiny. I was strong for a fourteen-year-old, and I had great reflexes. He put the fear of the Fates in me, saying that squandering the gifts they had given me would anger them. He also told me that I needed to use these gifts to do good and not waste them on stupid behavior that causes much more harm than I'd realized. Then he listed all the potentially catastrophic consequences of my so-called pranks, shaming me and making me feel smaller than a flea. After the scolding was done, he clapped me on the back and promised to put me on the right path."

Onegus had done just as he'd promised, and Bowen had discovered that being a protector and a savior was much more satisfying than leading a bunch of delinquent hoodlums.

"Didn't you want to be a healer at some point?"

Bowen shrugged. "I like helping people. If I weren't built for fighting, I would have turned to medicine."

Leon snorted. "You're not studious or smart enough for that. Can you see yourself sitting on your ass for sixteen hours a day and poring over books?"

"You've got a point. Perhaps I could have been a paramedic. This reminds me that I need to talk to Onegus about putting all the Guardians through some basic medical training. Firefighters are trained paramedics, and if we ever need to pull a similar operation again, our lack of knowledge could give us away."

"We probably won't." Leon climbed the steps to the front porch and knocked on the door with his foot. "And if we do, we can take Julian with us. The training would take too long, and we have more important things to do. But maybe it should become part of the curriculum for the Guardians in training."

"Good thinking. We don't need more than one person who knows what to do if a human gets injured. Margaret was lucky that Safe Haven had a nurse who helped her. If not for Shirley and the morphine shot she gave Margaret, she would have suffered needlessly. I don't think she would have made it to the hospital without passing out."

"You could have thralled her."

"True, but it would have been a damn intrusive thrall."

Margaret

Bowen was back.

Through the slightly opened bedroom door, Margaret heard him and Leon unloading groceries in the kitchen, and Ana commenting on what they'd bought.

She should have closed the door. The only reason she hadn't was the insane soundproofing of the house. When closed, no sounds penetrated the door or the walls, and the bedroom felt like a tomb.

She should have opened the window and closed the door, but it was too late to do it now.

If she got out of bed, Bowen would know that she was still awake, and she wanted to pretend to be asleep. That way, the decision to either join her in bed or sleep on the living room couch would be his, and she wouldn't have to invite him or comment on it or do anything at all. She could just pretend to sleep.

Damn, she was such a coward.

But it wasn't entirely her fault. Bowen was sending her mixed signals and confusing her. He claimed that he wanted her, but other than a few kisses, he hadn't initiated anything.

Maybe Ana was right, and they just needed to have sex and get it out of the way. They both wanted it, but they were both too reserved to go for it.

And then there was the cast.

Margaret had no clue how to maneuver around it, and even if they found a way, the sex would be awkward at best. That wasn't what she wanted, not for herself and not for Bowen.

She'd had enough awkward sex to last her a lifetime, even if it hadn't been more than a handful of times. Perhaps Emmett had done her a favor by spiking the wine he'd given her. It had taken care of the awkwardness, or maybe just her memory of it.

Roger, damn him all to hell, had been her first lover, and before he'd turned abusive, the sex had been quite good. After, she'd been too terrified to enjoy it even when he hadn't hurt her.

As the door opened a little wider, Margaret closed her eyes and forced her breathing to come out deep and even. She hadn't fooled Bowen, though.

"Would you like some tea?" he asked quietly.

Damn his immortal super senses.

"Sure." She opened her eyes and pushed up on the pillows. "How did the meeting go?"

Standing in the doorway and leaning against the doorjamb, the light from the living room framing him in a halo, Bowen looked like the warrior he was—big, strong, a rock she could lean on.

"As expected." He smiled. "Did you manage to rest?"

"A little. I can't fall asleep." She ran her hands over the mattress on both sides. "The bed is incredibly comfortable. I don't know what's keeping me from falling asleep."

Liar. She knew perfectly well what it was. She was too nervous about the sleeping arrangements.

"The tea will help." He pushed off the doorjamb. "I'll be right back."

Combing her hair with her fingers, Margaret arranged the blanket, so it covered her breasts. Her nightgown wasn't see-through, but without a bra, her breasts were a little saggy. They were still nice, nothing to be embarrassed about at her age, but Bowen had most likely seen nicer.

Also, it was cold in the room, and her nipples were standing at attention.

When he returned a few moments later with two teacups, she smoothed her hand over the blanket. "You can turn the light on if you want."

"I don't need it." He handed her the chamomile tea and sat on the bed next to her. "Do you?"

He'd left the door open, so the light from the living room was spilling in, and it was enough to see by. "No, I'm good." She took a sip from the tea. "It's just what the doctor ordered."

Had he left the door open on purpose?

"Anastasia told me that you were concerned about the sleeping arrangements."

She was never going to speak to Ana again. How could she?

"There are only two bedrooms." She looked down at the cup in her hands. "It's not that I don't want you sleeping in the same bed as me. It's just that we haven't been intimate yet, and it seems awkward."

Bowen

"It doesn't have to be." Bowen reached for Margaret's hand. "Forget about what you think the rules are. You and I don't have to follow any of them. We can share a bed and just hold each other, or we can spoon, or we can lie on our backs and tell each other bedtime stories. And if we feel like kissing, we kiss. And if we feel like touching each other, we touch. I have absolutely no expectations. All I want is to be with you."

That got a smile out of her. "I want to be with you too. If not for the damn cast..." She lifted her eyes to him. "It's the cast, right? That's why you are holding off?"

He nodded. "I might be weird that way, and I know that most guys would have found a way to work around it, but I'm too afraid of hurting you." He lifted her hand to his lips and kissed it gently. "I want our first time together to be special, and I can wait patiently for the cast to come off." He smiled sheepishly. "Frankly, not so patiently, but I'd rather wait. There is only one first time, and I don't want to shortchange it for either of us. Are we on the same page?"

"I feel the same way. You know that I'm attracted to you, and if not for my injury..." Margaret lowered her eyes. "I'm not the type who is bold enough to initiate. I wish that I was assertive like Ana, but I'm not." She lifted her eyes to him. "I can't make the first move." She swallowed. "It will have to come from you."

It was her way of letting him know that he had her permission, but Bowen needed it verbalized better.

"That's perfectly fine with me." He kissed her hand again. "As soon as this cast comes off, the wait is over, and you are mine. Deal?"

She chuckled nervously. "Deal. I'm just...not sure that you really want me. I mean, most guys are not that patient."

Bowen arched a brow. "You think?" He took her hand and put it over his raging hard-on.

Her eyes widened. "Oh, my."

As Margaret's feminine scent intensified, his shaft responded by twitching against her hand.

She looked nervously at the opened door. "That's just... wow."

"Leon and Ana are in their room. They can't hear us." He removed her hand and gave it a little squeeze. "Do you still think that I'm not attracted to you?"

She licked her lips. "Now, I think that I want to do something about it." She sounded breathy. "May I?"

Her intention was clear, and as he imagined them pleasuring each other orally, his fangs started to elongate, and his venom glands swelled.

Margaret's breath hitched. "Your eyes are glowing."

He smiled, flashing her his partially elongated fangs. "Are you sure that you're ready for all that I am?"

She hesitated for a split second. "Yes."

Her yes hadn't sounded convincing, but as the smell of her fear mixed with that of her arousal reached his nostrils, the predator in him clawed to be let up to the surface.

That wasn't good.

If he didn't take the edge off before getting in that bed with her, he might do something he would regret, or worse, he might hurt her.

Leaning down, he kissed her forehead. "It was a long day, and I need a shower. You have until I come out of the bathroom to decide whether you are absolutely sure about being ready for me. If you are not, that's perfectly okay. We can do all those things that I've mentioned before. Spooning, or cuddling, or telling each other bedtime stories."

"Oh, Bowen." She lifted her hand and cupped his cheek. "How can you be so sweet?"

"Sweet?" He curled his lips back, letting her get a good look at his fangs. "I'm trying to do the right thing by you, but I'm still a predator. You should never forget that."

"I won't." She lifted on the pillows, letting the blanket slide down and expose the swell of her ample breasts. "I like that you are a fierce warrior. I feel safe with you because I know you will never use your strength against me, only for me. You can protect me until I transition and become strong enough to protect myself."

There would never be a situation in which Margaret would need to defend herself. That was his job.

"There is no safer place for you than this village, and as long as you are with me, which I hope is forever, I will protect you."

Margaret

Long moments after Bowen had gone into the bathroom, Margaret's heart was still pounding against her ribcage.

He hoped that she would be with him forever?

As what?

His life partner or just a fellow resident of the village?

She shook her head. That was stupid.

Back in the cabin, Bowen had said that they had found love there, and that he believed they were destined for each other. Perhaps it was time she stopped doubting his feelings for her and whether she was worthy of him.

She might be a broken doll who was held together by strings, but for some reason, the Fates deemed her worthy.

She knew next to nothing about statistics, but there was no way that their meeting hadn't been guided by a higher power.

The Fates had arranged for her to meet Bowen.

Thinking back to the woman who'd told her about Safe Haven, Margaret had a feeling that she hadn't been who she'd claimed to be. Perhaps the Fates that the clan believed in took over mortal bodies on occasion or compelled them to be their mouthpieces.

She wondered how Ana had first learned about Safe Haven, and if she'd also encountered someone who'd told her about it. Except, these days the Fates didn't need to use people to deliver their messages. They had the internet at their disposal, and instead of sending a human, or speaking through one, they could manipulate technology, sending the right Facebook ads or YouTube videos to those they wished to influence.

Wow, that was a profound realization.

What if those meddling Fates had helped create those channels of communication precisely for that purpose?

And that led her to another more disturbing thought.

Anyone with the right resources could do that through social media. As a novice, she might have paid more attention to the way it worked than those who had been using it since its inception, noticing that the ads she saw were definitely custom-tailored to her interests, and so were the videos YouTube suggested for her. She could see how easy it could be to take it a step further and use it to promote agendas that had nothing to do with commerce.

Margaret shook her head. That wasn't what she should be thinking about right now. What she needed to decide was whether she wanted to get intimate with Bowen tonight, or wait until the cast came off so they could make love no holds barred.

On the one hand, he excited her like no man ever had, and she wanted him. But on the other hand, she wanted to enter their relationship whole, and give it all she had. If she transitioned successfully, they would have eternity ahead of them and there was no need to rush things. They'd known each other less than two weeks, and although for some it might have been considered long enough, for her, it really wasn't even if she wasn't injured.

She'd let Roger take her virginity two weeks after meeting him, and that hadn't ended well for her. Bowen wasn't Roger, but it wasn't about him.

It was about her.

Margaret was no longer that naive eighteen-year-old girl who'd thought that her body was the only thing she had to offer. She might not be much of a catch, but she was wise and experienced enough to know that the love and companionship she brought to the table were no less valuable than sex, probably more.

Hey, how was that for a new-found self confidence?

She was making progress.

Perhaps she should write it down and later design a workshop around it.

Theoretically, that all made sense, but as the bathroom door opened, and Bowen stepped out with only a towel wrapped around his hips, logic flew out the window, and desire took over.

He was such a magnificent male.

She wanted to run her hands all over those defined muscles, feel that warm, smooth skin under her fingers, and kiss every inch of him.

He smirked. "Like what you see?"

"Like is too mild of a word," she breathed. "You are a god."

"Just an immortal." He sauntered over to the dresser and started opening drawers. "Where did you put my briefs?"

For a moment, she contemplated not telling him. If he couldn't find them, he would have to come to bed naked.

He looked at her over his shoulder. "Did you hide them on purpose?"

She shook her head. "I didn't. But maybe I should have."

Turning around, he dropped the towel. "Should I keep looking? Or should I get in bed?"

"Bed." She licked her lips. "Definitely get in bed."

Cassandra

It was after midnight, but Cassandra couldn't fall asleep. Her late lunch with Onegus had left her unnerved for several reasons. First, it had been the talk about her mother's murky past and Onegus's offer to investigate it, and then it had been the kiss goodbye that had left her hot and bothered.

Perhaps she should take the edge off with her neglected battery-operated boyfriend. Would it count as being disloyal to Onegus?

She snorted. Bob didn't count, and neither did her fingers, especially since she would be fantasizing about Onegus while pleasuring herself.

When her phone buzzed on the nightstand, a smile spread over her face. No one other than Onegus would be texting her in the middle of the night.

Lifting the device, she read the message. *Are you awake?*

She answered. *Yes.*

Her phone rang a moment later. "What are you doing awake after midnight?"

"Waiting for you to call." She pushed up on the pillows, dragging the blanket up to cover her bare shoulders. "How did it go with your mother?"

"We had a cup of coffee together, chatted for a little bit, and said good night. She was tired."

"Did you tell her about me?"

"Yes."

"What did you tell her?"

"That I met a sexy lady who is gorgeous, talented, smart, and has impeccable taste."

"What did your mother say to that?"

"That you must have great taste because you chose me."

Cassandra rolled her eyes. "Now I know why you are so full of yourself. It's your mother's fault."

"Isn't it every mother's job to think her child is the best there is?"

"I guess. Where are you now? Are you still at work?"

"I'm in bed, but I can't fall asleep."

"Why?"

"I can't stop thinking about you and how your lips tasted when I kissed you goodbye earlier today."

"How did they taste?"

"Like more. Are you naked?"

Cassandra laughed. "You sound like a pervert."

"Are you?"

"No."

"Can you get naked?"

"Quite easily. All I have on is an old T-shirt."

"No panties?"

"Nope."

He hissed. "Take it off."

"I'm not activating the camera."

"I'm not asking you to. My imagination can fill in the details."

"Oh, yeah?" She tugged the T-shirt up over her breasts, exposing them. "What did I just do?"

"Did you bare your beautiful breasts?"

"Good guess."

"Play with them."

She rimmed her left nipple with her finger. "I can only do one at a time because I'm holding the phone."

"Activate the speaker."

"Nah-ah. My mother might hear you."

"Right." He sounded disappointed.

"Are you naked?" She flipped the tables on him.

"I always sleep in the nude."

Imagining all those rippling muscles, she licked her lips. "Are you playing with yourself?"

"I wouldn't call it playing."

"What would you call it, then?"

"Strangling the snake, slapping the salami, waxing the eel, having a tug of war with a Cyclops."

She laughed. "I haven't heard any of those except for the salami one."

"I have plenty more. Choke the chicken, polish the knob, the five-knuckle shuffle."

"That's funny, but not very sexy."

"I agree. I'd much rather hear about what your fingers are doing."

"Nothing yet." She trailed her hand down her belly. "I'm inching my way down south."

He groaned. "Are you wet?"

"I don't know. I need to check."

She'd been aching since that kiss, so yeah, she was wet. Slipping a finger down her moist folds, she bit on her lower lip as she circled her throbbing clit.

Her hips arched of their own accord.

"Well, are you?"

"Very," she said on a hiss.

"Are you fingering yourself, Cassy?"

"Ah-hum." Sliding her fingers deep, she stifled a moan.

Imagining that it was Onegus's hand and his fingers that were plunging inside her, she repeated the move, but her own slender fingers couldn't compare to his, couldn't deliver the same kind of pleasure.

Trailing her hand back up, she cupped her breast and squeezed, then lightly pinched her nipple.

"Talk to me, Onegus. Tell me all the naughty things that you want to do to me."

"It will be my pleasure."

As his masculine voice whispered in her ear, Cassandra smoothed her hand down her belly until the tips of her fingers reached her moist center.

Spreading her legs wide, she closed her eyes and listened to his voice, imagining that he was there, doing all those naughty things he was describing in detail, and when she careened over the edge, it had been Onegus's hand that had brought the release.

On the other side of the line, she heard him groan, and as she imagined his strong hand pumping his manhood, his essence erupting and landing on his taut stomach, another release tore through her.

Kian

"It's too early in the morning for a meeting." William walked into Kian's office with two tall cups of coffee in his hands.

"The Sanctuary people are arriving today, and some of the Scots arrive later tonight. I need to get everything out of the way as early as I can."

"My brain isn't fully awake before ten." He handed Kian one of the cups.

"That's because you work until two o'clock at night." Kian took a sip before putting the cup down. "How is the Kra-ell language coming along?"

"Slowly but surely." William sat down and put his briefcase on the conference table. "I put two of my assistants on it, but we are dependent on Emmett providing us with word lists, and he's taking his sweet time."

"Obviously." Kian sat at the head of the table. "He doesn't want us to decipher it too quickly. Maybe I need to pay him another visit and issue some threats."

"What's the rush? I've already deciphered the email he sent to his former mistress."

"Amanda came up with an interesting idea. We could send Mey with Arwel and Jin to China, so she can listen to the walls of the Kra-ell's old compound. The problem is that she needs to understand what she hears, and for that, she needs to learn the Kra-ell language."

William arched a brow. "Did she agree to go on the mission?"

"I haven't asked her yet. She and Yamanu are joining us for the meeting today, together with Jin and Arwel. Given that Jin has already agreed to go and lend her particular talent to the mission if needed, I assume that Mey won't say no. It would be like going on a family vacation."

"Can I go?" William lifted the cup to his lips.

"Why would you want to?"

"I've never been to China. I'm curious."

Kian shook his head. "I can't risk you. You are irreplaceable."

"So are Yamanu and Arwel and Jin and Mey."

"Of course. Each individual is precious. But I meant strategically. You are the only one capable of deciphering the gods' tablet and understanding the technical instructions, and you are far from done with that. Without you, all that knowledge will become useless to us."

"Speaking of the gods' tablet." William pushed his glasses up his nose. "I discovered a few common words between their language and the Kra-ell's."

"I'm not surprised," Kian said. "They either come from the same place or have a common ancestor. Otherwise, they wouldn't be similar enough to humans and to us to be sexually compatible and produce hybrid children."

William nodded. "I have a feeling that the Kra-ell language is much older than the gods'."

As a knock sounded on the door, Kian rose to his feet and opened the way. "Good morning."

"Yeah, about that," Jin grumbled. "Any reason you summoned us at the ungodly hour of six-thirty in the morning?"

Arwel cast her a warning glance, but she waved him off.

Kian chuckled. "You have to forgive me. My schedule is a bit crazy during the celebrations."

Mey, always the polite lady, smiled apologetically for her sister and dipped her head in greeting. Next to her, Yamanu grinned happily as if an early morning Friday meeting was his favorite thing to do.

"Please, sit down." Kian motioned to the conference table.

"You are probably wondering why I called you here today." Kian returned to his seat.

"I can guess," Mey said. "You want me to listen to the echoes of conversations left by the Kra-ell in their old compound."

"Correct." Kian clicked on the remote, activating the large screen hanging on the east wall of his office. "This video was shot with a drone by one of Turner's contacts in China. As you can see, the compound is no longer occupied by the Kra-ell and is used as a boarding school for international youth. It's bilingual, classes are taught in English and Chinese, and its goal is to foster integration between Chinese and Western cultures."

"When was the school established?" Arwel asked.

"1991." Kian clicked the video off. "Unfortunately, digging out information about who occupied it before and what happened to them is impossible. Roni can't hack into the Chinese government records because he's unfamiliar with the encryption protocol they are using. I believe that in time he will crack it, but for now, boots on the ground is our best bet for finding out more information."

Mey pushed a strand of hair behind her ear. "Yamanu and I can pretend to be prospective American parents who want their children to learn about their Chinese heritage. The problem is that I can't listen to the walls when there are other people in the room. We'll have to infiltrate the place at night."

"That's not the only problem." Kian drummed his fingers on the table. "Even if you hear echoes of Kra-ell conversations, you won't understand what's being said. You don't speak their language or even Chinese."

Mey's face fell. "Then there is no point in me going." She glanced at Jin. "I was actually looking forward to sharing an adventure with you and Arwel."

"How good are you at learning new languages?" Kian asked.

Mey winced. "Good, but not good enough to learn two extremely difficult ones in a few weeks."

"You don't have to get fluent. All we need to find out is where the Kra-ell moved to. If you spend a couple of hours with Emmett every day until it's time to go, you can learn most of the words associated with moving, trips, addresses, etc. And the same is true for Chinese. Actually, he can teach you both."

"You mean Jin and me?"

"I meant Kra-ell and Chinese, but having Jin with you is a good idea. She needs the lessons just as much as you do."

Jin groaned. "I wish there was a chip William could implant in my head that would translate what I hear. I've spent months studying Mandarin, and all I have to show for it are a few badly pronounced sentences."

Rubbing a hand over his jaw, Yamanu smiled. "What if we get Kalugal to compel you to learn faster? Do you think it might work?"

Jin shook her head. "Forget about it. I'm not letting him do that to me. It's enough that I have to suffer through learning this accursed language voluntarily. I can't even think about being forced to do it."

"And I'm not looking forward to spending time with Emmett," Mey said. "Those people got rid of Jin and me as if we were garbage."

"It wasn't Emmett's doing." Kian leaned his elbows on the table. "He was treated as a lesser being by his own father. Besides, he's an interesting fellow, and you might enjoy his company. Aren't you curious to find out more about your parents? He might know who they were."

"I don't give a shit about our father or fathers, but our mother is a Dormant." Jin looked at her sister. "If we find out where they moved to, we might be able to rescue her."

Mey nodded. "Not only her, but also the other humans they keep enslaved." She let out a sigh. "I'm in. I'll do what I can to help."

"You will both have to wear earpieces," Arwel said. "And I will be there to keep an eye on Emmett and make sure that he behaves."

"What about Stella?" Jin asked. "She's traveled extensively in that area. She must know Chinese."

"She probably does, but she could only function as a translator. I don't know how helpful that would be. I need to think it through."

Margaret

After Bowen and Leon left for work, Anastasia stood with her back to the front door, her hands on her hips, and scanned the living room.

"Can you move and sit at the counter?" she asked Margaret.

"Why?"

"I want to push the couch closer to the wall." She looked at the fireplace. "Or maybe to the side. I don't like where it is."

"It's centered on the fireplace." Margaret used the crutches to push to her good foot. "Isn't that where it's supposed to be?" She collected her phone and her notes and hobbled to the kitchen counter.

"It's boring. This place looks like a hotel room. I want to make it feel homier."

"Perhaps you should wait for the men to get back and do the furniture moving for you."

"Nah." Ana waved a dismissive hand. "I'm strong now, and I'm getting stronger every day. I don't need help."

"Knock yourself out." Margaret touched the phone screen to wake it up.

Perhaps it was pointless to keep preparing the workshop she'd started working on in the cabin, but she had nothing better to do. Besides, if she were to get a job at the rescue center, or sanctuary, as they called it, she could modify the workshop to fit a mostly young female audience. Chocolate-making was sure to be a hit with the girls, but it would have to get approved by the therapist who was running the show.

Hopefully, she would like the idea.

The sound of Ana's phone pinging with an incoming message stopped her mid-shove. She left the couch in the middle of the living room to get it.

"We have visitors in fifty-five minutes," she said after reading the text. "Syssi and Amanda are coming over."

Margaret swiveled the barstool around. "Remind me who they are?"

"Syssi is the boss's wife, and Amanda is his sister. They both work in paranormal research, hoping to discover more Dormants."

"Are they scientists?"

"Leon told me that Amanda is a neuroscientist, but Syssi is an architect by profession. She started working for Amanda to learn more about her own paranormal talent, but after meeting Kian and transitioning, she decided to stay in the lab and help Amanda with the research instead of pursuing a career in architecture."

"Did they find many Dormants that way?"

"I don't know. We can ask them when they come over."

Margaret rearranged her skirt around her legs. "I wish I had something nicer to change into. I'm tired of wearing the same two dresses all the time." She chuckled. "I shouldn't complain. I've been wearing the equivalent of a uniform for nearly two decades. Those dresses are a vast improvement over that."

"You're waking up, discovering who you really are. Clothing is a form of self-expression." One corner of Ana's lips lifted in a smile. "Speaking of waking up. How did sharing a bed with Bowen go?"

Margaret felt heat rise up her cheeks. "It was nice."

"Just nice?"

It was the best night of her life, and given that what they could share had been limited by the cast, it was only a taste of what was still to come.

"That's all you are going to hear from me."

"Meanie." Ana shoved the couch back into place as effortlessly as if it was a chair. "The rearranging of furniture will have to wait for after the visit."

She'd become really strong. If Margaret had been that strong when Roger knocked her around, she could have beaten the crap out of him.

The thought made her smile.

Maybe after she transitioned and became as strong as Anastasia, she could go back and confront him.

Nah, he wasn't worth the aggravation. She was starting a new life with Bowen, she had her daughter back, and Roger was a pathetic loser she shouldn't waste even a single thought on.

As far as she was concerned, he was dead.

The lightness that filled her following that simple decision was like a breath of fresh air. She should forget that he'd ever existed, but that was impossible to do. They'd created Wendy together, and her daughter would always be a reminder of him. Thankfully, the resemblance didn't evoke any negative feelings. Wendy was beautiful, and some of it had come from Roger, but her character didn't resemble his in the slightest. She was pure sunshine and positivity.

Ana fluffed the pillows, unfolded and refolded the throw blanket, and took a step back to examine her work. "Maybe I'll just leave it like that."

Margaret rolled her eyes. "That's what I suggested."

"I should prepare some snacks." Anastasia walked into the kitchen. "I thought that they would come around noon, and I'd serve them lunch, but it's too early for that. Any suggestions?"

"Maybe some cut-up fruit and nuts would do as a mid-morning snack? Or you can just serve the chocolates Bowen got me along with tea or coffee. Everyone likes chocolate."

"I'll prepare a fruit and cheese platter and serve it with crackers."

"Even better."

Onegus

Onegus glanced at his watch. It was nearly noon, and he hadn't planned on calling Cassandra, but he had to at least hear her voice to ease the irritation crawling over his skin.

Only she could calm that incessant itch.

Last night, he'd kept her awake past one o'clock in the morning, and the memory of her stifled moans had kept him up much longer than that. His hand had been busy, bringing him one release after another, but nothing save for Cassandra's slender neck could ease the pressure in his venom glands.

Perhaps he could meet her for lunch somewhere?

He fired her a quick message. *Are you free for lunch?*

Her return text came several minutes later. *Sorry for the delay. I couldn't hear the incoming message over the din in this store. What do you have in mind?*

She was shopping?

Wasn't she supposed to be at work?

Instead of texting, Onegus rose to his feet, closed the door to his office, and called her. "Where are you?"

"In Glendale. I took the day off to get a new dress."

"Why Glendale?"

"That's where my favorite store is."

Glendale was about half an hour away, provided that there was no traffic, but it was Friday, which meant the worst traffic of the week.

With a sigh, he leaned back in his swivel chair. "What about shoes? Are you going to wear the same ones you wore to the gala?"

She laughed. "I'm starting to think that you are even more into shoes than I am. Do you have a shoe fetish?"

"Not really. I just have a thing for those particular shoes on those particular feet. Are you about done with shopping?"

"I'm an efficient shopper, and I only needed a dress. I already have the shoes and the jewelry."

"You could've worn the same dress too. I don't know why you bothered. I'm wearing the same tuxedo to the wedding that I wore to the gala."

"No one remembers your tuxedo, and no one cares if you wear it to every function until it falls out of fashion. But whoever saw my pictures from the gala in the gossip magazines would recognize the dress. I needed a new one."

"Is it sexy?"

"Obviously, but it's also classy and elegant. Don't worry, I'm not going to embarrass you."

"The thought never crossed my mind. Can you meet me for lunch in the same place we met yesterday?"

She didn't answer right away. "Is your place still full of people?"

"Worse. I had to give it up for an unexpected guest, and now I'm sleeping on a cot in my underground office."

That was a lie. He'd spent last night in the Guardians' apartment in the keep. The place was like a frat house, so he might spend tonight in one of the renovated cells in the dungeon, but he couldn't tell Cassandra about either.

"Why are you the one in charge of taking care of the guests? It would seem to me that it's beneath your station."

Ouch.

"I'm part of a team of people who are in charge of coordinating everything, but I'm not in charge of the hospitality part. I coordinate the security, which is a huge headache with so many civilians coming in."

"Now I get it." She chuckled. "You are in charge of security and only moonlight as the face of your family business."

"You've got it. My cousin, who is the real head of the business, doesn't do well in social settings. I'm considered the charming one."

"Oh, you are charming, which is great for attending the annual gala, but your day job explains your bossy attitude."

"You like my bossiness, which reminds me that I still owe you a spanking."

"Well, you can't do that over lunch in a public place, so it's not happening."

Had he imagined it, or had she sounded a little breathy?

The hellcat was intrigued, and he was hard as a hammer. "How can we make it happen?"

"Instead of going out for lunch, you can come to my house. I'm walking toward my car as we speak."

"What about your mother?"

"She has a nail and hair appointment at one o'clock, and she won't be done until at least three."

That was plenty of time, but he didn't want her to miss out on time spent with her mother if that was the plan. "What about you? Aren't you joining her for the nail and hair thing?"

"Mine is tomorrow." She chuckled. "I feel like I'm on vacation. I took the day off to go shopping, and tomorrow I'm getting pampered in a salon."

"Speaking of vacations. You still didn't give me an answer about going away with me."

"To that secluded cabin? That's not my idea of a romantic vacation."

"What about a trip to Paris on a private jet?"

"Now you're talking."

She thought he was joking.

Paris wasn't a good destination as far as inducing Cassandra somewhere secluded, but she was going to love it, and that made the trip worthwhile.

"I'm serious. After the family festivities are over, I can take you for a weekend in Paris. I'm sure you can swing that."

"You said festivities? Is there something other than the wedding going on?"

It was so like Cassandra to latch on to the irrelevant part of what he'd told her. "My cousin's birthday is the following Wednesday. But forget about that. What about Paris?"

"How soon do you need an answer?"

Onegus shook his head. With any other woman, it would have been an automatic and enthusiastic yes.

"We can talk about it when I come over to your place."

She laughed. "I don't think we will be doing much talking."

Margaret

"Margaret." The tall brunette looked as if she wanted to pull her into her arms like she had done with Ana, but the crutches gave her pause. "It's a pleasure to finally meet you." She offered her hand instead. "I'm Amanda."

The boss's sister, who was way too gorgeous to be a neuroscientist, and who was very obviously pregnant.

"The pleasure is all mine." Margaret smiled as she took the woman's hand.

"And I'm Syssi." The other pregnant lady offered her hand. "Welcome to the village." She shook Margaret's hand and then Ana's. "I apologize for not welcoming you yesterday. With the entire family gathering for the wedding, Amanda and I had prior obligations we needed to attend to."

"Perfectly understandable." Ana motioned to the couch. "Please, make yourselves comfortable."

Margaret made her way to the armchair and lowered herself into it gingerly.

As Amanda and Syssi sat on the couch, Amanda turned to Ana. "I didn't have a chance to congratulate you yet. How does it feel to be an immortal?"

"Awesome." Ana grinned. "I'm so strong now, and it's not just physical. I feel like I can conquer the world."

"Good for you," Syssi said. "Do you plan on finishing your law degree?"

Ana nodded. "Eventually. For now, I want to play house with Leon for a little bit."

"What about the voices?" Amanda asked. "Are they still bothering you?"

Ana hadn't mentioned them, and Margaret felt bad for not asking. The voices had been the main reason Anastasia had joined Safe Haven. They had been a major disturbance in her life.

"I think Leon banished them." Lifting both hands, Ana crossed her fingers. "May they never return. I certainly don't miss them."

"Interesting." Syssi tried to reach for a piece of fruit, but her huge pregnant belly was in the way. "Maybe the sole purpose of the voices was to get you to Safe Haven so you could meet Leon. The Fates play a very long game."

Ana rose to her feet and lifted the tray for Syssi. "Then it was worth the suffering, and not just because I met the love of my life thanks to the voices. If I hadn't met Leon,

I would have never found out about my dormant genes and wouldn't have turned immortal."

"About that." Margaret motioned for Ana to bring the tray to her. "How does it work?" She took a strawberry.

"The transition?" Anastasia asked.

"Yeah. I know that you received a transfusion. But what was in it?"

Syssi and Amanda exchanged glances, and then Amanda cast her a pitying look. "Bowen hasn't told you how a female Dormant transitions?"

She shook her head. "Is it different for males?"

"Oh, boy." Syssi groaned. "Should we tell her?"

That sounded ominous. "Please do. You are scaring me."

Amanda hesitated for about two seconds and then nodded. "Bowen should have told you, but with everything that was going on, he probably couldn't find the right time. Usually, it's the mate's job to do the explaining, but since you are a confirmed Dormant, I guess it's okay for me to tell you. You know about the fangs, right?"

"Of course." Margaret felt her cheeks heating up. Thankfully, her skin rarely reddened, and she was able to hide her embarrassment.

Last night she'd experienced her first bite, and it had been better than any drug she'd ever messed with. Bowen had pleasured her orally and then bitten her inner thigh, sending her on a trip no psychedelic could ever deliver, but it wasn't only about the intense pleasure and the chain of orgasms she'd experienced. The venom's lingering effects were therapeutic and invigorating.

Margaret felt better today than she'd felt in years.

"In addition to the venom's aphrodisiac and euphoric properties, it also acts as a catalyst, activating the dormant immortal genes." Amanda leaned forward. "Have you experienced it already?"

With all eyes on her, Margaret was sure that the rising heat was visible on her cheeks. "Yes."

"Did Bowen use protection?"

That was an intrusive question, but given Amanda's serious expression, Margaret figured that it was somehow relevant.

"We didn't get there yet." She pointed at her cast. "Bowen is afraid of hindering my recovery. Besides, condoms are not needed. Everyone in Safe Haven was checked for STDs, and I got regular contraceptive shots."

"I see." Amanda leaned back. "The reason I ask is that to induce transition, two things are needed. The venom bite and insemination. The contraceptive shot wouldn't have interfered with the process, but a physical barrier would."

Margaret couldn't believe that Ana had lied to her. Well, she could understand why Ana had done it initially, but she'd had plenty of time to correct the misconception after Margaret had learned about her transition.

She turned to her friend. "Did you make up the infusion part?"

"I received liquids intravenously, so I just went with your assumption." She chuckled. "I learned from Leon how to walk the thin line between not actually lying but not telling the truth either."

"You should have told me."

"I'm sorry. At first, I had no choice because I needed to keep it a secret, and later, I just assumed that Bowen had told you."

"In any case," Amanda continued. "I'm pretty sure that your knee has to heal before you can transition. The process is very taxing on the body, and we have learned from experience that a Dormant must be healthy before it can begin."

Syssi shook her head. "I don't think that a broken knee is the same as a body weakened by pneumonia. We should check with Bridget."

"It doesn't matter," Margaret said. "Anyway, Bowen is not going to have sex with me until the cast is off, and I'm in no rush. I can wait."

"You should see Bridget anyway." Amanda pulled out her phone. "Maybe Bowen's bite can speed up your recovery." She winked at Margaret. "How's that as an incentive for lots of fun time?"

Cassandra

"The Uber is here," Cassandra yelled from the first floor. "The guard just called."

"I heard the phone." Her mother came rushing down the stairs, her hair flowing behind her like a dark curtain.

"Have fun, Mom," Cassandra called after her. "And I'm sorry I couldn't drive you to the salon."

"That's okay." Geraldine threw the front door open. "Say hi to Onegus for me."

As the door closed behind her, Cassandra let out a breath. How had her mother known that she was expecting him? She hadn't told her about it, only that she needed to catch up on work. Had the mid-day shower she'd taken as soon as she'd gotten home given her away? Or was it her outfit?

She'd debated between a casual sundress and the black shorts she'd worn to their first date on the beach.

The dress was nicer, and Onegus appreciated her putting effort into dressing elegantly, but she remembered how he'd ogled her backside when she'd worn the shorts, so they won. A loose silk camisole with spaghetti straps went on top. It was dark blue, which allowed her to forgo a bra, and it draped very nicely over her small breasts.

It was a casual, slouch-around-the-house outfit, and Geraldine should have thought nothing of it.

Whatever.

Cassandra was a grown woman, and if she wanted to invite her boyfriend for an afternoon quickie, that was no business of her mother.

What she should be worried about was whether Onegus would make good on his promise to spank her and whether she'd allow it.

It was a sexy fantasy, and it got her tingly in all the right places. When her nipples stiffened, poking through the delicate fabric of her camisole, she cupped her breasts and breathed in and out slowly, trying to calm her raging hormones.

It didn't help, and as soon as the guard at the gate called to let her know Onegus was there, her breathing turned into panting.

Damn, she was like a cat in heat.

"Not a cat," she corrected herself. "A tigress." One that was about to pounce on Onegus as soon as he crossed the threshold.

When the knock sounded at the door, she threw it open, grabbed the front of his dress shirt, and yanked him down toward her.

Luckily, he didn't need to be told what to do next. Smashing his lips over hers, he cupped her bottom, lifted her up, and kicked the door closed behind him.

"Tell me that your mother is not home."

"She left a few minutes ago." Cassandra wrapped her legs around his waist, threaded her fingers through his tight curls, and attacked his mouth again.

He tasted of coffee and man, of desire and strength, and she couldn't get enough of him. His tongue swept in, plundering, and then he was carrying her up the stairs as if she weighed nothing while still kissing the living daylights out of her.

She expected him to tumble with her onto her bed, but instead, he pressed her against the quilt-covered wall, his body pinning hers, his manhood a hard length pressing against her core.

Letting go of her mouth, he traced a line down the column of her neck, licking, kissing, nipping. And when he clamped his teeth over the spot where her neck met her shoulder, she hissed, not from the slight ache, but from the surge of desire rushing through her. He let go, the hurt immediately soothed by a quick swipe of his tongue.

She had a fleeting thought that his teeth were damn sharp, but it eddied away as his lips traveled up her neck, kissing, his tongue licking, his hot breath tickling her ear.

Her breasts ached, needing the attention he was paying to her neck. Yanking the bottom of her camisole, she pushed it up, baring them to him in a blatant invitation.

Onegus groaned, and a moment later, she was hoisted higher on the wall, so her nipples were perfectly aligned with his hot mouth. He latched onto one, suckling it so hard that he made her see stars. Then he let go and soothed the ache with gentle swipes of his tongue.

How was he so strong? And how sexy was it that he could hold her up so effortlessly.

Onegus did the same with her other nipple, never halting the grinding movement of his hips and the press of that maddening hardness that Cassandra couldn't wait to feel inside of her.

She let her head drop back, saved from banging it hard thanks to the cushioning of the thick quilt she was pressed against.

Her mother would be tickled silly if she knew what her handiwork was being used for.

Perhaps a different mother would have been aghast, but not Geraldine. Heck, she might have made it especially for that purpose. After all, it had been her idea to hang it on the wall instead of using it as a bedspread.

With her camisole still bunched up under her armpits and hoisted up high, there wasn't much Cassandra could do other than thread her fingers through Onegus's hair. But that wasn't where she wanted to touch him.

She wanted to peel his clothes off, to kiss and lick every inch of his warm skin, and to run her hands over those perfect muscles it was stretched over.

"Let me down," Cassandra whispered.

Onegus let go of her nipple, looked up at her, then back at her straining nipples, and then up again. "Bed?"

"Oh, God. Yes."

Onegus

To bite, or not to bite, that was the question.

And the answer was a roaring, definitely bite.

Onegus had bitten Cassandra only once, had been inside her only once, and he needed to do both soon or he'd explode. He was a patient male with an iron will and firm control over his primal responses, but even he had his limit, and it seemed like he'd reached it now.

Fighting the urge to just toss Cassandra on the bed and rip those sexy-as-sin shorts off her, he laid her down gently and hooked his fingers in their waistband. Thankfully, there was enough stretch in the fabric to allow peeling them off her without bothering with the zipper.

She helped, lifting her magnificent bottom so he could pull them down. Her panties went along with the shorts, and as he tossed them on the floor, the only piece of clothing remaining on her was the bunched-up camisole.

Cassandra took care of that, yanking it over her head and tossing it on the floor to join her shorts and panties.

The lady wasn't shy, not with her body and not with anything else. Cupping her small breasts, she parted her legs, creating a perfect cradle for him.

"Your turn." Her hooded eyes roamed over his still fully-dressed body.

Smiling, he started on the buttons of his dress shirt, his fingers steady despite the urge to just rip the thing off. He lasted two buttons and then pulled it over his head and tossed it.

Cassandra sucked in a breath. "I will never tire of seeing you undress. You must train for hours every day to look that good."

His grin got wider. "Not really. I have good genes." Ones that she might be sharing. As he unbuckled his belt and dropped his pants, he might have flexed his abdominals a little.

Her eyes riveted on the bulge stretching his undershorts, Cassandra licked her lips. "Take them off."

"Bossy today, are we?" He hooked his thumbs in the waistband. "I still owe you a spanking, but luckily for you, I'm too impatient to get inside you to play games."

As he pushed the undershorts down and his shaft sprang free, Cassandra parted her legs even further and trailed one slender hand down to where she was already sleek and glistening. "Condom," she breathed.

"Right."

He'd almost forgotten, which wasn't like him. Unlike many other immortal males who thralled their human partners to think that they were using protection, Onegus had been using condoms faithfully ever since they'd come out on the market. Before the recent years of Dormant discoveries, it hadn't been about accidentally inducing a Dormant like what had happened to Eva. It had been about avoiding fathering a mortal child.

With Cassandra, however, it was a valid concern. She was almost certainly a Dormant, and he had no intention of inducing her transition without obtaining her consent first.

Bending at the waist, he retrieved his slacks and pulled a packet out of the pocket. "Do you want to put it on me?" He walked to the side of the bed, his shaft saying hello in person.

"Yes." Cassandra shifted up and took the packet from him.

"But first, I need a taste."

He tensed, and when she wrapped her hand around him, he hissed. Her grip was surprisingly strong, just the way he liked it, and when she flicked her tongue over the head, his shaft rewarded her with a pearly offering.

"Hmm." Cassandra licked it off while looking up at him. "Tangy." Leaning down, she took nearly one-third of his length into her mouth.

Taken by surprise, Onegus nearly came. Gritting his teeth, he held his fangs at bay with a herculean effort, fisted her hair to hold her in place, and pulled out of the wet heat of her mouth.

"Perhaps I should give you that spanking after all."

She looked at him with a challenge in her eyes. "Didn't you like it?"

"I liked it too much." He motioned at the condom. "Put it on."

"Yes, sir," she said mockingly before tearing the packet open.

The minx could really use a good spanking, but it wasn't going to happen today. Regrettably, he had no time to play.

Somehow, despite her long, elegant nails, Cassandra managed to sheath him expertly without tearing the condom.

When she was done, Onegus pushed her back on the pillows and climbed in between that inviting cradle. "I'm not going to be gentle."

"I don't want you to be." Her eyes issued a challenge.

The beast in him wanted to rise to that challenge and surge into her with one swift thrust, but he stifled the urge and teased her opening instead, coating his shaft with her juices. Looking into Cassandra's eyes, he pushed in slowly, letting her body dictate the pace.

"I need you," she panted, lifting her hips and urging him to go deeper.

With a growl, he drove into her, seating himself fully.

Cassandra cried out, and as her long nails dug into his back, scoring it, the slight hurt snapped the last of his restraint.

Giving in to his baser needs, Onegus pounded into her without holding back. It was dangerous to let go like that with a human, but he knew that he wouldn't last long, and she was strong enough to take it for a short while, especially since he was going to bite her in the end.

Any bruising he might cause would be healed by his venom.

Cassandra took all he had to give, her moans and mewls accompanying the banging of the headboard against the wall to create the erotic music of abandon.

His favorite.

With her scent flooding his senses and shredding the last vestiges of civility, his seed rose up in his shaft, and when he was about to climax, she turned her head, offering him her neck.

Sending a slight thrall into her mind, Onegus struck, biting hard.

Her body jerked under his, reaching the peak and hurtling over it at the same time his did.

When he was spent, Onegus retracted his fangs and licked at the bite marks, sealing them, and then gently pulled out. He was still hard as a club, but regrettably, he had no time to wait for Cassandra to come down from soaring on the euphoric cloud so they could go for a second round.

After disposing of the condom, he covered her with the blanket and took a moment to gaze at her blissed out, beautiful face.

Perhaps Cassandra felt him looking at her because she smiled, but she didn't open her eyes.

After getting dressed, he kissed her cheek, her forehead, her parted lips, but it was to no avail. She didn't wake up, was probably still soaring, and it wasn't fair to shorten her trip.

He'd call her later, maybe in a couple of hours, to check on her and tell her...what? That he was grateful? That she'd rocked his world? Some witty combination of the two that his mind was too hazy at the moment to come up with?

Hopefully, by the time Cassandra woke up, he would figure it out.

Bowen

"I'm leaving," Bowen told Leon as he returned from escorting guests to their suites. "You'll have to catch a ride back home with one of the guys."

Leon cast him a worried look. "What happened?"

"Amanda made an appointment for Margaret to see Bridget, and Margaret wants me to go with her."

"Did you get permission from the boss?"

"Of course."

Their shift was less than half over, but he'd texted the chief and asked to be released earlier. Onegus had accepted his request on the condition that Bowen found a Guardian to trade shifts with.

"Who is taking over for you?" Leon asked.

"Mason. He agreed in exchange for me taking over half of his night shift."

It was a steep price to pay, especially after last night and this morning. It had been revelatory to share a bed with Margaret, and he would have loved to do the same tonight, but he would have to settle for spending just half of it holding her in his arms.

"Is it about her cast?"

"Among other things." Bowen grimaced. "Amanda also explained the induction and subsequent transition processes, and Margaret wants to find out whether her healing injury is an obstacle."

"You didn't tell her what's involved?"

"When? There was no time."

Leon arched a brow. "You could have told her last night."

"Margaret was tired."

Leon's brow hiked even higher. "Really?"

If the guy was waiting for details, he could keep on waiting. "I'll see you later." Bowen headed to the elevators.

His mother's flight had been delayed, and she'd arrived only an hour ago. He'd barely had time to tell her a condensed and highly edited version of how he'd met Margaret and the story of her being Wendy's mother. Naturally, Elise couldn't wait to meet Margaret and wanted to come to visit right away. After explaining that Margaret was still shell-shocked and needed time to wrap her head around her new reality, he'd managed to convince his mother to wait until the wedding.

That reminded him that Margaret needed something nice to wear for the event, but he had no time to take her shopping, and it was too late to order online. Some items could be delivered overnight, but he doubted it included clothing.

Amanda could probably loan her something. Margaret was a little shorter and a little slimmer, but maybe Amanda had a dress that could fit her.

Except, he wasn't close enough to the princess to ask her for a favor. Who else was tall and slim but more approachable?

Sari. He'd gotten pretty friendly with her during the crisis with David's parents. She wasn't as slim or as tall, and her wardrobe wasn't nearly as robust as Amanda's. Besides, she'd probably brought with her only what she needed for the visit. Perhaps he could ask her to talk to Amanda on his behalf.

Nah. He was overcomplicating things. He would just take Margaret shopping after the doctor's visit. Hopefully, she wasn't too picky and would be quick about it.

When he parked the golf cart in front of Leon and Anastasia's house, he had a plan. He climbed the steps to the front door and knocked.

Anastasia opened the door. "Why did you knock?"

He shrugged. "It's your house."

"The four of us entered it yesterday evening for the first time together. For now, it belongs to all of us."

He found Margaret in the bathroom, brushing her hair. She turned and smiled at him. "Did I get you in trouble with your boss?"

"Not at all." He pulled her into his arms, lifted her, and sat her down on the counter. "It was torture to be away from you. Thank you for providing me with an excuse to come home early." He took her lips in a long, passionate kiss. "Are you mad at me for not telling you about what it takes to start your transition?"

She shook her head. "There was no time. Besides, it sounds like much more fun than an infusion, which is what I thought I was going to get."

He rested his forehead against hers. "I can't wait for this cast to come off."

"Neither can I."

"Let's see what Bridget says. Maybe it can come off sooner than we thought." He lifted her into his arms and carried her out to the golf cart.

"Amanda said that your bite can speed up my recovery." Margaret rearranged her dress over her legs and then waited until he got behind the wheel to whisper in his ear, "That's one hell of a bonus on top of the most intense pleasure I've ever experienced."

The grin that spread over his face stayed there until he parked the cart in front of the clinic. He had to force it off so he wasn't caught looking like a fool.

"It's embarrassing to be carried in," Margaret said softly.

"But it's more efficient. Besides, I enjoy it."

"So do I."

After last night, things had changed between them, and they were all good. Margaret was much less reserved, and she finally seemed to be embracing what they shared.

"Good afternoon," Bridget greeted them. "Let's go in there." She pointed toward a patient room. "You can set Margaret down on the exam table."

After he had done as she'd instructed, Bridget politely kicked him out. "You can wait in the front room or you can wait outside on the bench. I'll call you when I'm done."

"Can't he stay?" Margaret asked.

The doctor shook her head. "I'm going to remove the cast, and knowing how overprotective mates are, I'd rather Bowen wasn't there when I cut it off you."

"Oh." Margaret paled. "I wasn't expecting that." She cast a worried look at Bowen.

"I promise to behave." He crossed his arms over his chest. "I'll stand next to the wall and won't move from there."

Given her grimace, Bridget didn't like it, but she nodded. "One growl and I'm kicking you out."

"Deal."

Margaret

"I feel so light." Margaret lifted her leg. The cast was off, replaced by a light brace, and the doctor had said that it was okay to put weight on the foot of the injured knee.

"Are you up to doing some shopping?" Bowen carried her back to the golf cart only because she was missing a shoe.

Margaret laughed. "I don't think any store sells just one shoe."

"Very funny." Bowen set her down and hopped into the cart on the driver's side. "You need a dress for the wedding."

Her eyes widened. "Am I invited?"

"Of course."

"But you'll be working. What am I going to do there all alone?"

"You are not going to be alone, and I can be with you while keeping my eyes open for trouble and carrying concealed weapons. Being on duty only means that I can't get drunk. But since none of my friends can drink either, I don't mind." He cast her an amused glance. "You'll be missing out on lewd Scottish ballads."

"Can you sing me one?"

"You won't understand it."

"I want to hear you sing."

"Fine." He started so quietly that she could barely hear him over the wheezing noise of the golf cart's engine.

It still sounded beautiful to her. Bowen had a deep, masculine voice. Sexy, and as he got into it and upped the volume a little, his lilting accent and timbre raised goosebumps over her arms.

Now that the damn cast was off, there were no more excuses. Tonight, she was going to seduce him and make love to this magnificent male she could finally call her own and not feel like a fraud.

When the song ended, Bowen parked the cart in front of the house. "You can wait here while I get your other shoe and one of the crutches." He turned to her and smiled. "That's all you need."

She frowned. "You were serious about the shopping."

"I have to wear a tux to the wedding, and everyone is going to be formally dressed. You need an evening gown, and there are only two ways you can get one on such short notice. One is to go to the mall, and the other is to borrow a dress from Amanda. The selection in her closet is probably better than any high-end boutique's, and it's all designer stuff."

"I can't ask Amanda for a dress. I barely know her. Do I really have to go? I don't know the bride or the groom, and they don't know me."

"You are my mate. Of course, you have to come. Besides, I promised my mother that she could meet you at the wedding. That was the only way I got her to agree not to come to the village this evening."

Margaret's throat constricted.

Damn, she'd been so sure that she would never be gripped by panic again, but here it was. First of all, Bowen had called her his mate. That was a big deal. And then he'd reminded her about meeting his mother.

Breathing through it, Margaret forced herself to relax.

She wasn't wary of meeting Bowen's mother. Not after what she and Bowen had shared. The sense of panic was a knee-jerk reaction stemming from her old self-doubt.

Something had changed in her last night.

Maybe it was the way Bowen had worshiped her body, or the incredible pleasure she'd experienced, or maybe it had been the bite's effect or the venom's, but she felt like a new woman.

She was happy and hopeful in a way she hadn't felt since before her parents had died and her world had dimmed.

She hadn't realized it up until now, but she'd lived in darkness long before ever meeting Roger. Perhaps her despondency had drawn him to her, or perhaps she'd been too numb to notice how horrible he was. Margaret had no doubt that she would have never fallen prey to him if her parents had been alive and her world had been whole.

Turning to Bowen, she put a hand on his arm. "I need a dress, shoes, makeup, and a visit to a hairdresser. Can we manage all that in one afternoon? I want to look good when I meet your mother."

Bowen grinned. "I'll make it happen." He leaned and cupped the back of her neck. "You are beautiful to me as you are, but if you want a new hairdo, you are going to get one." He smashed his lips over hers.

The kiss was interrupted when the door opened and Anastasia stepped out. "Are you going to smooch for much longer? I want to know what the doctor said."

Reluctantly, Bowen let go of Margaret's lips. "Couldn't you have waited a few more minutes?"

Ana crossed her arms over her chest. "I was worried that poor Margaret would suffocate. She is still human, you know."

"Not for long." Margaret lifted her leg to show Ana the new brace. "The doctor said that my knee is mostly healed and that I can walk on this leg. She also prescribed as many venom bites as Bowen can manage to speed up my recovery."

A grin spread over Ana's face. "That's awesome. We need to celebrate with a bottle of wine." She uncrossed her arms.

"Later," Bowen said. "I'm taking Margaret shopping for an evening dress and to a hair salon."

Ana's eyes sparkled with excitement. "Can I come? I planned on wearing the black dress Amanda got me, but if you are going shopping, I might as well get something fancier."

Bowen didn't look happy, but Margaret lifted her hand to stop him before he could refuse. "Of course, you can come. I need your style expertise. Mine is terribly out of date."

Bowen

Bowen had expected to suffer through the shopping expedition with Margaret and Ana, but it turned out to be not as bad as he'd thought it would be.

Sitting in the food court, he was reading an article on his phone when he was interrupted by a call from Leon.

"How is it going?" his friend asked, a note of amusement in his voice.

"Better than expected. Your mate is an experienced shopper, and she's helping Margaret choose the dress and everything else. All I have to do is wait for them to be done."

He'd given Margaret enough cash to cover even the most extravagant gown along with everything else she needed. Naturally, she'd been shocked at the amount, saying that she wouldn't spend even a fraction of that, and once she got a job, she was going to pay him back.

To avoid further arguments, he'd nodded, but he had no intention of ever accepting her money. He had plenty, and it made him feel good to be able to pamper her. Fates knew that she deserved it after the miserable life she'd had.

"Have they been to the hair salon yet?" Leon asked.

"No." Bowen glanced at the time. "They have an appointment in less than half an hour, and the receptionist promised to have them out of there in an hour. My torment is almost over." Not that he was suffering.

"Which mall are you at?"

"The Oaks."

"I could join you there for dinner."

"It will have to be something quick. I need to get back for the night shift."

"Onegus is a bastard. He knows your situation. He should have just given you the time off with no trade-off."

"Not his fault. He told me to find someone to trade with, and Mason agreed to take over the rest of my day shift only if I took the first half of his."

"You'll be back by three in the morning. That's not so bad."

"Yeah. Margaret will be asleep, but at least I can wake up with her in my arms."

Bowen interpreted the silence that followed as Leon debating whether he should ask him about last night. Thankfully, his friend had more tact than that. "Anastasia told me that Bridget removed Margaret's cast and gave her a brace instead. That's good news."

"Yeah. She said that the knee is healing nicely."

Leon hesitated for another moment. "Then there are no more obstacles in the way of Margaret's transition. You can start the process."

Bowen's shaft hardened at the thought, but then as worry washed over him, it deflated. "I didn't tell her yet."

Leon chuckled. "Ana said that Amanda did that for you."

"She told her what's involved, but she didn't warn her about the risk. Margaret doesn't know that it can potentially kill her."

"It won't. The Fates didn't bring you together only to end it that way. You are a good guy, Bowen. They wouldn't do that to you."

"That's all superstition, and I can't put my faith in it. The risk exists, and I need to tell Margaret about it."

"Naturally. But I disagree with your lack of faith. We haven't lost a Dormant to transition yet. Not Andrew, who was forty at the time of his transition, and not even Turner, who was forty-something and not in good health. I think that we have enough circumstantial evidence in favor of affirming the Fates' involvement. It's not a superstition when it's proven true time and again."

Bowen raked his fingers through his hair. "What if Margaret gets scared and refuses to go through with it? She told Anastasia that she didn't want to live forever. That life was hard and sad and that she couldn't understand why anyone would want to prolong the misery."

"A lot has happened since."

"That conversation took place yesterday morning. How much could have changed for her since then?"

There was another pause. "Last night changed things for both of you. I could tell that just from looking at you and Margaret this morning at breakfast. She seemed like a different woman. There was a sparkle in her eyes that hasn't been there before, and her smiles were genuine rather than forced or polite. She looked happy. Hopeful."

Bowen had seen that too. And her excitement about getting a new dress and a hairdo was like a breath of fresh air. Before, Margaret hadn't wanted anything for herself.

It saddened him to think that after spending half of her life in Safe Haven, she had nothing worth retrieving from there.

"I'll tell her about the risk tonight before I leave for the shift."

"If you want, you can tell her over dinner, so Ana and I can support you if needed."

That wasn't a bad idea. "I might take your advice on that. Do you want me to check which restaurants are in the vicinity and make a reservation?"

"Nah. I'll do it. Knowing you, you'll choose a hamburger joint."

"As you wish. Make it for seven-fifteen in case the hair salon takes a little longer than expected."

"No problem. Any preferences?"

After the hamburger joint comment, he wasn't about to make any suggestions.

"Whatever you choose is fine."

"Good deal. I'll text you the name and address."

Eleanor

"Let's go over the schedule." Arwel dropped a yellow pad on the coffee table.

Eleanor snorted. "What happened to the scheduling software you were testing?"

"Too much work." Arwel pulled out a pen. "It takes me less than five minutes to write it down, and there are no glitches where everything I worked on disappears because I pressed the wrong key."

Eleanor glanced at the monitor, checking on Emmett, who was supposed to write a dictionary of basic Kra-ell words, especially those that had to do with travel and locations. Kian wanted it done yesterday, which meant that her time with Emmett had been cut to nothing. Her job was to bring him food and leave right away, so he could work on the Kra-ell-English dictionary.

Peter opened the fridge and pulled out a bottle of water. "When are you heading out to China?"

Arwel cocked a brow. "Can't wait to get rid of me?"

Peter twisted the cap off and straddled a chair. "This is my first command. I'm eager to start."

The five of them were gathered around the small dining table in Arwel's suite, which served as their makeshift conference table. It was an intimate setting that she preferred to the one in Kian's office. For some reason, every time Eleanor participated in a meeting over there, she felt like she didn't belong. Here, everyone treated her as part of the team, and it felt good.

Jay cast him a look that Eleanor couldn't decipher. Was he mad that Peter had gotten promoted ahead of him? Or did he just doubt Peter's ability to be in charge?

Eleanor's first impression of Peter had been that he was a light-hearted, take-it-easy kind of guy who didn't take the initiative unless he was forced to. But she'd learned that there was more to him.

Perhaps Jay didn't know Peter as well as she did.

"Kian wants the team to leave after the guests are gone." Arwel leaned back in his chair. "My last day here is going to be next Friday, and I'm only working the first half of the day tomorrow." He picked up the yellow pad. "We need to work out a schedule for the wedding. Since it's right here in the keep, you can take turns. I suggest dividing it into one-hour shifts, so each of you gets to enjoy at least some of the party." He glanced at Eleanor. "By the way, several of Kalugal's men are invited to the wedding, so that's an additional level of security."

Great. If Greggory was one of those who were invited, she'd pass.

Alfie grimaced. "You think? I'd say that they are an additional level of complication."

"They pledged alliance to the clan, and it was cemented by Annani's compulsion. And unlike most of our civilians, they are trained warriors. I say that's an asset and not a liability."

"You're a head Guardian," Alfie said. "So you must know best."

As the two continued to argue and then Peter and Jay added their comments, Eleanor tuned them out.

She'd planned on attending the wedding, or at least some of it if possible. It would have been a great opportunity to mingle, maybe dance with some of the males and see if she responded to any of them.

Getting to know Emmett better, Eleanor was no longer distraught by her attraction to him, but she would've preferred to bond with a pleasant immortal clan member instead of the enigma who might be putting up an act to win her over to his case.

The problem was that she didn't have a date, which would have been fine as long as Greggory wasn't there. But if he was invited, the last thing she wanted was to see him dancing with other females and enjoying himself while she played the role of wallflower.

What if no one invited her to dance?

"I'll cover the wedding," she blurted. "You guys can go and enjoy yourself."

Arwel shook his head. "I can't leave you alone in charge of Emmett. Besides, why don't you want to attend the wedding?"

"Because someone decided to invite some of the ex-Doomers at the last moment, and Greggory might be one of them. I don't want to watch him having a splendid time with the clan females and gloating over my single status."

Peter put a hand on her shoulder. "We can go together and pretend to be a couple. Would that work for you?"

"Thanks for the offer, but no. That would defy the purpose. I planned on checking out other men, but with you by my side, no one would dare to approach me."

Alfie snickered. "They wouldn't dare even without Peter pretending to be your date. You're a scary female."

She flipped him the finger.

"What about Emmett?" Jay asked. "I thought the two of you were getting cozy."

"We're getting to know each other, but we are far from cozy. Besides, I want to keep my options open. Emmett is definitely not the guy of my dreams."

"Of course he's not." Peter wrapped his arm around her shoulders. "I am."

He was teasing, but there was a tiny kernel of truth in his words. The attraction was there, and if not for Emmett's magnetic pull, she might have given Peter a chance.

Except, their attraction to each other was so mild that there was no chance that they were fated mates.

She was female, and he was male, and that created an unavoidable sexual tension, but it was nothing either of them would write home about, so to speak. They were good friends, and they were sharing a home, which they weren't using at the moment because of the assignment in the keep.

Casting him a grin, she leaned into his arm. "Back to the schedule issue. I can guard Emmett on my own, and you can all enjoy the wedding without missing a thing. If you are worried about me being alone with him, I won't even go inside. We can give him a large meal before you guys leave, so I don't have to go in at all. And if there is an emergency, I can call one of you to come over."

Arwel nodded. "Since we will be right here in the keep if you need us, I'll consider that. But if I let you guard him alone, I don't want you opening his door under any circumstances, is that clear?"

"Crystal."

Margaret

As the hairstylist swiveled Margaret's chair to show Anastasia the final result, Ana gasped. "Wow. You look like a model."

The stylist joined Ana to admire her work. "You have a beautiful facial structure, but the dark hair made your cheeks look too hollow. The blond highlights soften your face."

"Thank you." She smiled at the stylist. "I'm glad I listened to you about that."

"And I'm glad that you are happy with the results."

"Your hair looks gorgeous too," Margaret returned Ana's compliment. "The guys' jaws are going to drop when they see us." She took the crutch that had been resting against the stylist's work counter and pushed to her feet.

It felt so good to actually walk instead of hobbling, to wear leggings instead of a dress, and to have shoes on both feet. New shoes that were black ballet flats instead of the white sneakers or snow boots that she used to wear in Safe Haven.

Anastasia grinned. "Bowen is going to faint." She lifted the shopping bags off the floor. "Let's go get him."

At the sight of those bags, guilt speared through Margaret.

Since the evening dress she'd gotten had been on sale and not nearly as pricy as Bowen had expected, Ana had convinced her to get some new everyday clothes, and once she'd started, she'd just lost it and bought a whole new wardrobe. Leggings, blouses, T-shirts, and jackets. Bras, panties, and shoes. It was good that Ana was an immortal now and had the strength to carry all of their purchases.

"I went overboard," Margaret said after paying for her hair. "I'm so embarrassed."

Ana snorted. "You think that's a lot? You've only spent a fraction of what Bowen gave you."

"It's still more than I've ever spent on myself. I'm writing down every penny he spends on me, and I'm going to pay him back as soon as I have a job." She groaned. "At the rate I'm going, I'll owe him a year's salary."

"Drama much?" Ana cast her an amused look. "Before Safe Haven, I would spend twice as much as you did today on every shopping run. You didn't buy that much, and everything you got was on sale. Besides, Bowen will never accept money from you, so you can just forget it."

"I'll make him take it. I don't want to be dependent on a man ever again. Not even Bowen."

Ana's eyes softened. "Oh, Margaret. I get why you feel that way, but if you say those words to Bowen, you are going to offend him. You're bundling him together with the likes of your ex. Don't do that."

Margaret swallowed. "I'm not. But I really want to be independent. How can I phrase it so it won't sound as if I'm comparing Bowen to Roger?"

Ana shrugged. "Just accept what he gives you for now, and as soon as you start earning an income, use your own money to buy groceries and things for the house. Don't make a big deal out of it. That's my advice."

"I don't want him to think that I'm a leech."

"Bowen will never think that. It makes him happy to buy things for you. It's his way of showing that he cares."

As they neared the food court, Margaret spotted Bowen sitting at a table, reading on his phone.

"Poor guy. He must be bored out of his mind."

"Shhh." Ana put a finger over her lips. "Don't let him hear you," she whispered. "I want to surprise him."

Margaret rolled her eyes. "Yeah, good luck with that. Bowen is a Guardian, and even while reading, he's alert and paying attention to what's going on around him."

A split second later, she was proven right as his head whipped around, and his eyes widened upon seeing her.

A grin spreading over his face, he pushed to his feet and strode toward her.

"Stunning." He leaned and kissed her cheek. "Did you get a facial too?"

"No, it's an illusion created by the highlights." She fluffed her hair.

"I don't think so." His eyes roamed all over her, taking in the new outfit, the shoes. "It's everything together." He smoothed his hand over the sleeve of her new blouse. "I'm so glad that you bought more things for yourself. I should have suggested it, but I didn't think you'd have enough time."

"I'm going to…" She was interrupted by Ana clearing her throat.

"Leon is waiting for us in the restaurant," Ana said. "We should go."

Margaret closed her mouth.

Bowen took all the shopping bags from Ana, freeing her to thread her arm through Margaret's. "Are you okay to walk to the car?"

"I'm fine." She leaned on Ana's arm just a little.

The truth was that her body was tired, and she ached in multiple places. But she was also excited, energized, and hopeful. If not for the brace, she would have had a spring in her step.

Less than ten minutes later, Bowen parked the car in front of the restaurant.

Leon, who had secured a table out on the patio for them, rose to his feet and gawked the entire time it took them to reach him.

"You two look like you've stepped out of a fashion magazine." His eyes darted from Ana to Margaret and back to Ana.

Chuckling, Ana leaned and kissed his cheek. "Let's order some wine. We need to celebrate the cast removal."

Next to Margaret, Bowen tensed for some reason. Was he apprehensive about what that meant for them? It wasn't likely.

Last night, he'd proven to be not only a confident and dominant lover, but also superbly skilled. A man like him would never feel shy about taking that final step.

He pulled out a chair for her and took the crutch, leaning it against the patio's railing. "Do they serve whiskey here? I'm not a fan of wine."

"I can check." Leon waved the waiter down. "Do you have whiskey in your bar?"

The guy smiled and then listed all the brands they carried.

Bowen didn't look impressed by any of them, but he ended up ordering a Jack Daniels. Leon chose the same, while she and Ana ordered a glass of wine each.

The appetizers arrived together with the drinks, and after the toasts had been made, Bowen reached for her hand and looked into her eyes.

"There's one last thing I need to tell you." He glanced around at the other diners and then leaned closer to her. "The transition is difficult, and it gets more dangerous the older the Dormant is. For Anastasia and Wendy, the risk was minimal, but it's significantly higher for you."

She frowned. "What's the worst that can happen?"

"You might not wake up." When she sucked in a breath, he squeezed her hand. "It hasn't happened yet. All the Dormants we induced have transitioned successfully, and some were older than you. But I can't start your induction before making you aware of the risk."

"Do I have a choice?"

"It's entirely up to you. No one will force you to attempt transition."

"What's the alternative? Will I be allowed to stay in the village as a human?"

He nodded. "Kian has relaxed the rules lately, and now parents of transitioned Dormants are allowed to stay in the village. And as Wendy's mother, you qualify for that exemption. As for me, I love you, and I want to be with you. But if you choose not to risk your life for the chance of immortality, I will not try to persuade you. I'll take whatever years you can give me."

Margaret swallowed. "Can I take a day or two to think it through?"

"Take all the time you need. This is not a decision that should be taken lightly."

Annani

"Why didn't I think of inviting strippers?" Amanda accepted the virgin strawberry daiquiri Onidu handed her. "What kind of a bachelorette party is it without alcohol and strippers?"

Annani exchanged knowing smiles with Ronja. It did not matter that Ronja was younger than most of the immortal women in the room. She was a mother, and therefore had more in common with Annani and Alena than with the rest of the boisterous attendees of Sari's bachelorette party.

It had been decided to make the party alcohol-free on account of the three pregnant ladies and Lisa, who was still underage. Having the girl there also meant that the others needed to keep the sexy comments to a minimum, which would have been a problem if the girls got drunk.

There had been some grumbles, but no one was too upset about the lack of alcohol.

Syssi snorted. "Knowing Anandur, he's planning another performance to entertain us."

The men were at David and Sari's place, celebrating David's last day as a bachelor, and Annani had no doubt that the alcohol was flowing freely over there.

Wonder cast Syssi a mock angry look. "The only one Anandur strips for these days is me."

Hiding a smile, Syssi sipped on her virgin drink.

"We don't need strippers," Jacki said. "We have a full schedule of fun activities." She donned the colorful turban she'd brought for the occasion. "Who wants to have her fortune told first?" She sat on one of the big pillows thrown in the center of the living room and crossed her legs, pulling a fake crystal ball to nestle between them.

Her pregnancy was still in the early stages, so even if she got a real foretelling, it would not harm the child, but that was most likely not going to happen. Jacki's visions were rare, even more so than Syssi's.

Tonight, she was providing entertainment and nothing more.

"Sari is the bride," Amanda said. "She should go first."

Sari shook her head. "Miranda is dying to find a true-love mate. She should go first."

Her assistant got to her feet and lowered herself gracefully to the other pillow. "Tell me my fortune, oh great seer."

"Did you bring an object for me to touch?" Jacki asked.

Miranda removed a bracelet from her wrist and handed it to Jacki.

Closing her eyes, Jacki waved it over the plastic ball that was made to look like crystal. Humming, she swayed from side to side as if she was entering a trance.

"She's good," Ronja whispered in Annani's ear.

"I see a long journey," Jacki said. "To a faraway land. Lots of sand, the sun is blindingly hot, and in the distance, the ocean shimmers. A handsome man emerges from the water, his long dark hair plastered over his muscular chest, his green eyes blazing with desire." She opened her eyes. "For you, Miranda."

"When?"

Jacki lifted her hand and brushed it over the crystal ball. "Ten moons."

"Yay." Miranda clapped her hands, but then her smile slid off her face. "Does that mean none of Kalugal's men is the one for me?"

Jacki shrugged. "The future is always changing, and nothing is set in stone. Perhaps the gorgeous Aquaman will emerge from the water for someone else."

"Aquaman?" Miranda squeaked. "Did he look like Jason Momoa?"

Jacki smiled. "Yeah, he kind of did."

"Then it's worth the wait." Miranda pushed to her feet. "Onidu, another virgin margarita over here."

"Yes, mistress." He bowed.

"Who's next?" Jacki asked.

"I am." Veronica, one of Sari's good friends, jumped in before anyone else could volunteer. "I want Superman. The latest one. Henry Cavill."

Stifling a laugh, Jacki extended her hand. "An object, please."

She told two more fortunes before Ronja decided to take the hot seat.

"I don't have any particular requests." She crossed her legs and put her hands on her knees.

"Do you have an object for me to touch?"

Ronja pulled a compact mirror out of her purse. "I got this as a present from my first husband." She rubbed her hand over the engraving. "Michael gave it to me for my nineteenth birthday." Her expression turned wistful. "I loved Frank dearly, and he was a much better husband to me than Michael ever was, but Michael was the true love of my life, my passion, my obsession, and also the one who caused me the biggest pain. Regrettably, he didn't love me as much as I loved him." She cast an apologetic glance at Lisa. "I hope that you are not mad at me for saying that."

A tear slid down Lisa's cheek. "I can't get angry at you for telling the truth. The heart chooses who it wants to love, even if it's the wrong person."

Ronja nodded. "Even though Michael was much older than me, he was either immature, or just incapable of loving as fully and as completely as I was. Back then, I was young and naive, and I hoped that my love would be enough for both of us." She smiled sadly. "Now that I'm older and smarter, I know that's not how it works." She took in a deep breath. "What I want to know is whether I will ever experience that kind of love again, and more importantly, whether it will be reciprocated with the same fervor."

As Jacki closed her hand over the mirror and her eyes drifted shut, Annani straightened in her chair. Would Ronja's foretelling be real, or another one of Jacki's acts?

Jacki's forehead furrowed. "I can't see the man that will make your heart soar again, but I can sense that one was fated for you. You will know love again."

Ronja smiled. "I hoped you would see Aquaman or Superman in my future." She turned and winked at Lisa. "But I'll settle for loving again. Not right now, I'm not ready yet, but sometime in the future." She looked at Annani. "One is never too old to love, right?"

Annani nodded. "Never."

Kian

"Help yourself to the second finest cigars." Anandur placed the box on the coffee table. "Opus X."

"Why not the finest?" Kalugal reached into the box, pulled out one, and handed it to David. "The soon-to-be former bachelor goes first."

"Cuban cigars are banned in the United States," Kian grumbled.

"So?" Kalugal pulled out another one for himself. "You can get them on the black market."

"There are some online sellers that supposedly carry them, but you never know what you're actually getting." Kian slid the balcony doors open and stepped out. "Most are counterfeits."

Kalugal and David followed, and soon all ten were crowding the small balcony, with Okidu making rounds and refilling everyone's whiskey glasses.

Leaning against the glass railing, David puffed on his cigar. "Can you tell me more about the Kra-ell social structure?"

"You know the basics already. What else do you want to know?" Kian asked.

"I'll tell you what I know, and then you can fill in the blanks." David puffed on his cigar. "They are a different race of immortals who need blood for nutrition and have the ability to compel. They are relative newcomers to earth, and their society is matriarchal like the clan's. For every four Kra-ell males, only one female is born, so they don't form couple relationships. Instead, they live in small tribes, with two to four females sharing a group of males in a communal harem."

Kian tapped on his cigar, the ash falling into the big glass ashtray Okidu had put on the outdoor table. "Their compulsion or thralling abilities vary in strength from one individual to another, in the same way that ours do, they are long-lived, and they are genetically similar to us, but that's where the similarities end. Their society is very different than ours or any of the human cultures that I'm familiar with."

David smiled knowingly. "Then you are not familiar with the Mosuo."

"I've never heard of them."

"Their society is structured very much like that of the Kra-ell, and they are a subgroup in China. I remembered reading about them a long time ago, and when I heard about the Kra-ell and their society, I was reminded of the Mosuo and decided to refresh my memory."

Kian cocked a brow. "That's interesting. Maybe there is a connection."

"That's what I thought, but after reading more about them, I don't think there is. The Mosuo, or the Na as they call themselves, live in the Yunnan and Sichuan provinces, which are close to the border with Tibet. The women head the households, and inheritance is through the female line, but they leave the politicking to the males. That wasn't always the case, and in the past the matriarch was also the political head of the community. Still, even today, the matriarch, the Ah Mis, has absolute power over everyone in her household, assigns jobs to every member, and controls all the money."

Kian took a puff of his cigar. "So far, that sounds loosely similar to the Kra-ell. What about their mating habits?"

David smiled. "I saved the best part for last. The Mosuo men are primarily used as breeders. After the coming-of-age ceremony, which occurs at the age of thirteen for girls and boys..." David paused for emphasis. "The girls are given a private bedroom that is called the flowering room, and they can start inviting partners for what's called Walking Marriages. Those are basically sexual encounters, and the men are supposed to come at night and leave in the morning. Any resulting children stay with the mother. The fathers are granted visitation rights, but they are more involved with raising the children of their sisters and aunts in their own matriarch's house than they are with their own."

"That sounds a lot like the Kra-ell," Anandur said. "Why do you think they are not related? They could have picked up the customs from a neighboring compound."

"Because the Mosuo's tradition is thousands of years old, and the Kra-ell are supposed to be newcomers."

"Emmett thinks that his group arrived relatively recently." Kian lifted his empty glass for Okidu to refill. "But he deduced it rather than knowing it for a fact. Also, his group might not be the first one. It's possible that others came before."

"What are the Mosuo's religious beliefs?" Kalugal asked.

"The Mosuo have a hybrid faith. The Daba is their original religion, which has been handed down through the generations for thousands of years. It's based on the worship of a mother goddess and on their ancestors, functioning as both religion and oral history of their people. In recent years, Buddhism has gained ground in the Mosuo society, but it was adapted to suit their culture."

"The Kra-ell believe in a mother goddess." Kian took a puff of the cigar. "The leaders of their communities are supposed to be the goddess's embodiments. I need to ask Emmett if they also worship their ancestors."

Kalugal handed his glass to Okidu and extinguished his half-smoked cigar. "The ancestor worship is a big part of Confucianism and Taoism. It might have influenced the

Mosuo beliefs in the same way that Buddhism did later. To me, that sounds too much like the Kra-ell for it to be a coincidence. The Chinese society is very patriarchal by nature, and for the Mosuo to develop such a divergent system, there must have been a strong outside influence." He smiled at David. "Your next task is to find out whether the Mosuo have vampire legends."

"As far as I know, they don't." David rubbed a hand over his jaw. "But they have an interesting legend regarding dogs. First of all, unlike other Asian cultures, eating dogs is strictly forbidden, and dogs are considered important members of the household. According to legend, long ago, dogs had much longer lifespans than humans—they lived to be sixty, while humans lived only thirteen years. At some point, humans traded lifespans with dogs in exchange for worship. During the coming-of-age ceremony, young Mosuo pray before the family dogs."

"Perhaps it's a loose reference to attaining longevity," Kalugal said. "Legends and myths get twisted over the millennia. It might have started as something else."

"Where did you say their communities are located?" Kian asked.

"The Sichuan and Yunnan provinces are on the eastern border of Tibet. Sichuan is more or less in central China, and Yunnan is to the south."

Kian glanced at Kalugal. "I think we should send a team to investigate that region as well."

Kalugal shook his head. "Even if the Mosuo were influenced by the Kra-ell, it happened thousands of years ago. What do you hope to find there?"

"Maybe there are some interesting archeological finds that would provide us with clues." Kian smiled at Kalugal. "That's actually your field of expertise. Perhaps you could do some digging."

Kalugal's eyes gleamed with interest. "Indeed."

Syssi

After Jacki's fortune-telling, it was Callie's turn, and Syssi was grateful for the change in atmosphere.

Ronja's admission about her first husband having been the love of her life had been a mood downer, and more than one discreet tear had been shed. It must have been devastating to love a man who hadn't loved her back, and who'd cheated on her left and right. Syssi couldn't imagine the pain.

Callie emerged from the kitchen, followed by Okidu and Onidu, all three carrying trays loaded with the ingredients she'd prepared.

"This is going to be very simple." Callie pointed to the tray she'd put on the dining table. "We are going to prepare beautiful canapés and then eat them."

Amanda clapped her hands. "Perfect. I'm hungry."

For the next half an hour, they assembled small sandwiches, and then demolished them in less than ten minutes.

"That's the problem with cooking as an artistic expression," Amanda said. "In contrast, my contribution to this lovely evening is going to be a keepsake." She started pulling small bags from the large box Dalhu had hauled in before joining the men for their party. "Every bag contains several sheets of high-quality drawing paper and a packet of charcoals. All we need now is to choose a model, and I volunteer." She took her jacket off. "I can pose in the nude."

"Don't you dare." Syssi laughed. "Keep your clothes on. Besides, it's Sari's party, so I think she should pose."

Sari graciously agreed, pulling a barstool into the center of the living room. "Just so we are clear, I'm volunteering to be the model only because I can't draw for the life of me, and I'm not posing naked."

"That's a shame," Amanda grumbled. "You have a beautiful figure."

Sari dipped her head. "Thank you. But the clothes stay on."

They spent the next hour drawing and laughing at each other's fumbling efforts, and when everyone was done, Lisa's sketch was chosen as the best.

"I want to keep all of them." Sari collected everyone's sketches, insisting that each of them sign her creation.

"You should have Dalhu draw your portrait," Amanda said as she handed over hers. "You and David can come to his studio in the village, or you can just send him a photo to work from."

"I don't want to trouble him." Sari put the collection of drawings into the box the kits had come in.

"It's karaoke time." Wonder pushed to her feet. "I need help setting it up."

"I'll help you," Amanda offered. "I have lots of experience with these machines."

Syssi vaguely remembered Amanda buying a karaoke machine to entertain the all-female crew of the *Anna*. Alex's yacht had been used for trafficking young women that the corrupt immortal had been thralling into a stupor and selling for profit.

Back then, none of them could have anticipated that rescuing trafficking victims would become one of the clan's main humanitarian efforts. But the Fates must have started them on the path with that yacht.

When everything was set up, and Amanda took the microphone, singing along to Journey's *'Don't Stop Believing,'* everyone joined her.

Well, everyone save for Annani, who shifted closer to Syssi. "I was thinking," the goddess whispered in her ear, "that I like Ronja a lot, and I think that she deserves another chance at love."

"She sure does."

"Perhaps she should attempt transition after all."

Syssi turned to look at her mother-in-law. "I would have loved for Ronja to have another chance, and she'll get it, but not as an immortal. She can't transition at her age."

Annani smiled mischievously. "Perhaps with the help of my blessing, she can."

Syssi stifled the incredulity that threatened to show on her face. Annani's blessing was a great morale booster, but it couldn't guarantee a successful transition.

It wasn't as if she could argue with the goddess, though. That privilege was reserved for Annani's children, and perhaps in this case, also Bridget, who had medical training to back up her position. Then again, Annani regarded Syssi as her daughter, so perhaps she was allowed to voice her doubts, as long as she kept it respectful.

"As powerful and as generous as your blessings are, I'm not sure even that would be enough to pull Ronja through the transition. But I'm not an expert. Bridget is probably the one you need to talk to."

Syssi was kicking the can down the road, but she wasn't in a position to argue with the goddess, while Bridget had the authority to back up her argument. The doctor would no doubt shoot Annani's idea down and save Ronja from nearly certain death.

"You are right," Annani acquiesced. "I need to consult Bridget."

Margaret

It had been difficult to say goodbye to Bowen when he left for his second shift of the day. Margaret felt guilty. If she hadn't been such a wuss, she could have gone to the clinic with Ana and waited for Bowen to come home.

But then he would have been too late to take her shopping, and she really needed an evening dress if she was to attend the wedding. Besides, she had a wonderful time.

When a knock sounded on the front door, Leon rose to his feet and opened the way for Wendy and Vlad.

"Is that you, Mom?" Wendy pretended not to recognize her.

"It's me." Margaret flipped her hair back and smiled. "Just improved."

"I'll say." Wendy sat on the couch next to her. "I don't know if it's the hair color or the clothes, but you look ten years younger."

The smile slid off Margaret's face. "Thank you. But it doesn't change the fact that my body is thirty-eight years old, and that transitioning is dangerous for me. Potentially deadly."

As everyone went quiet, Margaret felt bad for ruining everyone's good mood. She waved a dismissive hand. "I'm sure that everything will be okay. It's just that I didn't know that until a few hours ago, and it was a little bit of a shock to learn it."

"Does that mean you decided to go for it?" Anastasia asked.

"I don't know." She pushed a strand of hair behind her ear. "What do you think I should do, Wendy?"

Her daughter pursed her lips. "I say, go for it. Thirty-eight is not old, and I have no doubt that you will transition successfully." She turned to Vlad. "You said that so far, every Dormant who started transitioning has made it through."

Vlad nodded. "Correct." He glanced at Margaret. "But some had a really difficult time. I remember that Turner was in a coma for two weeks. Maybe even longer."

Leon chuckled. "That bastard would have wrestled death and won. He doesn't accept defeat."

"Who's Turner?" Margaret asked. "I keep hearing that name."

"It's a long story," Leon said. "Syssi's brother knew him from his special ops days, and when the clan needed to find a kidnapped clan member, he brought him in to help. Naturally, no one suspected that Turner was a Dormant, but he needed to be in the know in order to help us out. Kian gave the guy the bare minimum of information, but Turner is a brilliant bastard. He figured out that Andrew had turned immortal, and he demanded to be induced. The problem was that he had cancer, and that needed to be taken care of first. Kian sent him to Bridget for evaluation, the two fell in love, and the rest is history."

The shortened version left a lot out, but Margaret could ask Bowen to tell her the whole story some other time. Right now, she was more interested in how Turner had transitioned despite the cancer.

"Female immortals don't have fangs and venom. So, who induced Turner?"

"Kian," Vlad said. "Because he's Annani's son, he's the purest immortal we have, and his venom is the most potent. He was Turner's best chance. Also, Annani gave Turner her blessing, which many believe was what helped him pull through."

"A blessing?" Margaret whispered. "Does the goddess have healing powers?"

Leon and Vlad exchanged glances, and then Leon lifted his hands in the air. "Maybe. All I know is that every time she gave her blessing to a transitioning Dormant, it helped."

"Can I petition her to help me?"

Leon nodded. "It would be best if you started your transition while she's here. But since she's supposed to leave a week after Kian's birthday, I doubt that you'll make it in time. Still, if your transition gets dicey, Bowen can plead with her to fly over and give you her blessing."

When the silence that fell over the room was interrupted by another knock on the door, Wendy pushed to her feet. "That must be Stella and Richard." She walked over to the front door and opened it.

"Hello, everyone." Stella swept into the living room with Richard in tow. He was holding a humongous satchel that Margaret was sure had been custom-made. There was no way something that size and that embellished was sold in stores. It had Stella written all over it.

"I brought outfits and accessories galore." Stella stopped in front of Anastasia. "I love the hair." She turned to Margaret. "Yours too."

Wendy laughed. "Are we having a costume party?"

"Something like that." Stella took the satchel from Richard and plopped it on the coffee table. "I heard that you bought evening gowns for the wedding, but I bet that you didn't buy anything for Kian's bimillennial birthday, which is Wednesday. I thought that you could model my designs."

No one had mentioned the birthday, or that Kian was two thousand years old. Margaret hadn't met him yet, and now she was dying of curiosity.

Wrong phrase. She shouldn't mention the word dying in regard to anything until she transitioned successfully.

"Are we even invited to the birthday?" Ana asked.

"Of course." Leon wrapped an arm around her shoulders. "Everyone is. I should have thought about it when you told me that you were shopping for a dress for the wedding."

"Don't worry about it." Stella waved a hand. "I have it covered."

"Is it going to be as formal as the wedding?" Margaret asked.

"A little less."

As Stella started pulling dresses out of her satchel, Richard opened the sliding door to the backyard. "That's our cue, guys."

"Right." Leon walked to the kitchen. "I'll get the beers."

When the sliding door closed behind the men, Stella fluffed out a colorful dress. "This one will look great on you, Margaret. Try it on."

"Now?"

"Yeah." Stella unfurled another one and tossed it at Ana. "Right now, Sari is having her bachelorette party at the building across from the keep, and we were not invited." She pouted. "I figured we could have a party of our own."

"Splendid idea." Ana draped the dress over her shoulder. "I'll try on this beauty and then bring out the wine."

Stella gave her the thumbs up and then pulled a red dress out of the satchel. "I saved the best one for you." She handed it to Wendy.

As the three of them headed to the bedroom to change, Margaret felt tears prickle the back of her eyes.

Happy tears.

Grateful tears.

Life just didn't get any better than this. She had her daughter back, a great guy who loved her, and friends who were like family.

This was worth living for.

"I'm going to attempt the transition," she told Wendy.

"Oh, Mom." Wendy pulled her into her arms. "I've never doubted that you would, not even for a moment. You are a fighter."

Onegus

"Thank you." Onegus took the garment bag from Connor. "You're a life saver. I wouldn't have made it to the village and back on time."

"My pleasure." Connor put a paper bag on the desk and pulled out a Tupperware container. "Have you eaten yet?"

Onegus's mouth watered. "I didn't have time."

"That's what I thought. Dig in." Connor took a look around Onegus's spartan office. "You should spruce this place up a little. It's depressing."

"It's just temporary." Onegus motioned for his roommate to take a seat. "Can I offer you a beer?"

Connor shook his head. "I'm saving the drinking for the wedding. How is your lady getting here?"

"I'm sending one of the Guardians to pick her up." He opened the container and lifted one of the turkey wraps Connor had prepared for him.

"I can do that if you want. I know that your men are all busy guarding our guests."

"That would be a great help. Thank you." Onegus put the wrap down and pulled out his phone. "I'm texting you her address. Just be careful with what you tell her. She doesn't know anything yet."

Shaking his head, Connor glanced at the small fridge that served as Onegus's printer stand. "I think that I'll have that beer after all." He got to his feet and pulled a Snake Venom for himself. "Do you want beer or water?"

"Water. I'm on duty."

"Naturally." Connor put a water bottle on the desk and sat down with his beer. "How are you going to explain to Cassandra what she's about to see?"

"I hope she won't notice. People will have to keep up the pretense because of the human servers, so it's not like she's about to witness a lot of weirdness."

Connor arched a brow. "The servers will clear the banquet hall when Annani enters to preside over the ceremony. Do you think Cassandra will not notice a glowing goddess?"

"I plan to get her tipsy by then." Onegus twisted the cap off the bottle and took a long swig. "Hopefully, she will not notice the peculiarities, and if she does, I'll thrall the memory away."

There was no way Cassandra could miss a glowing goddess, but maybe he could convince her that it was a trick of the light?

"Right." Connor arched a brow. "And how are you going to get her tipsy while overseeing security?"

"Good point. You're seated next to her." Onegus saluted with the bottle. "You'll need to do that for me. I'll also ask Jackson, Roni, and Nick to keep offering her drinks."

"Why don't you just tell her? You must know by now that Cassandra is your one and that she is a Dormant."

"I suspect that she is, but I have a plan for when and how to tell her, and it's not during the wedding."

His eyes glowing with interest, Connor leaned forward. "What's your plan?"

"I'm trying to convince Cassandra to come with me to Paris after the festivities." He shook his head. "I was sure she would be thrilled and that I'd get an enthusiastic yes. But Cassandra is unlike any other woman I know. She said that she needs to think about it."

"And once she agrees, and you take her to Paris, how are you going to tell her?"

"I don't have all the details figured out yet, but I'm thinking a honeymoon suite in an exclusive hotel and a dinner for two on the suite's balcony."

"That's so romantic." Connor snorted. "I bet it wasn't your idea."

"It was Ingrid's. How did you know it wasn't mine?"

"Because you would have taken Cassandra to the cabin and thought that it was the most romantic getaway ever."

"I did suggest that. She got so mad that I had to invite her to the wedding to compensate. She thought that I didn't want to be seen with her, and that's why I chose a secluded cabin for our weekend getaway."

Connor leaned back and crossed his arms over his chest. "She thought that you were a player."

Nodding, Onegus pointed with the wrap at Connor. "The cabin was also Ingrid's idea, but that was a mistake. Next time, I'll come to you for advice."

"As you should. Let me ask you something. After you tell Cassandra the truth over a romantic dinner on the hotel suite's balcony, how are you going to keep her from running out and telling everything to whoever is willing to listen?"

"I didn't get that far. I'll figure something out."

Kian

"This is so nice." Syssi leaned on the cushion Kian had put on her chair. "I love these family gatherings. I wish we all lived in the same place."

Annani reached over the dining table and patted Syssi's hand. "What makes them special is that we do not have them often. It takes a special celebration for us all to congregate in one place. If we were all living in the village, it would not have been as fun."

Kian agreed wholeheartedly, but he was smart enough to keep his mouth shut. Coming from his mother, it wasn't going to offend anyone, but if he dared to say something like that, his mother and sisters would think that he preferred them in small doses. Not that they would be wrong. Other than Alena, they all had big personalities, and having them all in one room was too much.

"Thank you for a lovely breakfast, Mother." Sari pushed to her feet. "But we have a wedding to get ready for, and the hair and makeup team is on its way." She looked at David. "You can stay for a little longer if you wish."

"I'll come with you." He rose to his feet.

"You are not allowed to see me before the wedding."

"That's a silly superstition. But if you want, I can stay in the bedroom and read while you are getting ready."

She smiled at him. "You know that I like you near me at all times."

Jacki leaned over and kissed Kalugal's cheek. "I'll see you tonight." She followed Sari up. "Thank you for inviting us, Clan Mother." She bowed to Annani.

Ronja, Lisa, and Alena also said their thanks and goodbyes, and then the five of them left to meet the beauty team in Sari and David's apartment.

Syssi and Amanda had opted out of the pre-wedding preparations and were going to change into their bridesmaids' dresses at home.

Annani, naturally, didn't require any preparations. There was no improving perfection. She never applied any makeup or styled her hair.

"How is Ronja dealing with Bowen finding his mate?" Annani asked.

"I'm not sure she knows." Syssi adjusted the pillow at her back.

"I thought that there was something going on between them, but I'm starting to doubt it." Amanda put her empty coffee cup down. "Ronja didn't even ask where he was and what he's been doing during the time he was gone."

Annani let out a relieved breath. "Good. I like her, and I do not want to see her hurt again. Ronja deserves a break." She looked at Kian. "Is there anyone else other than Bowen who's showing interest in her?"

"I'm not the right person to ask. Matchmaking is Amanda's department."

"She's friendly with many people," Amanda said. "But as far as I know, she isn't interested in anyone."

"That is a shame." Annani motioned for Ojidu to refill her coffee cup. "I would like her to attempt transition."

Kian had a feeling that was where Annani had been going. "Regrettably, she's too old, and it's too risky."

Annani leveled her eyes at him. "I will be there for her. I will give her my blessing, if needed, more than once."

Translation, his mother was willing to give Ronja more than one transfusion of her blood to help her transition. It might be enough, and it might not be. The risk was too high in his opinion. Besides, Ronja hadn't expressed an interest in transitioning.

Then again, as far as she knew, it wasn't an option for her, so she might have just resigned herself to mortality.

In any case, as much as Kian would have liked for his mother to have her new friend around forever, he wasn't willing to risk Ronja's life for that.

"Even if that was in the cards, Mother, Ronja needs to find a mate first," he said gently. "And she doesn't seem ready to get involved with anyone yet. She's still grieving for her husband."

"Yes, well." Annani dropped a cube of sugar into the coffee Ojidu had refilled and stirred it with a small silver spoon. "Normally, a year of grieving is to be expected, but Ronja is not getting any younger." She looked at Amanda. "Perhaps you can find her someone? You are so good at matchmaking."

"I'll see what I can do," Amanda said without much conviction.

If Annani noticed, she didn't let it show. "I will talk with Ronja and gauge her interest. Perhaps she has noticed someone but did not think it was appropriate for her to befriend a male so soon after Frank's passing."

"I'm so happy for Wendy," Syssi changed the subject. "Finding her mother must have brought her so much joy."

"I've thought of something," Dalhu said.

He usually spoke so rarely that everyone turned to hear what he had to say.

"If Emmett had sex with Margaret during the years she lived in Safe Haven, and I assume that he did, then it's proof that the Kra-ell don't have the ability to induce transition in Dormants." He looked at Kian. "From what I heard, everyone in there was checked for STDs, and the women received contraceptive shots. Therefore, there was no need for anyone to use condoms."

Kian had already deduced as much.

"What about the bond?" Amanda asked. "Perhaps Margaret didn't transition because there was no bond between her and Emmett."

Dalhu shook his head. "That's my point. We can't be sure that a bond is needed. Eleanor transitioned without a bond, and so did Eva."

"I've given it some thought." Amanda crossed her arms over her small belly. "Maybe it's only needed for those whose genes are highly diluted."

"Like me?" Syssi challenged.

"I don't think yours are weak. You are a strong seer, and Andrew is the only infallible lie-detector the clan has."

Syssi grimaced. "At least Andrew's gift is useful. My visions are mostly useless. The only time they were actually helpful was when I summoned a vision to find Ronja and Frank."

"You also saw the Kra-ell in a vision." Kian took her hand. "Once our baby is born, you can go back to training with Madam what's-her-name. What she taught you seemed to help with locating David's parents."

"Madam Salinka," Syssi reminded him.

"Yes, her."

"You want me to go back to training with her?"

"Only if you want to."

Cassandra

"You look so beautiful and classy." Misted with tears, Geraldine's eyes were full of pride. "My Cassandra." She wiped at them, smearing her mascara.

"Oh, Mom." Cassandra dipped her head and kissed her mother's cheek. "You always say that, and you always cry when you do."

Her mother wiped at her cheek even though Cassandra's lipstick was the kind that didn't come off. "That's because it's true, and seeing the amazing woman I raised fills my heart with pride and joy. But you still didn't tell me what's the occasion." She trailed her eyes over the floor-length black evening dress. "You are not dressed for just a date on the town."

It was so like her mother to get all emotional and yet notice everything. Despite her memory issues, there was no fooling Geraldine Beaumont.

"It's a private event, and Onegus made me promise not to tell anyone about it. I even had to lie to Kevin and tell him that I needed a day off because of a doctor's appointment. I couldn't tell him that I needed to go shopping for a dress for another event."

Geraldine was no stranger to secrets, and she didn't press for details. "Is Onegus picking you up?"

"He's sending someone. The event is so secret that he couldn't even tell me where it is."

Her mother glanced at her small evening purse. "I hope you have your phone with you."

"I'm sure he'll ask me to put it in airplane mode."

Geraldine waved a dismissive hand. "That doesn't prevent it from being tracked. He'll probably ask you to turn it off completely."

Cassandra narrowed her eyes at her mother. "How do you know that?"

"I read it in one of my billionaire romance novels and then checked the internet to see if it was true. It was."

As the house phone rang, Cassandra kissed her mother's cheek one more time. "That's probably Connor. Tell the guard to let him in."

She opened the door and walked out. The guy was doing Onegus a favor. She couldn't expect him to get out of the car and escort her out of her house like a prom queen.

Except, Connor was a gentleman, and as soon as he pulled up to her house and killed the engine, he got out and offered her his hand. "Hello, Cassandra. It's a pleasure to finally meet you."

"Same here." She shook his hand.

Connor matched how she'd imagined a score composer would look, only much more handsome. His shoulder-length dark brown hair curled at the bottom, framing a slim, smiling face with lush lips and merry blue-gray eyes. With her stilettos on, she was a couple of inches taller than him, which meant that without shoes, they were about the same height.

He opened the passenger door for her. "Onegus apologizes for not being able to pick you up himself."

"Does he?" Cassandra slid into the seat, careful not to snag her long dress.

"He would have if he weren't so busy."

"I want to tell Josie that I met you in person, but Onegus made such a big deal out of keeping this wedding a secret that I don't know what I'm allowed to disclose."

"You'd better not mention it." He smiled at her tightly. "I'm sure we will have many more opportunities to meet that you could tell Josie about."

She'd expected Connor to make light of Onegus's worries about the risk from some ancient enemies of his clan, but Connor seemed just as concerned.

As they reached the downtown area, Cassandra was surprised when Connor turned into the parking structure of the same building Onegus had brought her to.

"The wedding is in this building?"

"No, we are just using it for parking. A shuttle will take us to the venue."

Two guards stood at the entrance, and Connor stopped next to them. "This will take just a moment." He lowered the window. "Good evening, gentlemen."

The guy ignored Connor and looked only at her. "Who's your guest, Connor?"

"This is Cassandra, the chief's friend."

The guy nodded. "Good evening, ma'am." He motioned for Connor to move on.

"Onegus is the chief?"

Connor arched a brow. "He didn't tell you?"

"He told me that he's overseeing security for this wedding. What is he chief of?"

"You will have to ask him. It's not my place to say."

She rolled her eyes. Everything was steeped in so much mystery, and she wondered if it was really necessary.

On the way down the spiraling interior lane of the parking structure, she'd seen two more guards, and that was in addition to the cameras mounted on the walls in intervals of no more than ten feet.

"That's some serious security."

Connor cast her an apologetic sidelong glance. "Better safe than sorry, right?" He smiled. "Or the term that is now in vogue, out of an abundance of caution."

"In general, I'm all for caution, but this seems fit for a presidential visit."

For some reason, Connor found her answer amusing.

"Yeah, it does, doesn't it?"

The lowest level of the parking garage had its own gate, but it parted as soon as Connor pulled up to it. Did he live in the building?

Onegus had said that he and Connor shared a house, and that he was staying in the building only temporarily. Had he lied about that?

"How did the gate open? Do you have a sticker that allows you access?"

"I don't, but there is a camera up there." He pointed. "The people in the security office were notified of my arrival by the guards at the entrance. They read the car's license plate and opened the gate for me."

"Oh."

As he pulled in and the gate started closing, another car arrived, and the gate retracted once more.

Watching it in the rearview mirror, Cassandra didn't notice Onegus until Connor stopped the car.

He opened the door for her. "Good evening, gorgeous." He offered her a hand up.

Scanning her from head to toe as she straightened, Onegus let out a whistle. "I'm going to be the envy of every bachelor attending the event. How am I going to manage security tonight while keeping them away from you?"

Smiling, she leaned and kissed his cheek. "Don't worry about me. I'll put on my resting bitch face, and no one will dare to approach me."

"Don't forget me," Connor said. "I'll keep Cassandra safe."

"Come on." Onegus took her hand. "Let's find you a good seat before the transport gets full."

"What transport?" There were no buses or limousines waiting to shuttle guests from the parking garage to the venue.

"It's through that door." Onegus tugged on her hand.

Perhaps there was another garage on the other side or a corridor leading to the garage of the adjacent building.

Behind them, merry voices and the staccato of heels hitting concrete announced more guests arriving. Curiosity getting the better of her, Cassandra looked over her shoulder.

Two couples, but she wasn't sure who was with whom. The women were both beautiful and beautifully dressed, and they were holding hands. The two men walking behind them were no less good looking, and they were talking about some building project they were involved in.

"Are those relatives of yours?" she asked Onegus as he opened the door.

He glanced at the four. "Everyone attending tonight is in some way extended family. Even those two." He motioned with his chin at the men.

She wondered what he'd meant by that. Perhaps the men were more distant family. Second and third cousins. Or perhaps they'd just married into the family.

"Your chariot, ma'am." Onegus waved his hand at the so-called transport.

It was a long golf cart that looked like a golf limousine. She couldn't see inside, but it was long enough to seat eight people. The canopy enclosing the interior was decorated with ribbons and flowers and glitter, and a large banner hung at the back that said 'Sari and David are getting married.'

She chuckled. "That's my chariot? Does it turn into a pumpkin at midnight?"

"The celebration will last long into the night." Onegus offered her a hand up. "It can't turn back into a pumpkin before five o'clock in the morning."

He climbed in behind her, and the two of them sat at the back. Connor got in next, and then the four who had arrived behind them.

The driver's seat was separated from the back by a partition, just like it would be in a limousine, and the decorations covering nearly every inch of the canopy made it impossible to see what was outside the cart.

One of the women turned around with a face-splitting grin and offered her a hand. "Hi, I'm Gwen."

"Cassandra." She shook the hand she was offered. "It's nice to meet you."

"The pleasure is all mine." Gwen cast Onegus a knowing smirk. "Good luck."

"With what?" Cassandra asked.

"Taming Onegus, of course." She winked.

When he glared at her, Gwen giggled and covered her mouth with her hand.

"Ignore my nosy cousins." He took Cassandra's hand and held it in his lap. "It would seem that they've already started drinking."

Onegus

During the ride in the golf cart, Cassandra had chatted with Gwen and Elaine about this and that, the two doing an admirable job of keeping her too busy to notice where the cart was going, while avoiding incriminating topics.

When the cart finally stopped at the keep's underground garage, Gwen wiped invisible sweat from her forehead and mouthed behind Cassandra's back, *you owe Elaine and me for this.*

He dipped his head in acknowledgment.

"Where are we?" Cassandra asked.

The entire elevator bank was decorated for the wedding, with flowers and balloons and banners.

He pressed his thumb to the elevator button. "It's a portal to a fairytale land."

"It would appear so." Cassandra's forehead furrowed. "Did the button just scan your finger?"

"It did."

As the doors opened, he ushered her inside. Even the interior of the cabin hadn't escaped the attention of the overenthusiastic decorators. A large poster hung over the mirror with a picture of Sari and David kissing inside a big cutout heart, but just their silhouettes, so no one outside the clan could guess who they were.

Cassandra gave the poster a perfunctory glance before turning to him. "So, if I want to call the elevator, I can't?"

"Correct."

"What about them?" She waved her hand at Connor and the rest of their group.

"Every member of the family has their fingerprints taken and inputted into the system. They can all summon the elevator."

And that even included Kalugal's men, which Onegus wasn't entirely comfortable with, but he was aware that his feelings on the subject were irrational.

They didn't pose a security risk.

If they had, they would have never been admitted into the village. But they were former Doomers, and he could never bring himself to trust them completely and without reservation.

"You are really taking security measures to the extreme."

Connor chuckled. "You've seen nothing yet."

"Show me." Cassandra looked up at Onegus. "Unless I'm not allowed to know that either."

She was irritated, and the energy swirling just under the surface was starting to crackle. Hopefully, it wouldn't affect the elevator's mechanism. If her energy operated like Sylvia's, just without the control, it might damage electronics.

Thankfully, they reached the banquet hall level without incident, and as the elevator doors opened, the noise of music and conversations was a welcome distraction.

Onegus put his hand on the small of Cassandra's back and led her to the table he'd chosen for them.

Sylvia and Roni were already there, and so were Nick and Ruth. Sharon, Robert, Jackson, and Tessa hadn't arrived yet.

The seating arrangement covered three objectives. First of all, except for Connor, every male at the table was mated, so no one would flirt with Cassandra. Secondly, most of them were either young immortals or newly transitioned Dormants. They were the least likely group to make Cassandra suspicious because they knew what to be careful about. And thirdly, he'd asked Sylvia to keep an eye out for Cassandra's strange energy and see if it felt similar to hers.

He'd explained the situation to them and had asked for their cooperation. Nick, who had attended Eva's wedding while still human, had been drunk through the entire party thanks to Jackson. He promised to goad Cassandra into doing the same, or at least getting tipsy.

Pulling a chair out for her, Onegus made the introductions. "Sylvia, Roni, Nick, and Ruth." He helped push her chair back in place. "Please meet Cassandra, my girlfriend."

The round table was too big to reach over and shake hands, so they either dipped their heads or waved as Onegus said their names, and Cassandra smiled and waved back.

The term girlfriend seemed so wrong in the context of what Cassandra was to him, but that was what she expected him to say.

As he sat down next to her, she put a hand on his thigh and leaned closer. "Are they your cousins?"

"Sylvia and Ruth are, while Roni and Nick are their partners."

Partners was a much better term than boyfriends, and maybe if he used it enough when talking about members of his family, Cassandra would deem it more appropriate than girlfriend as well.

"The reason I asked was that Roni seems familiar. I can't put my finger on it, but I know that I've seen him somewhere."

The kid had been on the news when he'd been caught hacking into the government confidential records, but Onegus didn't remember whether Roni's picture had been made public. If it had, Cassandra might have seen it. After the clan had helped him escape, there had been an APB on him, but he doubted it had been available for civilians to see.

"He might look like someone you know." Onegus sighed. "I wish I could stay, but I need to continue making rounds until all the guests arrive." He pushed to his feet. "Can I get you something from the bar?"

"No thanks." Cassandra reached for the water pitcher. "I'll stick to water for now."

"Allow me." Connor took it and poured her a glass.

"Who drinks water at a wedding?" Nick asked. "And a Scottish wedding at that. Everyone has to get drunk." He filled Cassandra's wine glass to the brim. "That's the tradition."

She lifted her eyes to Onegus. "Is it?"

"I'm afraid so." He patted her shoulder. "I'll be back as soon as I can."

Eleanor

Alfie leaned over Eleanor's shoulder to look at the screen. "He's still reading?"

"What else do you expect him to do?"

She'd been watching Emmett for hours, waiting for the moments when he lifted his eyes to the surveillance camera, his intense gaze seemingly caressing her.

Did he feel her eyes on him?

Was that why he glanced at the camera every so often?

"He can watch television, play video games, or do some exercise." Alfie pointed to the pull-up bar he'd hung over the bedroom doorway.

He and the other Guardians used the contraption to do endless pull-ups, and even Eleanor had gotten in some during her shifts.

"You can't give him one of those because he could use it as a weapon."

"True, but he can do push-ups, lunges, and sit-ups. All he's doing is sitting on his butt all day and reading. At this rate, his muscles will atrophy."

That would be a shame. Emmett wasn't as buff as Alfie or the other Guardians, but he was lean and toned, just the way she liked it.

"Do you want to go in and keep him company?" Alfie asked.

Frowning, she turned to look at the Guardian. "I delivered his dinner two hours ago. I have no reason to go in again."

Arwel had decided against leaving her alone to guard Emmett, and Alfie had volunteered to stay with her. Apparently, the guy didn't like parties, and he didn't mind missing the wedding. Still, Peter had warned them to be extra careful. Everyone else was at the wedding, and although they could get to the dungeon level in minutes, no one wanted their fun interrupted.

Alfie shrugged. "I thought you wanted to spend time with him."

They all knew about her plan to befriend Emmett, and they also knew that her interest in him was not only professional. But Eleanor wasn't an exhibitionist, and there was no way they would let her be with him without the surveillance.

"I do," she admitted. "But I can't."

"You can." Alfie put a hand on her shoulder. "I'll keep an eye on you."

She snorted. "Are you hoping for a porn show?"

His smirk was confirmation enough. "I've watched you with him. He wants you, and you want him. What are you waiting for?"

She grimaced. "Privacy. I'm not an exhibitionist."

Alfie plopped down on the couch next to her. "I wish I could give you that, but it's not safe. The sound is already muted because I don't want to wear the damn earpieces all day long, but I have to watch."

She sighed. "I know."

"There is no camera in the bathroom…"

Eleanor cast him a disgusted sidelong glance. "That's gross. I'm not that desperate."

"It doesn't have to be. I've taken women into club restrooms—ladies' rooms, mind you, not the men's. Those are just as gross as you imagine. I've done it in closets, pantries, hallways, dark niches, you name it. It was exciting, for them and for me." He waggled his brows. "You should try it."

She shook her head. "The ladies' room might be cleaner than the men's, but it's still gross."

"You can always find at least one clean wall, and I'm sure that Emmett keeps the bathroom clean. He's not the messy type."

She'd noticed and liked that about him.

"I can't believe I'm having this conversation with you."

Eleanor was slowly losing her human inhibitions and adopting the immortals' attitude toward sex. Most of the change had occurred during the mission with Peter and Leon. To be treated as part of the team, she needed to act like a Guardian, and the only female example she had was Kri. The woman was as direct and as blunt about sex as any of the guys. Thankfully, the Guardians weren't crass or lewd. But they were unapologetic about their sexuality, and sometimes their talk still made her uncomfortable.

"Who else could you talk to?" Alfie waved a hand. "We are the only ones here, which is a golden opportunity for you to do what you want. I doubt you'd have the guts to go for it with Arwel or Peter watching."

He was right, but she really didn't want her first time with Emmett to be in the tiny bathroom.

"There must be another way. If it's okay for me to have sex with him in the bathroom, where you can't see us, then why not do it in the bed while you are not looking? I don't see a difference as far as security goes, but it will make a big difference to me."

Frowning, Alfie scratched his stubble. "Maybe there is a way. I can turn the screen brightness all the way down, so when you turn the lights off, I won't be able to see anything. And if you sense trouble, just say lights on."

She snorted. "If I can. The one time that Emmett bit me, I was helpless to do anything. I felt paralyzed."

Alfie's expression turned exasperated. "Do you want to do it or not? I can solve all your problems by going in with you. I wouldn't mind a threesome."

"Right." She narrowed her eyes at him. "Even if I was into that, how would you hold a gun while participating?"

His smile was lupine. "Oh, I know precisely how I would do that. Do you want me to describe the scene to you?"

She lifted a hand to stop him. "No need."

It was as if he had planted the image in her head, and she could see it. Her on all fours with Alfie in front of her, holding a gun trained on Emmett, who was thrusting into her from behind.

Alfie's nostrils flared, and his lupine smile turned into a hyena grin. "Evidently, you caught my drift."

Cassandra

As the guests continued to arrive, Cassandra realized what had been bothering her about Onegus's family. They all looked to be around the same age—mid-twenties to mid-thirties.

Where were the parents? The grandparents?

Perhaps Onegus's family had a respect-your-elders tradition, dictating that the young people had to be on time while the older generation arrived later. A Korean friend told her that she wasn't allowed to leave the dining table before anyone older than her, even by a month, was either done or gave her permission to leave. Different cultures had different traditions.

There were almost no children either.

She'd seen one cute toddler girl running around, one teenage boy who looked to be fourteen or fifteen, and one couple came with a stroller. But that was less odd than the missing elder generation. It was after nine in the evening, and the event hadn't started yet, so it made sense that nearly no one had brought their kids. The two exceptions probably couldn't find a babysitter for tonight.

When and if Cassandra got married, she would have a day wedding, so all the children could attend. A family should celebrate together, the young and the old.

Leaning closer to Connor, she asked, "Where are all the old people?"

"Gone," he deadpanned.

She rolled her eyes. "I'm serious. Where are the mothers and fathers, uncles and aunts, grandmothers and grandfathers? Were they not invited?"

Connor shrugged but didn't offer an answer.

"More wine?" Nick refilled her glass without waiting for her response.

Roni, who'd been eyeing her with the same curiosity she'd been eyeing him, rose to his feet. "Wine is boring. I'm going to the bar. Can I get you anything?" he asked her.

He hadn't asked anyone else.

Were they all trying to get her drunk for some reason?

"Thanks, but I'm fine with the wine." She lifted the glass to her lips and pretended to take a sip.

Maybe she should dump it in one of the flower arrangements and pretend to be drunk, so they would show their hand.

"I'll ask the bartender to mix you the same drink Sylvia and Ruth like."

So that was why he hadn't asked them. He knew what they wanted. Cassandra felt silly for being so suspicious, but she couldn't shake the feeling that something wasn't right, and it wasn't only about the missing older generation.

"Thank you. I'll give it a try."

As Roni walked away, a stunning brunette sauntered toward their table. She had a gorgeous face, eyes of such vivid blue that they must have been contact lenses, and lips that were painted red. The dress she wore was an Oscar de la Renta gold-hued gown from his latest collection. Cassandra had seen it in a fashion magazine and had ogled it, but the only way she would have bought it was if she found it in her favorite, used designer attire boutique. It cost a small fortune, and it was too showy even for the gala she'd attended.

The Grecian style loose gown was fit for the goddess-like creature wearing it.

It accentuated rather than tried to conceal the woman's pregnant belly, and it was also definitely the original and not a knockoff.

"You must be Cassandra." The woman sat on the chair Onegus had vacated. "I'm Amanda, one of Onegus's many cousins." She offered Cassandra her hand.

"Hi." She shook it. "I love your dress. Oscar de la Renta, right?"

"You have a good eye." Amanda grinned. "I'm so happy that Onegus is dating a fashionista. I will finally have someone to play with." She leaned closer and smoothed her hand over the skirt of Cassandra's dress. "And yours is a Versace. I had one just like it, but I donated it to charity." She smiled sheepishly. "I tire of outfits after wearing them only a few times, and I donate them to charity, so I don't feel as guilty for buying them in the first place."

Cassandra felt her ears heat up, and it had nothing to do with the wine. Well, perhaps the wine was partially responsible for her reaction, turning it from mild to exasperated.

Her anger wasn't directed at Amanda, though. She was mad at herself.

The gown was indeed Versace, but it was a three-year-old one that she'd bought second-hand. Most people wouldn't have noticed, but Amanda was precisely the type of woman who would.

Unlike the gala dress, which had been made by an unknown designer, the one she was wearing now was recognizable by anyone who followed fashion shows and magazines.

She should have considered that Onegus's family was rich, and that some of the ladies were bound to be fashionistas like Amanda. The best way to deal with that was not to try to cover it up, but to own it and turn it to her advantage.

Cassandra had nothing to be embarrassed about. In fact, she was proud of herself for being frugal. It wasn't as if she couldn't afford to buy the latest Versace. She just didn't want to spend so much on a dress that she would wear only once.

"It might be yours." Cassandra smoothed her hand over the straight skirt. "I got it in my favorite secondhand designer attire boutique."

For a long and awkward moment, Amanda and everyone else around the table didn't say a thing. Averting their eyes, they were probably desperately searching for something non-offensive and politically correct to say.

As the silence became oppressive, Cassandra took pity on them. "I like designer clothing. I love the precise cuts, the luxurious fabrics, and I get pleasure from wearing something that was created by a true artist. I just don't like the price tags attached to those beautiful outfits. Finding them on sale or buying a gown that was used only once satisfies the bargain hunter in me as well as the fashion junkie. It's a win-win." She smirked. "It gives me immense satisfaction knowing that I'm dressed to the nines but at a fraction of the cost."

Amanda laughed. "You have to meet my sister-in-law. Syssi can't stomach paying more than a couple of hundred for an outfit. The only time I saw her lose her cool and raise her voice at me was when I took her shopping in an exclusive boutique and bought her an entire wardrobe." She stood up and motioned for Cassandra to join her. "Come. I'll introduce you."

Reluctantly, Cassandra followed, expecting to be led to one of the nearby tables. Instead, Amanda kept walking toward the front of the banquet hall and stopped in front of a long, rectangular table, the only one in the room that wasn't round.

The bride and groom's family table.

"Everyone, this is Cassandra, Onegus's date for this evening and probably for many more to come." She walked up to the most beautiful man Cassandra had ever seen and put her hands on his shoulders. "This is my brother, Kian."

The god-like creature dipped his head in greeting but didn't smile.

Cassandra felt like offering a curtsy, but she stifled the impulse and forced a smile. "It's a pleasure to meet you."

"And this is his wife, Syssi." Amanda moved to a very pregnant blonde, who was smiling broadly and seemed like a sweetheart of a person.

"Nice to meet you, Cassandra," Syssi said. "I've seen your and Onegus's pictures in the gossip magazines, but you are even more impressive in person than in those articles."

"Thank you." Cassandra fanned herself. "You are making me blush." She looked at the other couples sitting at the family table. "Where are the bride and groom?"

"They are getting ready," Amanda said. "My sister Sari is the bride, and my other sister Alena is with her and the other bridesmaids." She rubbed a hand over her belly. "I figured that Sari had enough bridesmaids already so the pregnant ladies could sit this one out." She winked at Syssi.

The woman winced. "I can barely walk. I feel like a beached whale."

Cassandra laughed. "When are you due?"

"In three weeks."

"Good luck."

"Thanks." Syssi smiled. "I can't wait to meet my daughter."

"I bet."

The eyes of the terrifying god-like creature sitting beside Syssi softened, and he draped a gentle arm around his wife's shoulders. "All in good time."

"Anyway," Amanda said. "I wanted the two of you to meet because you have something in common."

Syssi arched a brow. "We are both artistic?"

"Well, yes, that too. But I'm referring to being frugal. Cassandra manages to look fabulous without spending a fortune on it like I do."

That was a nice way to put it.

Syssi chuckled. "No one spends as much as Amanda does. And in my case, it's hard to look fabulous when I'm the size of a whale."

"You're beautiful," her husband said.

"He's right." Cassandra offered the couple her best smile. "I should go back to my table. It was nice meeting you."

When Amanda escorted her back to her companions, the waiter arrived with another round of drinks for everyone.

"I ordered you a lychee martini," Roni said.

Cassandra grimaced. "It looks tasty, but I'm already a little tipsy. I don't think I should drink anymore."

"It's tradition to get drunk at a Scottish wedding." Amanda patted her shoulder. "Regrettably, Syssi and I will have to remain sober. You'll have to drink for both of us."

Lifting the goblet, Cassandra smiled. "When in Rome and all that. To the happy couple." She took a small sip.

Kian

Kian watched Cassandra leave with Amanda and wondered who she reminded him of. Shuffling through two thousand years of memories wasn't an easy task, and after a couple of minutes, he gave up.

He might have seen her face in an advertisement back in the day.

Cassandra was a beautiful woman, and according to Onegus, she'd modeled for the cosmetics company she was still working for. So, it was possible that Cassandra simply reminded him of her younger self.

The thing was that her attitude seemed familiar as well.

She was confident to the point of being arrogant, and unlike most people, she hadn't been intimidated by him. No wonder that Onegus had fallen for her.

The chief needed a strong woman to stand up to him.

Onegus fooled most people with his easy smiles and his charm, but he was the chief of Guardians for a reason. He was a true commander, a great strategist, and he was also a stubborn bastard who didn't yield to pressure and didn't take bullshit from anyone. Not from Kian and not from Turner.

Cassandra was his match. The language she used was polite and eloquent, but she was a straight shooter who didn't mince words.

"Did you feel it?" Syssi asked.

"Feel what?"

"The energy coming off Cassandra." She smoothed her hand over her hair. "I felt my hair stand up on end."

"It didn't. You must have imagined it."

"I felt it too," Kalugal said. "But then I might have reacted to her feminine beauty."

"Do you miss your bachelor days?" Syssi asked.

"Not at all." Kalugal straightened in his chair. "So, who's the lady, and why did Onegus invite a human to the wedding?"

"He thinks she might be a Dormant, and he wants Sylvia to check out her power, or at least that's the excuse he gave me. He thinks that the energy Cassandra has is similar to Sylvia's, but she doesn't know how to harness and direct it."

Kalugal looked confused. "Does Cassandra know that she's a potential Dormant?"

"She doesn't." Kian took a sip from his water goblet. "Onegus didn't tell her yet. He figured it was safe to bring her to the wedding because other humans would be here as well, and we couldn't do anything overly suspicious anyway."

Kalugal leaned back and pursed his lips. "Onegus could've asked me to compel her silence. Heck, even Eleanor could have done it. Why risk it?"

Kian put down his goblet none too gently, and some of the water splashed out. Stifling a curse, he wiped it off his sleeve. "He gave me some bullshit explanation about not being ready to involve others in his business. But by inviting her here, he involved all of us."

"I'll ask Lisa to sniff her," Syssi said. "I wish she was here."

Lisa and Ronja were part of Sari's entourage of bridesmaids, which was the size of a small army. His sister had a big heart, and she wanted to honor as many of the females close to her as she could. He suspected that Amanda and Syssi had bowed out so others could take their place.

That reminded him that he and Kalugal needed to take their places. Glancing at his watch, he turned to his cousin. "It's time." The groomsmen were supposed to meet outside the banquet hall in a few minutes.

He leaned and kissed Syssi's cheek. "Don't cry."

She got emotional at weddings, and the pregnancy made her even more vulnerable. Usually, Syssi found comfort in his arms, but he wouldn't be near her to offer it during the ceremony.

"I won't." She smiled at him. "Sari and David are already mated. This is just a party."

"Try to remember that when Annani makes her speech." His mother had a talent for tear-jerking.

"Don't worry." Syssi affected a wider smile. "Go already." She gave him a gentle push. "Stop hovering over me like a mother hen."

Pushing to his feet, he turned toward the room's double doors. Brundar and Anandur were already waiting for him there, not to guard him, but to join the other groomsmen.

"I wish Lokan was here," Kalugal said as they walked toward the door.

"Yeah, me too." Kian actually meant it. "And your mother as well. I wish there was a way to convince her to leave your father."

Kalugal sighed softly. "It's a lost cause. I stopped trying a long time ago."

"Do you still talk to her?"

"Twice a week."

"How is she?"

"Same as always. Loving, gentle, and totally misguided."

Cassandra

"So, I told the wife," Sharon leaned back and crossed her arms over her chest. "Your husband is not cheating on you with his secretary. He's cheating on you with his business partner."

Cassandra was still waiting for the punchline to Sharon's story. What did it matter who the husband cheated with?

"What did the wife say?" Roni asked.

"She rolled her eyes and said that she'd known the two had been lovers since college. She didn't mind, and the woman was so happy that he wasn't schtupping the secretary that she paid us a bonus."

Cassandra shook her head. "So, she didn't mind the one lover, but hired your firm to investigate whether there was a second one?"

"Yep," Sharon confirmed. "Humans are strange." She leaned toward Robert. "I can hardly stand it if Robert so much as looks at another woman with appreciation."

He wrapped his arm around her shoulders. "I only have eyes for you, my love."

Connor chuckled. "Let me guess. The partner was a guy, and that's why the wife was okay with it."

Cassandra was still stuck on Sharon's use of the word humans. Was that the new politically correct term for people? Cassandra couldn't for the life of her imagine what was wrong with 'people,' but these were strange times. Perhaps someone had decided that the word people was racist?

Could be.

After all, people might be from different ethnicities, but they were all human. She needed to remember that.

"Some people can be polyamorous," Tessa said. "Personally, I can't imagine living like that, but for some, it comes naturally."

Cassandra let out a breath. Apparently, the word people was still okay.

For now.

"Like the Kra-ell," Nick said and then winced. "I mean the Krall in the game."

"What game?" Cassandra asked.

"Have you heard about the Perfect Match Virtual Adventures Studios?" Ruth asked.

"I've heard about them, and I thought that it was all a big hype. Virtual technology is amazing, but it is still far from being realistic."

"It is very much so," Roni said. "If you ever get tired of Onegus, give it a try. It's pricey, but you can cram a two-week vacation into three hours. It's hard to beat that when you have a busy job."

"You don't have to dump Onegus to try," Sylvia said. "You can do it with him. Roni and I did it together, and it was the most fun we've ever had. We chose the winter spy adventure."

Roni smiled at his girlfriend. "We were already together when we went on the virtual spy adventure, but Cassandra and Onegus are not there yet." He turned to Cassandra and winked. "After all, it's called the Perfect Match for a reason. The software can find you a better match than him."

Roni had a sarcastic sense of humor that resonated well with hers. She lifted the wine glass Nick had just refilled and pretended to take a sip. "If things don't work out with Onegus, I'll give it a try."

He still hadn't made good on his promise to introduce her to his mother. In fact, he hadn't come to check on her at all. He'd said that he would join her after all the guests had arrived, but it seemed like every chair in the banquet hall was filled, and Onegus was still a no-show.

"Jackson and I need to give it a try," Tessa said. "But I'm scared. What if I don't like the adventure?"

"The technician is there to monitor you," Sylvia said. "If you get distressed, they will wake you up."

As the group continued discussing the wonders of virtual adventures, Cassandra listened with only half an ear. Not that the subject was boring, but observing her young companions was more interesting.

They were all about the same age as the snowflakes in her creative department, but they were completely different kinds of people. They all seemed to have busy careers, and Jackson, who looked no older than twenty, ran his own successful business.

The kid worked even harder than she did, and yet he couldn't be happier. He was excited to see his business grow and had no problem with the long hours he had to put into it. Naturally, his girlfriend wasn't happy about him working all of the time, but she accepted it as a temporary situation only until Jackson's business got big enough for him to delegate more of the work to others.

Cassandra had a feeling that Tessa would be waiting a long time. The guy's ambition would drive him to open yet another business and then another. At some point, though, he might get tired of the race and slow down.

The thing was, none of them complained about having to work too hard or about slights and offenses in the workplace, and for the first time in a very long time, Cassandra felt comfortable to speak her mind without having to double-check every word.

In fact, she felt like she was among longtime friends.

"Why aren't Vlad and Wendy sitting with us?" Tessa asked.

Jackson leaned back to scan the other tables, his chair perching precariously on its rear legs. "I see them sitting with Stella and Richard, Wendy's mom, Bowen, Leon, and the new girl. I don't know her name. Stella's mom is with them as well, as are Bowen and Leon's mothers. They have a full table." He leaned back.

Mothers? Cassandra glanced in the direction Jackson had looked, but she could see no one older than thirty-something. They either had an in-house plastic surgeon, or she'd stumbled into a nest of vampires.

She looked at her nearly empty glass. Perhaps she'd had too much to drink already, and her vision was blurry.

"Why isn't your mother sitting with us?" Tessa asked.

Jackson shrugged. "She decided to sit with Kalugal's men to keep them company so they wouldn't feel out of place. You know how she is. My mother always finds someone in need of help."

Cassandra emptied what was left of her glass. If mothers were supposed to sit with their children, then why wasn't Onegus's mother sitting at their table?

It wasn't that she particularly wanted her there, but she had to wonder why Onegus had chosen to seat her elsewhere.

Who had he thought to protect?

Her or his mother?

Margaret

Bowen's mother, a lovely woman named Elise who looked unnervingly young, held on to Margaret's hand as if she was afraid to lose her. "I'm giddy with joy that my Bowen found a mate." Using different words, she'd said the same thing at least ten times.

Margaret wondered if Elise would have been as happy if she knew about her past—a drug addict who had abandoned her baby daughter and hadn't gone back to look for her.

Wendy had forgiven her, but Margaret still had a hard time forgiving herself.

If what they had said about Emmett was true, then it really hadn't been her fault, but even that wasn't enough to eradicate her guilt. She should have fought harder.

Wendy had called her a fighter, but she wasn't. The best term Margaret could apply to herself was a survivor.

Leon's mother, Rowan, was more reserved than Elise. She snuck glances at Ana, and the two chatted a little about how Leon and Ana had met, but Rowan wasn't holding Ana's hand or gushing how happy she was that Leon had found a mate.

It was ironic. Leon had snagged himself a young, beautiful heiress, who was well educated and had no skeletons in her closet, but his mother wasn't overjoyed. Bowen was saddled with a former drug addict, abuse victim, and child abandoner, and his mother couldn't be happier.

Fate had a twisted sense of humor.

"Where is Eleanor?" Ana asked Leon. "I want to say hi, but I don't see her."

"She volunteered to guard Emmett," Bowen said.

Stella huffed out a breath. "I'm not surprised. Greggory is here, and he's sitting next to Vanessa. Eleanor would not have liked seeing that."

"Can you tell me more about Eleanor?" Leon's mother said. "I was under the impression that Kian wasn't at all happy to let her into the village, and now she's assigned guard duties?"

Bowen answered Rowan. "Eleanor helped Leon and Peter get Anastasia out of Safe Haven, and she was also instrumental in unmasking Emmett Haderech, the cult's leader. She's proven herself as not only trustworthy but also capable. Kian authorized her inclusion in the Guardian training program."

Stella snorted. "He must be desperate for new trainees to let her into the program. I don't trust her."

"Why?" Margaret asked. "I met Eleanor, and she might be rough around the edges, but she was nice to me, and Peter seemed to like her."

"Peter likes everybody," Elise said. "He has a good heart."

Margaret smiled at Bowen. "No one has a better heart than your son."

"I know." Elise smiled. "He was such an unruly child that I still can't believe what a good male he became."

Bowen had been a troublemaker?

"Is that true?" She looked at his smiling eyes.

He nodded. "I'm afraid so." He leaned, kissed her cheek, and then whispered in her ear, "If the Fates bless us with a child, I hope it will be a girl. I don't want to put you through what my mother had to endure."

Margaret was still reeling from the idea of having a child with Bowen when Elise said, "I heard that, and it's nonsense. You were a sweet boy who had a couple of hellion teenage years. I wouldn't have traded you for anyone. Margaret already has a wonderful daughter. I'm sure she wants a son."

"Well, in that case, whatever the Fates decide is fine with me." Bowen wrapped his arm around Margaret's shoulders.

Desperate to change the subject, she blurted, "Emmett is right here in the keep, right? Can I see him?"

Next to her, Bowen tensed. "Not tonight, that's for sure. Kian or Onegus have to approve it, and then you will need to wear earpieces that will nullify his compulsion."

"I've met him," Stella said. "He's not as bad as I thought he would be. He's polite, even charming."

"Villains often are," Ana said. "At least in movies. And being handsome doesn't hurt either."

Stella's mother, who was a very different person from her daughter, arched a brow. "Why did you go to see the cult leader?"

Margaret wanted to know that too.

For some reason, Stella glanced at Vlad before answering her mother. "Kian wanted me to help with the interrogation."

Vlad seemed relieved to hear her answer.

Was Stella hiding something?

"In what way?" Vlad's grandmother asked.

Margaret stifled the need to shake her head. None of the immortals looked old enough to be the parents of adult children, and definitely not anyone's grandparents, and yet some of them were ancient. Bowen included.

It was difficult to wrap her head around that.

"I speak Chinese, Stella said. "Both the Mandarin and Cantonese dialects, just not very well. I know enough to get by. But as far as I know, no other clan member does."

"Morris speaks it," Bowen said. "I don't know how well, though."

"He's fluent," Richard said. "He's teaching Mey and Jin Chinese in preparation for their trip."

Margaret shook her head. "Why did Kian need someone who spoke Chinese to interrogate Emmett?"

"There is still a lot you don't know about him." Bowen took her hand.

"Can you tell me?"

Bowen and Leon exchanged glances, and then Bowen shrugged. "You are a clan member now, so there is no reason to keep it from you. But now is not the time. Besides, I don't have all the details either. Only those who were involved with the interrogation do."

"I will fill you in," Stella said. "Just not tonight. This is a time to celebrate and rejoice."

Cassandra

Connor tapped Cassandra's arm. "Onegus is heading this way, which means that the ceremony is about to start."

She looked over her shoulder, hoping to see him walking toward her with an older woman that looked like him. Instead, he was holding a drink in each hand. The one with the lychees floating inside was probably for her, no doubt another attempt to get her drunk.

They were all drinking like fiends, but none of them seemed to be even tipsy, while she'd had to watch her step returning to the table. Then she'd had a martini, which had been delicious, and now her head was spinning.

She'd better not mention his mother and blurt out something that would sound bitchy. Besides, it wasn't as if she was eager to meet the woman. In fact, Cassandra would gladly skip it.

Perhaps Onegus was planning to introduce them after the ceremony?

That actually made sense even to her alcohol-addled brain. He'd been too busy before, and now that everyone had arrived, the ceremony was about to start.

"Thank you." She accepted the drink he handed her. "Are you free to finally join me?" There had been more bite to her words than she'd intended.

Watch the bitchy tone, Cassandra.

"Yes." He pulled out the chair next to her and sat down. "Now that everyone is here, I have the place locked down, so my team and I can sit down and enjoy the ceremony."

Lockdown sounded ominous; had Onegus locked the doors to the banquet hall?

"You shouldn't have done that. It's a fire hazard to lock the doors with so many people inside."

"The doors are not locked. The lockdown refers to the entry to the building."

Glancing at the closed doors, she noticed that all the servers were gone. "What's going on?"

"It's just a security measure," Onegus said. "We had every member of the serving staff thoroughly searched for bugs and weapons, but you never know what our enemies might come up with. This is just one more precaution to safeguard the bride and groom and the head of our clan."

"You mean Kian?"

Onegus cocked a brow. "Did you meet him?"

"Amanda took me to the family table and introduced me to her brother and sister-in-law."

"That's good." Onegus's expression and tone didn't match his words.

Was he upset that someone else had introduced her to his boss?

As the music was silenced, everyone turned to look at the closed doors, and a moment later they were opened by two burly men in tuxes.

A hush fell over the room.

It was as if they were all holding their breath, and Cassandra wondered whether it was in anticipation of the bride and groom. Perhaps their tradition didn't include the wedding song.

A small woman in a long white dress walked through the open doors, or rather floated because she moved with such fluidity that it didn't look like walking at all.

Was that the bride?

The dress looked more like a priestess's robe than a wedding gown, and the woman didn't wear a veil over her mane of flaming red hair, or hold flowers in her hands, and she glowed.

Cassandra wanted to rub her eyes to make sure that she wasn't hallucinating, but that would have ruined her makeup, so she just peeled them as wide open as she could and gaped.

It must be a trick of the light. Someone was shining a soft spotlight on the woman, or rather girl because she couldn't be more than eighteen, and the shiny fabric of her robe-like dress must be reflecting it, making it look as if her skin was glowing.

She wanted to ask Onegus who the beautiful angel was, but it was so quiet in the room that a needle dropping would have been heard. Cassandra barely dared to breathe, let alone whisper.

The woman floated up the three-rung platform at the back of the room, turned to face the guests, and lifted her arms. "It is with boundless love and joy that we gather here to celebrate my daughter and David's joining."

Cassandra closed her eyes and let that angelic voice wash over her.

Someone must have slipped her a roofie because she was hallucinating for sure. Angels weren't real, and the girl on the dais couldn't be anyone's mother.

But what if she was a priestess? Priests called everyone son or daughter, right?

Yeah, that made more sense than someone slipping her a roofie. Her boyfriend was the head of security. No one would dare to do that to his date.

The priestess just happened to be the most beautiful female Cassandra had ever seen, and she also happened to possess an angelic voice.

After all, the woman had no wings, and despite the glow, there was no halo floating above her head.

"Let us welcome Sari and David with the musical composition they chose for this joyous moment."

As the soft instrumental music started playing, the doors opened once more, and the groomsmen entered. She recognized Kian and the guy who had been sitting next to him at the family table. The other four were also inhumanly handsome, but next to those two, they looked almost ordinary.

All the members of Onegus's family could star in a soap opera. It was a shame that *The Bold and the Beautiful* title was already taken. It would have been a perfect fit for them.

When the men were in position, standing on the lowest rung to the priestess's right, the bridesmaids entered, and Cassandra stifled a surprised sound. One of them was an older woman who looked like a real mother, and one was a teenage girl.

Finally, some semblance of normality.

Perhaps she wasn't hallucinating after all, and Onegus's family weren't all beautiful vampires who never aged.

When all eight bridesmaids took their places to the priestess's left, all eyes turned to the banquet hall doors.

The music changed to another classical piece that Cassandra had never heard before, and the couple entered together holding hands.

The bride was gorgeous like her sister, but in a softer way. She was shorter, rounder, and her hair was auburn and not black. Her dress was simple and elegant, with no lace or embroidery or anything shiny. Just a perfectly cut bodice with a skirt that flared from the knees down and a train that trailed on the floor several feet behind her.

Cassandra had seen a similar dress at the Oscar De La Renta show, but this one was even more beautiful and had probably been custom-made for the bride.

Departing from tradition, the bride wore no veil and held no flowers. Her groom was a handsome blond man, who was grinning from ear to ear as if he'd won the lottery.

The couple walked up to the second rung of the platform and looked up to the priestess.

During the processions there had been several murmurs, but everyone hushed again, waiting for the priestess to start the ceremony.

Margaret

Margaret stared at the goddess, willing her jaw to close. She wanted to see Ana's reaction, to say something to her friend who was sharing this revelatory moment with her, but to do that she would have to tear her eyes away from the glowing otherworldly being up on the dais.

When the door was opened once again and the groomsmen entered, murmurs started and some of the magic eddied, enough for Margaret to slide a quick glance at Ana.

Her friend was gaping just as stupidly as she was, but she still felt Margaret's gaze on her and turned to look at her. "Un-freaking-believable," she whispered. "The goddess is actually glowing."

Next to Ana, Leon and the other immortals smiled indulgently. Richard, however, nodded in understanding. "She's magnificent and terrifying to behold," he whispered. "But when you get to know her, the fear goes away. Annani is kind and friendly."

Taking another look at the goddess, Margaret could believe it. Annani looked like an ethereal angel, and her smile was benevolent, but her mane of fiery red hair hinted that there was a little bit of the devil in her as well.

The goddess's expression wasn't haughty or condescending, but Margaret wasn't convinced that it was all about Annani's love for her people. Annani radiated power, and she gobbled up their adoration, feasting on it in a similar way Emmett had done in Safe Haven.

Margaret wondered what Annani would have done if her people weren't as enamored with her, if they rebelled, or if they refused to follow the path she'd carved for them.

Would she have resorted to compelling them against their will like Emmett had done?

Under the tablecloth, Bowen reached for her hand and gave it a gentle squeeze. "You have nothing to fear from the Clan Mother."

He must have smelled her fear.

It was difficult to adjust to the new world she was living in, with immortals who could sniff her emotions, hear her heartbeat in another room, and perform other feats she couldn't even imagine.

She cast him a small smile and squeezed his hand back.

With Bowen by her side, she shouldn't fear a thing except for the goddess. He would protect her from everything and everyone, but he was as helpless against that immense power as she was.

As everyone in this room was, or perhaps in the entire world.

Well, that couldn't be true. The goddess had existed for over five thousand years, and if she was that powerful, she could have prevented wars and saved millions upon millions of people.

Annani probably wasn't powerful enough to smite entire armies, but she could have eliminated some of the leaders, the worst offenders in human history, and prevented the slaughter of so many.

Perhaps she couldn't do even that?

Maybe she was forbidden to tamper with destiny?

"Why are you suddenly so sad?" Bowen asked in a whisper. "This is a joyous occasion."

She waved a hand. "Don't mind me. Sometimes my mind wanders in twisted paths."

Across the table, Anastasia nodded.

As the music changed, the doors opened again, and the bride and groom entered holding hands. People smiled and waved at the couple, some offering air kisses as they walked by, but no one rose to their feet.

Come to think of it, they hadn't done that to honor the goddess either.

Maybe they had done away with that tradition because Annani was tiny. If everyone stood up, only those on both sides of the pathway would have seen her.

When the couple took their position on the platform, the music stopped, and the goddess lifted her arms again.

"It gives me great pleasure to have nearly my entire clan here to celebrate Sari and David's joining. They are blessed to have such a big, supportive, and loving family." She smiled down at the couple standing before her. "Are you ready to pledge your eternal love to each other?"

"We are," her daughter answered and turned to her groom. "Would you like to go first?"

He nodded. "I love you, my Sari. I wish there was a word stronger than love to express the depth of my feelings for you, but since there isn't, love will have to suffice. I, David, son of Ronja and Michael, pledge everything that I am to you, my life, my love, and my unwavering support."

Margaret wiped away a tear. It was such a simple and yet heartfelt pledge, and what made her tear up was the knowledge that nothing short of a major disaster would put a stop to that love. Immortals bonded forever, and abuse was unheard of in the clan. Hopefully, that would never change.

The groom pulled a ring out of his pocket. "Are you willing to share your life with me forever?"

"Yes, my love."

He slipped it onto her finger.

"My turn." Sari took his hands. "I, Sari, daughter of Annani, sister to Kian, Alena, Lilen, and Amanda, pledge myself to you, David, son of Ronja and Michael, brother to Lisa and Jonah. I will love you and support you and do my best to make you happy." She pulled a ring off her thumb. "Are you ready to share the rest of your life with me?"

"I am."

She slipped it onto his finger.

As the crowd erupted in deafening cheers and applause, the couple kissed, and the goddess waited patiently.

When they parted, she took her daughter's hand and then David's and put them one on top of the other. "May the Fates smile fondly upon this joining and shower your home with love, happiness, and as many children as your hearts' desire."

Onegus

There were too many people around to discern Cassandra's scent, but Onegus could feel the crackling current under her skin intensifying. He kept casting her sidelong glances, trying to gauge her response to the glowing goddess standing upon the dais, but her expression was guarded. Her body was a better barometer of her feelings.

As soon as the ceremony ended, he would have to thrall her.

Right now, there was too much going on for her mind to be calm enough for him to be able to penetrate it.

"May the Fates smile fondly upon this joining and shower your home with love, happiness, and as many children as your hearts' desire."

As soon as Annani let go of Sari and David's hands, everyone got to their feet, applauding and cheering the now officially joined couple.

Next to him, Cassandra clapped while swaying on her stilettos, but as he reached to steady her, she cast him a withering look.

When the cheering and clapping subsided, Gerard made a rare appearance.

"I need everyone to calm down and take their seats so my servers can do their job. *Bon appétit.*"

In typical Gerard style, the request bordered on rude.

"That's my cousin the chef," Onegus said in Cassandra's ear. "Do you still want to meet him?"

Her eyelashes fluttered, and she looked at him down her nose. "His attitude doesn't scare me." She leaned closer, so her face was only a couple of inches from Onegus's. "I know how to deal with pricks like him." She lifted her hand and brought her thumb and forefinger together. "I can make him feel this small."

Onegus stifled a chuckle. Cassandra was way past tipsy and all the way to drunk.

"I'd sure like to see you cut the mighty Gerard down to size. But I don't think even you can do that. Kian avoids confrontations with him."

She arched one perfectly shaped brow. "That's because Kian cares. I don't." She started to push to her feet.

This time, Onegus couldn't contain the chuckle. "Sit down, Cassy. The servers are coming with dinner."

Glancing at the side doors that were opened to allow the servers in, she huffed and sat down. "It was a beautiful ceremony, and Gerard shouldn't have been allowed to come out and talk to the guests like that. Shame on him."

Next to her, Connor snickered, and their other dinner companions were all trying not to laugh. Thankfully, Cassandra was too drunk to notice or that energy swirling inside her would have unleashed its destructive power on Gerard's fancy china.

Perhaps she'd been too drunk to notice a glowing goddess?

"That priestess was something else." Cassandra lifted her water goblet and took a sip. "How did she make her skin glow? Did she smear sparkly lotion all over her skin? And that huge red wig was so over the top." She rolled her eyes. "Where did you find her? Hollywood?"

The first one to lose it was Sharon. Hiding behind Robert's broad shoulders, she giggled uncontrollably. Then Tessa joined in, and soon everyone except for Cassandra and Onegus was laughing.

He tensed, expecting plates to crack and glasses to explode. Instead, Cassandra waved a hand. "It wasn't that funny, but at least now I know I'm not the only drunk at the table."

The others took their cue from her comment and started pretending they were inebriated. Connor even started a lewd Scottish ballad, but he was interrupted by the flurry of servers who descended on their table like a flock of ravens, placing an artfully presented first course in front of everyone.

"What is that?" Cassandra eyed the culinary masterpiece suspiciously. "I don't know if I should eat it or take it home and put it on a shelf as a decoration."

Roni sniffed at the creation in front of him. It was shaped like a rooster, and by the smell, it was made from cheese and slivers of carrots, apples, green onions, and some other stuff that Onegus wasn't sure about.

"It has cheese in it," Roni said. "The rest are veggies and fruits."

Cassandra still stared at hers. "I can't eat that. It's too pretty."

"What I want to know is who made over seven hundred of these roosters." Sylvia lifted her plate to take a closer look. "There is no machine that could do that."

"Maybe Gerard had the Odus make them," Tessa suggested.

When Jackson threw a warning look at her, she covered her mouth. "I meant Oompa Loompas or gizmos."

Apparently, Cassandra was too drunk to notice the slip, and as Jackson lifted his rooster to his mouth and took a bite, she did the same.

Her eyes rolled back. "I forgot how good Gerard's creations are. He's forgiven."

Laughing, Onegus wiped nonexistent sweat off his forehead. "What a relief. The prick gets to cook another day."

Emmett

As the door to Emmett's cell started to swing open, he glanced at his watch. It was after nine at night, and no one ever visited him this late.

Eleanor.

He smelled her scent even before she stepped into his cell, one of the Guardians no doubt standing outside to make sure that he didn't make a run for it.

As if he were stupid enough to try it.

"Good evening, Eleanor. What a nice surprise." He looked her over.

She still wore the same clothes she'd had on when she'd brought in his dinner, and she had two large paper cups in her hands.

"Hi." She waited for the door to close before joining him on the couch.

"I didn't bring you blood. But I thought you would enjoy some wine."

"I thought that I smelled wine." He reached for the cup. "Where did you get it?" He removed the plastic lid and took a sniff.

It smelled like good wine, which made drinking it from a paper cup even worse, but as the saying went, beggars can't be choosers.

"I swiped it from the kitchen." Eleanor flicked the lid off and lifted the cup. "Cheers."

"What are we drinking to?"

"Us."

"I'll drink to that." He tapped her cup with his.

While he sipped and savored, Eleanor gulped at least half of the large cup in one go.

"What's troubling you?" He regarded her with concern.

"Why do you think something is troubling me?"

"Do you usually gulp large quantities of wine?"

She looked at her cup. "No, but this one is good."

He doubted she'd even tasted it. "Talk to me." He reached for her hand. "We are friends, right?"

Eleanor glanced at the bed, then shook her head. "I'm not good at this."

He could sense her nervousness and wondered what had caused it. She wasn't fearful, just apprehensive.

"Good at what?"

"The whole seduction part."

She wanted to seduce him?

"What about the watchers?"

"It's only Alfie, and he's busy watching a movie." She glanced at the camera. "If we rotate the couch so its back is to the bed, it will block some of the camera's view." She avoided his eyes.

He had a feeling that she wasn't telling him the truth, but he didn't know about what.

Was it a trap?

Perhaps she'd been asked to seduce him so they would have a recording of him drinking from her?

But what could they possibly want it for? Obviously for leverage, but against whom?

"Even if we do that, and Alfie can't see what's happening on the bed, he will know what's going on and come to put a stop to it."

She shifted her eyes to him. "Why would he want to do that? I'm allowed to have sex with whomever I want."

"Even a prisoner whom you're guarding?"

Maybe someone had put her up to it to get her in trouble. She'd admitted to not being liked or trusted by many of the clan members. Someone might have devised a plan to get her kicked out of the training program, and if that happened, she would no longer be allowed to visit him.

He couldn't afford to lose her.

Eleanor's smile was tight. "The clan has its own laws, and human rules don't apply. It's not like I'm abusing my station to get you to do something that you don't want to."

"It could be interpreted that way. I don't want you to get in trouble."

She eyed him from under lowered eyelashes. "Perhaps you just don't want me?"

Releasing control over his fangs, he let them punch out and smiled. "Do you really think so?"

"That doesn't prove anything. You might be hungry or just crave a snack."

He shook his head. "You're an immortal. Use your sense of smell."

"I'm not good at interpreting smells."

"Then interpret this." He pulled her hand and pressed it against his erection. "Males can't fake arousal, Eleanor."

She sucked in a breath and ordered, "Dim lights!"

The system responded to her demand, dimming the lights, but Eleanor wasn't happy with it. "Dim lights by seventy-five percent."

"What are you doing?"

She leaned closer. "Making it much more difficult for Alfie to see us." She cupped his cheek. "Kiss me, Emmett."

Eleanor

As Eleanor stared into Emmett's dark eyes, she saw the hesitation and then the decision made.

He closed the distance between their mouths, not in a rush but with deliberate slowness, as if giving her time to change her mind. And then his soft lips were on hers, kissing her gently, as if she was fragile, precious, and then he withdrew and looked at the door.

"No one is coming to stop us, Emmett," she breathed. "Kiss me again."

He brushed a finger down her cheek. "I liked seeing you all flushed, wanting me." His finger trailed down her neck, stopping at where her pulse was beating wildly.

In the semi-darkness, his eyes flashed red, and his elongating fangs gleamed white. He looked like a beautiful demon, and an exquisite shiver of fear rippled down her back.

His finger continued its downward track. "Are your nipples hard, Eleanor? Shall I check?"

Her eyes closed, she couldn't breathe, couldn't respond, only pant in anticipation of his touch.

"Are they?" he whispered against her ear.

"Yes," she managed to hiss.

He nuzzled her neck, his tongue flicking over her pulsing vein. Was he about to bite her?

Her breath left her throat in a whoosh, her core spasmed, and moisture soaked the gusset of her panties.

Eleanor wanted Emmett to take her to his bed, to strip her naked and run his hands over every inch of her skin, but they hadn't moved the couch to block the camera's view yet, and she didn't want him to know that Alfie wasn't watching. As much as she wanted the sex, she didn't trust him yet.

He must have read her thoughts. Moving faster than she could process, he lifted her in his arms and shifted her to the bed, then turned the couch so its back was partially blocking the camera's view.

"I've fantasized about you naked in my bed for so many nights." He tugged her T-shirt up, and when she lifted her arms, he pulled it off her.

The red glow in his eyes eerie in the darkness, he gazed at her for a long moment before hooking his fingers in the elastic of her yoga pants. "Did you wear them knowing that I would take them off?" He pulled them past her hips.

She shook her head.

"I think you did." He pulled them all the way down and then tossed them over the back of the couch. "Gorgeous." He smoothed his hands over her outer thighs before dipping in, his thumb brushing over the soaked gusset of her panties.

"So ready for me. So lovely." Emmett leaned down and kissed her through the fabric. "Your scent is intoxicating." He moved the gusset aside and pushed a finger into her, then withdrew it and pushed back with two.

Eleanor was a hair away from climaxing. If he only touched the throbbing bundle of nerves at the apex of her thighs she was going to tip over.

Instead, he pulled her panties down her thighs, and then tossed them aside. Her bra was next, and then she was bare and didn't know whether to cover her breasts with her hands or let his eyes feast on her.

"Beautiful," he hissed. "Even more so than I imagined."

"I want to see you too."

His smile was conceited. "Have you imagined me naked when lying in bed alone at night?"

"Yes."

He started on the buttons of his shirt. "Have you been touching yourself, imagining that those were my hands and my fingers pleasuring you instead of your own?"

She searched her mind for something witty to say, but all that came out was the truth. "Yes."

He shrugged the shirt off, and she gasped.

"Do you like what you see?"

"You're beautiful." She didn't care that his ego was already inflated enough.

Emmett was perfect. His chest was all smooth, lean muscles and completely hairless.

Not bothering with the zipper, he pushed his jeans down his lean hips, and then he was standing in front of her in his boxer briefs, a massive erection obscenely stretching the fabric.

Eleanor licked her lips. "Take them off."

"Not yet, dove." He climbed on the bed and sprawled on top of her.

Dove? She was no dove. She was a bird of prey.

Lifting her head, she nipped at his lower lip.

He smiled, his fangs gleaming white. "A dove with teeth." He gripped her hands and pulled them over her head. "Do you want to wrestle with me, my little dove?"

She tried to pull her hands out of his grip, but it was like trying to break free from iron manacles.

"I didn't think so." He kissed her with surprising gentleness. "Don't fight me, Eleanor. Aggression spurs instincts I'd rather remained dormant." He kissed her neck, nipping at it lightly. "If you let me, I'll pleasure you for hours. But if you fight me, this will be over too quickly for either of us to savor."

It dawned on her then that Emmett might enjoy her assertiveness, but any sign of aggression reminded him of his mistress and his near-slave status in the Kra-ell community.

When she let her arms go slack, he released his hold and watched her with a wary expression, probably expecting her to strike again and not looking forward to it.

Emmett needed her human softness and her willing submission. He didn't want to have to fight her for it.

Eleanor's muscled body and assertive attitude might have painted her as a hard woman, but there was a soft core hidden deep inside of her that the tough exterior protected.

Looking into his cautious expression, she made her decision.

Tonight, she would give Emmett access to that soft interior, and if he treated it with care, she might give him access to it again.

"Kiss me." She smoothed her hands up his arms, her touch gentle and caressing.

With a sigh that sounded like gratitude, he brought his lips to hers and licked into her mouth. He kept kissing her until she writhed under him, rubbing her aching nipples against his hard chest and her core against the tremendous bulge straining against the confines of his cotton briefs.

Emmett

When Eleanor had bitten him, bringing out the Kra-ell savage in him, Emmett had fought against the instinct driving him to conquer and subdue.

He'd learned a long time ago that he preferred human females' softness and submission to the Kra-ell females' aggression, their sharp fangs and claws, their thirst for blood, their sadistic need to inflict pain, and the flip side of it, their masochistic need to be overpowered by the male.

It was a vicious dance that didn't allow for any feelings of closeness, or even fondness. It was primal and animalistic, deeply satisfying physically, but just as deeply disappointing emotionally.

Perhaps it was the fault of the human genes contributed by his mother that he didn't enjoy the Kra-ell savage sex games. Emmett enjoyed giving pleasure just as much as he enjoyed receiving it, and although he'd never been in love with any of his human partners, he'd been fond of most.

If he didn't like a female's personality, he didn't take her to his bed, and he definitely hadn't invited any rotten apples to join his community.

As he let go of Eleanor's lips and looked down at her, he found her staring at him with softness in her eyes, an acceptance that stirred something in his heart.

Eleanor knew who he was, what he was, and yet she accepted him, blood-sucking and all.

And then she lifted her hand and cupped his cheek. "You are so handsome."

He cocked a brow. "Even with the fangs?"

Her eyes became hooded. "Especially with the fangs. I know what these babies can do."

"In good time, dove." He slid down her body and licked at her nipple. "First, I want to taste you." He looked up at her. "Will you allow me to do that?"

She nodded, and as her thighs parted, her feminine scent hit him with a force that nearly knocked him out.

Licking her other nipple, he trailed his hand down her belly to the trove of pleasure between her legs.

As his fingers gently brushed over her wetness, her hips jerked upward, and she hissed, "I'm so close."

He pushed up and took her lips, licking into her mouth while his finger breached her entrance.

Eleanor moaned, her hips undulating to get more of his finger inside her. If he could make her come just with his fingers, he could make her come again with his tongue, preparing her to accept his size.

Adding another finger, he pressed his thumb to her clit and nipped her lower lip.

"Emmett," she groaned as a release washed over her.

"I love hearing you say my name." He kept stroking her, helping her ride out the aftershocks of the climax and watching her expression change from ecstatic to sated and content.

"I'm not done with you," he said when she opened her eyes.

"I know." She turned to him, her hand drifting down to stroke him over his briefs. "I want this inside me."

"Not yet." He slid down again and pushed her on her back. "Part your legs for me."

She obeyed without hesitation, and at the sight of her glistening sex, he dove down and treated himself to his first taste of her.

"Exquisite." He looked at her from in between her spread thighs. "Almost as good as the taste of your blood."

"Oh, dear merciful Fates." Her head dropped back on the pillows.

It did something to him that she was turned on by the thought of him taking her vein. The other females he'd been with hadn't known what was coming, and even though they had all orgasmed hard while he'd fed on them, it hadn't given him as much satisfaction because that first part, the wanting, the acceptance, had been missing.

He hadn't even realized that until now, until he saw the anticipation in Eleanor's eyes, heard it in her moans, and sensed it in the flare of her arousal.

She wanted him at her vein, craved it, and he couldn't wait to sink his fangs into her.

With a growl, he sealed his mouth over her sex, sucking, pulling, then licking and nipping, and back to sucking until she exploded over his tongue, her back arching like a bow off the bed. He didn't stop there, working her into another climax, and another, until she pushed on his head.

It took him less than a second to shuck his briefs, and then he flipped Eleanor's boneless body over and pulled her bottom up, baring her gleaming wet sex to him. Rising behind her, he gripped her hips and aimed his shaft at her entrance.

He wanted to spear into her with one mighty thrust, but even after all the orgasms he'd wrung out of her, Emmett feared that Eleanor might not be ready for his size. Pushing just the tip in, he waited for her response, and when she wiggled her bottom, he pushed in a few inches more.

Even with all the slickness, she was tight around him, but he couldn't wait a moment longer. Tightening his grip on her hips, he surged all the way in and then stilled as she whimpered.

Sweat beaded his forehead as he waited for her to adjust to his girth, and when she moved, encouraging him to do the same, the last of his control broke, and he pounded into her like a rutting beast.

It must have taken less than a minute for him to reach his climax, and as it erupted out of him, he let go of her hips, gripped her nape, and sank his fangs into her vein.

She orgasmed again, squeezing him tight, and as the first taste of her blood hit his tongue, he hardened again as if he hadn't just emptied a gallon of his essence into her.

Sucking and pulling, he started thrusting again, and as one orgasm after another rocked through Eleanor's body, Emmett had to remind himself to stop before he took too much.

With a Herculean effort, he retracted his fangs and sealed the puncture holes with a swipe of his tongue.

Her body slackened under him, and even though he could have climaxed again, Emmett pulled out, slid to the side, and tucked her into his chest.

Unfamiliar tenderness washing over him, he whispered in her ear, "Thank you."

Cassandra

Dinner took forever. Seven courses had been served, each one small but delicious. Cassandra was pleasantly full, but not overstuffed, and if not for her spinning head, she would have enjoyed herself greatly.

Good food and good company made for a pleasant evening. The only problem she had with her dinner companions was their insistence on getting and keeping her drunk. She'd never consumed so much alcohol, and at the rate she was going, she would soon pass out.

"Coffee, cappuccino, or tea?" the server asked.

"Coffee. Definitely coffee," she slurred.

"Same here," Onegus told the server. "After we are done with coffee and dessert, I'll introduce you to my mother."

She wanted to shake her head, but it made her dizzy. "I'm sorry, but I don't think I can meet her now. I need to sober up first."

"You're fine," he said dismissively. "As long as you can string three words together in the right order, you are not considered drunk."

"According to which country rules?"

"Scotland, of course."

"That's right." Connor lifted his umpteenth glass of whisky and downed it in one go. "The night is still young, and I can still talk without slurring my words." He lifted the empty glass, signaling for the server to refill it. "They should just leave a couple of bottles here."

"They serve fine whiskies," Jackson said. "The bar tab alone must have cost Sari a fortune." He chuckled. "I'm sure Gerard is not donating his services or the supplies."

"He's not," Sylvia said. "Amanda paid for everything."

"What does she do to afford all that?" Cassandra asked.

"She comes from money." Roni leaned sideways as the server placed a plate with cake and ice cream in front of him.

Cassandra chuckled. "So do all of you, but I don't see Tessa or Sylvia wearing the latest gowns by Oscar de la Renta. Did Amanda marry someone rich?"

Maybe she was the wife or daughter of the head of their clan. No, Kian was the clan's head, and she was his sister. Now, that made more sense. The five siblings inherited the empire. Or was it four?

Cassandra vaguely remembered the bride naming four people. Two brothers and two sisters.

Robert, who had hardly spoken more than two words throughout dinner, shook his head. "Amanda mated a simple soldier."

There was that word again, mated. Was it the new politically correct term for married?

"I get it now." Cassandra smiled at Onegus. "It has taken a few moments for my inebriated brain to connect the dots. Amanda is one of the five heirs of the clan's business empire. I've met Kian, but not the other two Sari mentioned. I know that the third sister was one of the bridesmaids. Was the other brother one of the groomsmen?"

"Lilen is no longer with us." Onegus's eyes clouded. "He has passed to the other side of the veil."

"I'm so sorry. When did it happen?"

"A very long time ago." His eyes turned hard.

She wanted to ask how Lilen had died, but Onegus had gotten upset, so she decided to drop the subject and divert the conversation to another topic.

"I bet there is a fascinating story behind Amanda marrying a simple guy. How did the incredibly rich and gorgeous heiress end up with a soldier?"

Suddenly, everyone got busy with their coffees and desserts and avoided her eyes.

"What? Did I say something wrong? Did the snowflake police deem the term to marry discriminating and it was replaced with mated?"

The term mate kept popping up, and the priestess had talked about a joining, not a marriage.

Damn, she should have figured it out. Unlike husband or wife, mate was a genderless term like partner or significant other.

"I'm not aware of marriage or to marry getting booted out of the English language," Onegus said. "Did any of you hear anything about that?" He looked at their dinner companions, who all shook their heads.

"Damn." Cassandra huffed out a breath. "I can never figure out which words they will oust next. But if that's not the reason for everyone clamming up, then what is?"

"Amanda's story is hers to tell." Onegus lifted the tiny fork and scooped a small piece of the cake. "You should ask her."

Eleanor

As Eleanor drifted down from the euphoric cloud she'd been floating on, she wondered how long she'd been out.

She was on her side, her back tucked against Emmett's front, the stickiness of their releases gluing them together.

His deep and even breathing suggested that he was asleep, which gave her time to think over the experience.

He'd taken her blood, this time she'd been aware of it, and it had been a little scary but still erotic as hell. The effect was the same as Greggory's bite, which meant that Emmett had injected her with venom before sucking on her blood, and that his venom was either the same as Greggory's, or similar enough to be indistinguishable.

She wasn't as lightheaded as she'd expected to be after having her blood depleted, and the sexual satiety felt different than what she'd experienced with Greggory. It was more complete, which was surprising since she and Emmett weren't a couple.

Maybe it had been the vulnerability that he'd let her see, dropping his usual swagger and easy charm to show her the scars of his past.

"Don't fight me, Eleanor," he'd said. "Aggression spurs instincts I'd rather remained dormant."

She wasn't sure what he'd meant by that, but she could guess. From the little he had told them, she'd garnered that the Kra-ell females were cruel, savage, and that they reveled in inflicting pain on the males who fought so hard for the dubious privilege of breeding with them.

Apparently, those sexual games were not cultural but rather instinctual, driven by biology, necessary to ensure the survival of the species. By weeding out the weaker males and choosing the strongest, the species continually improved, at least physically.

It was common in the animal kingdom, but it was counterproductive for an intelligent species. The more evolved the society, the less valuable brute strength was. Cunning, intelligence, the ability to form alliances and work productively with others, those were the traits of the most successful humans, not how much weight they could deadlift or how powerful their punch was.

The Kra-ell must have come from a primitive society, and the technology used to bring them to earth probably hadn't been developed by them. Maybe they had stolen it, or maybe they'd conquered a more advanced but less militant species and had taken their technology.

What if that species was the gods? Perhaps the group that had arrived on earth thousands of years ago had been refugees from a war with the Kra-ell?

"Are you okay?" Emmett kissed her neck.

She turned in his arms to face him. "I'm better than okay. I'm perfect." She kissed his lips lightly. "I thought that you were asleep."

"I was. Your loud thinking woke me up." When she frowned, he laughed. "No, I can't read your thoughts. But the energy you were putting out felt like intense thinking."

"You can sense that?"

"Only when you are in my arms, and I can feel any minute change in your body. What were you thinking about?"

Emmett sounded a little anxious, and Eleanor debated whether to share her musings with him. Perhaps later. The topic was not really suitable for pillow-talk. Besides, they both needed a shower.

"If you are anxious about your performance, don't be. It was perfect."

He looked at her down his nose. "Anxious? Why would I be anxious? I'm an excellent lover."

Eleanor stifled a chuckle. The Emmett she knew and loved was back.

Well, love was too strong of a word. She'd been burned one time too many to let herself fall into that trap again. She and Emmett could be friends, lovers, maybe even confidantes, but they weren't in love, and they weren't each other's fated mates.

"Yes, you are." She kissed the tip of his nose.

"I'm surprised none of your Guardian friends has come in with guns blazing. Did you strike a deal with them?"

She smiled. "What if I did?"

"Nothing. I just wondered how you pulled that off."

"It wasn't as difficult as we both imagined." She pulled out of his arms. "Let's get in the shower. I can't put my clothes back on without washing first, and I still have a shift to finish."

Cassandra

"Come on." Onegus put his arm around Cassandra's waist, his hand resting on her hip. "My mother has waited patiently for hours. She wants to meet you."

"Can we do it tomorrow? I can barely walk. Besides, I have a hard time being pleasant when I'm sober. I'm afraid I'll say something wrong."

He stopped walking and turned to her. "I find your company very pleasant. I can't imagine anyone thinking differently."

The smile that bloomed on her face was way too big for the small compliment, but that was what alcohol did. Her mind was mostly fine, she was still as sharp as always, but maybe not as quick. Her body, on the other hand, was a different story. The movements of her legs and arms were too large and uncoordinated, her smiles were too broad, her frowns too pronounced, and she was probably too loud as well.

"You are so charming, Onegus." She lifted her hand and cupped his cheek. "I could so easily fall in love with you. Are you going to break my heart?"

"No." He smiled tightly. "Your heart is safe with me."

"Promise?"

"I promise." He resumed walking. "It's the second table from Amanda's. The blond with the curly hair is my mother. Her name is Martha."

Cassandra narrowed her eyes to clear the blur, but it didn't help. Martha still looked too young. Heck, she looked younger than Onegus. Perhaps it was time to see an optometrist. She'd been getting headaches lately, and it was probably from straining her eyes at work.

When they got closer, the woman rose to her feet and smiled. "Hello, Cassandra. I'm so glad to finally meet you." She offered her a hand. "I'm Martha. Onegus's mother."

Her Scottish lilt was lovely, but there was no way she was his mother. Were they playing a joke on her?

"No, you're not." Cassandra shook the woman's hand.

Martha was tall, and she was in heels, so they were more or less eye to eye, and Cassandra took a good look at the woman's flawless, pretty face. There was not even one wrinkle, and nothing was sagging. Even if she had him as a teenager, Martha would have to be at least forty-five. Not that forty-five was old, and women that age might not have wrinkles or saggy jowls, but they didn't look like pretty twenty-five-year-olds either.

"I assure you that I am." Martha's smile melted away, and she turned to Onegus. "A little help?"

Help?

With what?

"My mother had me when she was very young, and she takes good care of herself." He smirked. "Like your mother. That's yet another thing that we have in common."

"I doubt that," Martha said.

Cassandra's forehead furrowed. "What do you mean?"

Martha shrugged. "I doubt that your mother is anything like me, or I like her."

At her side, Onegus tensed, and his hand on her hip tightened. Was that a warning?

She brushed his hand off and struck a pose, shifting her body sideways and moving her right leg forward in a well-practiced modeling pose. "How would you know? You've just met me, and you don't know my mother or me."

Martha smiled tightly. "What I meant was that your mother and I grew up on different continents and in different cultures. It wasn't a comment meant to reflect my opinion of you or your mother. I'm sure you are both lovely ladies. I just find Americans a little rough around the edges, a little too loud, and too casual in their dress and in their manners, and that includes members of my family who have moved here."

Talk about a stuck-up Brit.

The sizzling energy crawling under Cassandra's skin had been numbed by the alcohol, but the verbal sparring with Onegus's mother had upped the voltage and cleared Cassandra's head.

If Martha was anyone else, she would have torn into her, but the woman was Onegus's mother, so she had to smile and act civil toward her.

"Well, I hope my mother and I will change your mind about Americans. Perhaps we could all meet for lunch."

Geraldine could give any stuck-up Brit a run for her money, but with her memory problems and her made-up stories, Cassandra wasn't sure that it was such a good idea. But she had to put it out there and hope that Martha would decline politely.

"I would like that very much." Martha's smile was genuine.

Onegus let out a breath.

What had he expected? That she would bite his mother's head off?

"I was looking for you." Nick swaggered over with a large wine glass in his hand. "There is a punch bowl the size of a witch's cauldron in the antechamber, and it's the best I've ever had. It's made with lots of fine whiskeys. You have to try it." He took a swig from his drink and smacked his lips. "Delicious."

The young girl Cassandra had seen on the platform walked up to Nick. "Can I have some?"

"You're not old enough, sprite." He patted her arm. "Next year."

She laughed. "I'm not going to be old enough by then either." She moved closer to Cassandra. "Hi, I'm Lisa." She extended her hand.

"Nice to meet you." Cassandra shook it. "I'm Cassandra."

"I know." Lisa smiled, turned to Onegus, and gave him the thumbs up.

Cassandra rolled her eyes. Had the kid just given her the stamp of approval?

Well, at least there was that.

"When does the dancing portion of the evening start?" Martha asked.

"Given the change in music," Onegus said. "It's about to begin."

About a third of the chairs were vacant, but since no one was on the dance floor yet, Cassandra figured they were congregating in the antechamber and drinking punch. Damn Scots and their iron bellies. How could they drink so much and remain standing?

"Let's go." Martha threaded her arm through Nick's. "Lead the way to that punch, young man."

"I'm Nick," he said. "Ruth's mate."

"I know." Martha patted his arm. "Rumors about love matches spread fast through the clan, and they even jump over the ocean."

Love matches? Was there any other kind?

Well, duh. These people were rich. They probably married to make alliances with other rich people, either financial or political.

Cassandra did her best to walk properly, putting one stiletto-clad foot in front of the other. Despite having a somewhat clearer head, her body was still a little wobbly, and what was even worse, the current inside her was crackling like static electricity.

Holding it in would have been difficult under normal circumstances, doing so when her control was tentative required teeth gritting.

The damn static had been building despite her best efforts to tamp it down. Several petty annoyances had combined to create a volatile mixture that needed an outlet. She shouldn't have allowed it to build up like that, should have released it in small bursts, but it was too late for that.

Cassandra had to find a proper outlet and release it before she hurt someone. The problem was that a glass or a vase wouldn't be enough this time. She needed something that could absorb much more than her usual small blasts.

Perhaps she could excuse herself and go to the bathroom. Maybe a porcelain commode would do, or a large mirror. She would cause property damage, but at least no one would get hurt.

Onegus

That hadn't gone well.

Onegus should have known that his mother's strong personality would clash with Cassandra's.

It was ironic that he'd chosen a woman so similar in character to his mother. They were both alpha females, and therefore bound to lock horns. As a kid, he'd resented Martha's strictness, her haughty attitude, and her insistence on good manners. It hadn't been easy growing up as her son, but he had to admit that the things she'd instilled in him had served him well.

If not for his strict upbringing, he wouldn't have such strong self-control, the discipline that had helped him become Chief Guardian, and the manners that made him such a good stand-in for Kian.

In fact, compared to him, Kian was a brute.

But Kian was like that despite Annani's upbringing, not because of it. The Clan Mother hadn't been lenient with her sons or her older daughters. The only one who could get away with murder had been Amanda, who early on had figured out how to manipulate her mother and get anything she wanted.

"That's indeed a huge punch bowl." Martha stopped a good distance away from it. "I wonder what's in it."

"Lots of whiskey," Nick said. "But also champagne, orange juice, cranberry juice, some bitters, and cinnamon." He took another sip. "Maybe rum too."

"Sounds delicious." Martha eyed the long line. "Why is everyone here? The bar has plenty of other drinks."

"I don't know." Nick shrugged. "Maybe Gerard put something else in it that makes everyone crave it."

"Like what?" Cassandra asked.

"Magic." Nick snorted. "Although knowing that prick, it's something wicked." He let go of Martha's arm. "I need to find Ruth. She gets stressed in large crowds."

"Isn't she with Sylvia and Roni?" Cassandra leaned on Onegus's shoulder.

"Yeah, but it's not the same." Nick winked. "I'm her guy." He sauntered away without refilling his goblet.

"Are you okay?" Onegus asked quietly.

"My head's spinning." She looked up at him. "Can you point me in the direction of the lady's room?"

"I'll escort you." He was afraid she wouldn't make it.

"I can find it myself. It's not like you can go in with me."

"I can come with you," Martha offered. "You seem unsteady on your feet. How much have you drunk?"

Cassandra's energy surged, so much so that Onegus felt it sizzling against his arm.

"I lost count of how many drinks your son and his cousins kept pushing at me, but I assure you that I can get to the bathroom with no assistance from you or Onegus."

A clueless server stuck a tray with goblets full of punch in front of them. "Enjoy," he encouraged them to partake.

To Onegus's surprise, Cassandra took a goblet, and with a challenge in her eyes, brought it to her lips. "Nick said we have to try it."

"Indeed." Martha took another one.

"Well, I guess I have to taste it too." Onegus lifted the third. "Cheers." He clinked his glass with Cassandra's and then with his mother's.

"To many happy occasions," Martha said before drinking up.

"To the happy couple." Cassandra brought the glass to her lips.

She was still sipping on it when a guy backed into her to let a server through. The punch splashed over her face, not much of it, but enough to drip down her neck and into the neckline of her one-shouldered dress.

"Fruck," Cassandra cursed.

Thankful that she hadn't said fuck, Onegus took the goblet from her hand and waved a waiter over. "We need napkins."

"I'm so sorry," the offender apologized. He was one of the young Scots, and Onegus couldn't recall his name.

"I'll get you some napkins." He rushed off.

"Here." His mother pulled a handkerchief out of her small purse and handed it to Cassandra.

The waiter arrived at the same moment and handed her a stack of paper napkins.

"Thanks," Cassandra said to both and started patting at her neck and face. "The dress is ruined. Those stains are never going to come out."

"It's black, dear," Martha said. "No one is going to see the stains. You just need to fix your face." She took one of the paper napkins and lifted her hand. "You're covered with red and purple splotches."

Cassandra stayed her hand. "A napkin is not going to cut it. I'm sticky. I need to wash it off." She looked down at her cleavage and the sticky marks left by the punch.

"I'll take you to the restroom." Onegus put his hand on the small of her back.

He could take her to his office and let her use his private bathroom. She could take the dress off and shower if she wanted.

As the image of her standing naked in his shower flashed in his mind, he instantly hardened, a most inappropriate response given the situation. Cassandra was upset, his mother was standing right next to him, and people were watching them, curious about the commotion.

Cassandra

"I'll take you to the restroom." Onegus put his large hand on the small of her back.

Martha sneered. "Should we say our goodbyes now? I doubt the two of you will be back anytime soon."

From anyone else, Cassandra would have thought nothing of the suggestive remark, but coming from Onegus's mother, the woman who thought she was so prim and proper, it was annoying as hell.

Just another spark to ignite her barely contained energy.

She wished Onegus would hurry up and guide her to the bathroom, hopefully a private one.

His lips thinned for a brief moment, but then he smiled, and Cassandra realized that his charm was just one more weapon in his arsenal. It wasn't innate. It was practiced.

"I wish I could call it a night, Mother, but I need to be here to ensure all the guests get back to their respective lodgings safely."

"Of course." Martha smiled. "If you don't mind, I'll accompany you both to the ladies' room. I need to powder my nose as well."

Freaking great. That was the last thing Cassandra needed. How was she going to release the energy with Onegus's mother there? The one who had fueled it? If Martha was nearby, she would be like a magnet for it, and with how much Cassandra was packing, she would strike the woman dead on the spot.

"I'm going to take Cassandra to my old office. I have a private bathroom in there."

"Oh, well." Martha smirked knowingly. "Just be quick about it. I'm going to powder my nose and then join my friends on the dance floor." She sauntered away on her high heels, her curly, nearly white, blond hair swishing over her bare back, just skimming the top of her tight ass.

The woman was movie-star beautiful, and she was rich. No wonder she had a haughty attitude.

By now, the antechamber had partially emptied, with only a few people standing next to the tall round tables, chatting and sipping on their punch or coffee, some eating desserts on small plates. A server hovered nearby, collecting dirty cups, glasses, plates and used napkins.

"Thank you for the save." Cassandra smiled tightly.

Onegus arched a brow. "Save from what?"

Was he playing dumb? Or was he that clueless?

"Your mother. She's a bit much."

"I don't know what you're talking about. Other than that comment about Americans being uncouth, for which she apologized, she's been perfectly pleasant." He smiled sheepishly. "Or as pleasant as my mother can manage to be. She was doing her best."

If not for Cassandra's already elevated agitation, the tag-on at the end would have redeemed Onegus, but it was too little too late.

She could practically feel the last clamp holding her energy from erupting disintegrate. She was about to explode, and she needed a receptacle for the energy—preferably a sizable container, but there was no potted plant or statue in sight, not even one damn window.

Turning around, she had only enough time to focus her eyes on the punch bowl before the current zapped out of her with a force that had her staggering backward.

The bowl cracked, the thick glass holding up for a split second, and then it burst, big blue glass shards breaking off it and liquid spilling on the floor.

As before, Onegus shoved her behind his back, but this time they weren't close enough for the glass to hit him, or maybe the heavy weight of the thick glass had prevented it from getting airborne.

The disaster area was contained to the vicinity of the punch bowl, and the only one who got splattered was the poor server.

It didn't take more than a couple of seconds for a veritable army of broad-backed males to rush into the antechamber, Onegus's security team no doubt. Apart from their hard faces and muscled bodies, there was nothing to identify them as such. They were all wearing tuxedos and had run out of the ballroom, but the way their eyes quickly assessed the situation betrayed them as trained guards.

"How did that happen, boss?" One of them pushed a larger shard with his shoe toward the epicenter.

In the aftermath of the explosion, Cassandra felt faint, the blast emptying the excess energy together with what she needed to keep going. She held on to Onegus, her hand fisting the back of his tuxedo for support.

"No clue." Onegus wrapped his arm around her waist, propping her up. "I heard it crack, and then it just burst. I assume there was a flaw in the glass."

Cassandra sagged against his side, the relief further weakening her knees. He didn't suspect her. And if he did, he was covering up for her.

One of the men chuckled. "Perhaps the alcohol content was enough to erode the structural integrity of the glass."

Was that even a thing? Did glass even have structural integrity? Wasn't that a construction term?

A third guy offered another explanation. "Did anyone smoke near the bowl? Some idiot might have dropped a match into it."

"Given the alcohol content, the liquid might have caught fire, but there was none," Onegus said. "The thing would have burned, but I doubt it would have exploded. The bowl just cracked and then broke apart. Maybe it was the music. Sometimes a certain frequency can resonate with the glass. It's no big deal except for the cleanup."

"And the lost booze," someone bemoaned. "A lot of good whiskey went into that punch."

Cassandra wasn't an engineer, but even she knew that the bowl was too big and its glass too thick for the sound coming from the ballroom to shatter it. A noise cannon directed straight at it and tuned to its precise resonance frequency would have been needed.

Perhaps Onegus didn't know that, or maybe he was covering for her. Thankfully, none of the guys on his team knew that either.

Onegus

Onegus could feel Cassandra's body trembling with relief. If not for his arm around her, her legs would have given way.

"Liam, can you bring a chair out for Cassandra? She had quite a scare."

"I'm on it, boss."

"Roy. Get a cleanup crew here to clear the mess. Gerard has several people in charge of cleaning in the kitchen."

"Yes, boss."

Normally, he would have asked one of the Odus, but they were nowhere to be seen. He knew that Amanda wouldn't have excluded them from the celebrations, and she must have reserved seats for them. The Odus were treated as members of the family, and they were also an added level of security.

Perhaps they were helping Gerard and his crew in the kitchen. After all, the Odus were programmed to be helpful. Sitting around as guests would have probably fried their cybertronic brains.

Besides, Cassandra had just blown up the punch bowl. Until she learned to control her power, he didn't want the Odus anywhere near her. If anything happened to even one of them, Annani would be devastated.

Or worse, she might lose it and retaliate against Cassandra.

For now, he'd managed to cover for her, but he'd already told enough people about the power she possessed. It was only a question of time before someone figured out that the punch bowl hadn't exploded on its own.

Bridget came out of the ballroom and surveyed the damage. Finding the server, she walked up to him. "Are you hurt?

He shook his head. "Just wet and sticky. I was lucky that none of the glass pieces got me."

"Indeed." She walked over to Cassandra. "How about you? Are you okay?"

"She's just rattled," Onegus said.

Bridget threw him one of her withering looks. "I didn't ask you, now did I?"

"I'm not hurt." Cassandra rubbed at the punch stains on her chest. "This is from before. Someone bumped into me, and I got splashed."

Bridget nodded. "Then if I'm not needed here, I'm going back inside."

"Thank you for checking on us." Cassandra lowered herself to the chair Liam had brought for her.

"You're welcome." Bridget waved before going through the doors into the banquet hall.

"In case you were wondering, that was our family's doctor."

"I figured. She sounded like one." Cassandra pushed to her feet. "If you don't mind, I could really use the bathroom."

"Of course." He took her hand and led her out into the hallway.

"Do you still want me to use the one in your office?" She didn't sound like it was something she wanted to do.

"It's up to you." He leaned closer to her ear. "I'm sure my mother is done powdering her nose."

"I didn't see her coming back, but then I was a little distracted." Cassandra smiled nervously. "I just want to wash this stickiness off me, have a cup of coffee to clear my head, and then go dancing."

"Sounds like a plan."

As they headed in the bathroom's direction, his mother walked toward them together with Sylvia.

"We heard that there was an incident with the punch bowl," Sylvia said. "What happened?"

"It must have been defective," Onegus said. "The bowl cracked and then broke apart."

"Did anyone get hurt?" his mother asked.

Cassandra shook her head. "Fortunately, no one was standing near it when it cracked, and the glass was too thick and heavy to go flying."

Sylvia looked at her with knowing eyes. "You need to learn to control it. This time you were lucky, and no one got hurt. Next time you might not be."

Cassandra tensed. "I don't know what you're talking about." She pulled her hand out of Onegus's and walked into the restroom.

"Someone is in denial," Sylvia said.

"Not really." Onegus rubbed a hand over his jaw. "She's just pretending that it had nothing to do with her, and that's what she should be doing. Imagine what would have happened to her if someone other than us figured out what she could do."

His mother grimaced. "Don't remind me. I lived during those horrible times." She put a hand on his arm. "You should tell her who and what you are. It's not right to bring her into our midst and keep her ignorant. You need to ask Kalugal to compel her silence."

"First, I want to tell Cassandra what's at stake and offer her options. Compulsion is just one of the ways to protect our secrets, and it's not my favorite."

Cassandra

Cassandra leaned closer to the mirror and examined the neckline of her dress. Miraculously, the stain hadn't penetrated the fabric, and she was able to rub it off with one of the cloth towels she'd wetted. The spot was wet, but because the fabric was black, it was barely visible.

Onegus's haughty mother had been right about that.

Wetting another one of the small rolled-up towels, Cassandra wiped the sticky residue off her skin, then took a dry one to finish the job. Everything was back to normal.

Right.

How had Sylvia guessed that she'd had something to do with the punch bowl incident? She hadn't been there when it happened. If Onegus hadn't realized the connection, how could she?

Maybe the girl was a psychic?

Whatever. Sylvia, Martha, and whoever else wanted to pin it on Cassandra had no proof, and as long as she kept pretending innocence, she was safe. Circumstantial evidence might make people suspicious, but it was not enough to incriminate her.

Squaring her shoulders, she took one last glance at her reflection. Her hair was fine, her newly reapplied lipstick didn't have any smudges, and her eyeliner was still intact.

Tucking her evening purse under her arm, Cassandra headed out of the ladies' room.

Thankfully Martha and Sylvia were gone, and Onegus was waiting for her, leaning against the wall and looking sexily debonair.

"Was the operation successful?" He walked up to her.

She waved a hand over her dress. "Good as new."

"I'm glad." He took her hand. "Are you up for dancing?"

"Coffee first. And maybe another piece of cake." She was no longer tipsy, but she felt depleted and tired. A boost of caffeine and sugar was in order.

"Sounds good to me." He led her back to the banquet hall.

Several couples were dancing, but most of the guests were sitting around the tables and chatting over coffees, desserts, and more drinks.

Again, she was struck by how uniformly aged everyone looked.

"Does your family own a fountain of youth?"

He chuckled. "In a way."

"In what way? An in-house plastic surgeon? Or just good genes?"

"The second one." He led her to their table. "I'm actually over five hundred years old, but I aged extremely well." He pulled out a chair for her.

"Ha-ha. Very funny." Cassandra looked at Roni, who was smirking and trying to hide it. "Let me guess, you are one hundred years old and only look nineteen."

She could feel Sylvia's eyes on her, assessing, speculating, but she didn't turn to look at the girl.

"No, I'm actually twenty," Roni said. "Good guess, though."

"What about the priestess?" Cassandra pointed with her chin toward the family table. "She looks like an angel, so I guess she could be as old as time and only appears to be eighteen."

Amanda and the red-haired priestess were chatting animatedly, and other than being too beautiful to be real, she seemed almost normal now that the spotlight wasn't directed at her.

"Annani is not a priestess," Onegus said. "She is the head of our clan."

The girl was too young to be the head of anything other than a sorority.

"Did the previous head of your clan pass away, and she inherited the position?"

Sylvia pushed to her feet and tapped Roni's shoulder. "Come dance with me."

He looked as if he was about to protest, but the intense look she gave him didn't leave room for argument.

As Roni rose to his feet, the rest of their companions followed suit, including Connor who didn't have a date.

"I'm going to mingle." He winked before beating feet away from their table.

"Did I say something to chase them off?" she asked.

"They wanted to give us privacy."

"For what?"

Was it about her questions regarding the mysterious head of their clan? What was the story with her?

Was the woman a vampire?

The glowing pale skin, the flaming red hair...

Right. This wasn't a movie, and vampires didn't exist.

Onegus let out a long breath. "To talk. But this is neither the time nor the place for that. Can you stay and spend the night with me?"

She arched a brow. "On the cot in your office in the basement? I'd rather get a hotel room if you don't mind."

It dawned on her then, that when Onegus had offered to take her to his office to clean up in his private bathroom, he hadn't mentioned leaving the building.

She frowned. "Is your office right here? In this building?"

He chuckled. "It is, but we don't have to spend the night there. I can secure a better place with a proper bed."

That sounded like an invitation to share that bed with him, which was way better than the ominous, *we need to talk.*

"Do you want to go now?" she asked.

"I do, but I can't. I have to stay until all the guests leave. I have to make sure that everyone gets safely to where they are going to spend the night, and that could take hours." He lifted her hand and kissed her fingers. "Can you last that long? Or are you tired and want to go home? If you are, I can ask Connor to take you."

She was drained. The release had left her devoid of energy. But at least she wasn't drunk anymore, and she didn't want to go before hearing what he had to say.

"I'm fine." Cassandra rose to her feet and offered him a hand up. "Let's dance."

Onegus

"I think I'm done," Cassandra admitted defeat after almost two hours of nonstop dancing. "My feet are killing me. I have to sit down."

It was a wonder she was even standing.

Given the tremendous energy she'd expelled, she'd lasted much longer than he'd expected. Someone less stubborn would have given up a long time ago, but Cassandra didn't know that she'd been competing against immortals, who were twice or thrice as resilient. Her competitive nature had driven her to push herself to the limit.

"No problem." Onegus wrapped his arm around her waist and led her back to their table.

The only one there was Connor. Tessa and Jackson were still dancing, Sharon and Robert had gone home, and so had Roni and Sylvia. Ruth and Nick were sitting at another table, talking with Vlad and Wendy and their extended family, which now included Wendy's mother.

"As much as I love these Louboutins, I can't stand them for another moment." Cassandra kicked the shoes off and let out a relieved breath.

"Do you want me to rub your feet?" Connor offered.

She narrowed her eyes at him. "Not a good idea. But I will be forever grateful if you get me a cup of coffee."

"I'm on it."

Onegus wondered whether she didn't want Connor to rub her feet because that was too intimate for her, or because she thought that he would get jealous.

The truth was that he didn't want any man's hands on her, not even Connor's.

As soon as his roommate left, Cassandra shifted the chair to the side, lifted her feet, and put them on the next chair over. "If I'm breaking any British etiquette rules, I don't care." She wiggled her dainty toes.

His mother might think so, but he didn't.

"You can do as you please." Onegus pulled out the next chair over, sat down, and took one of her feet in his hands. "I don't have a lot of time, but I can squeeze in a quick foot massage."

Her eyes rolling back in pleasure, she sighed. "I might never let you go. A man who offers foot massages is a keeper."

That was a loaded comment.

Connor had made the same offer a moment ago, and she'd refused.

As Onegus's hands on Cassandra's feet stilled for a brief moment, she opened her eyes. "Did I scare you? Don't worry. I was just teasing."

He shook his head and resumed massaging her toes. "You've got it all wrong. Your comment made me wistful, not fearful. I like the idea of you holding onto me."

Her eyes softened. "Don't say things you don't mean."

He put her foot down and picked up the other one. "I never say things that I don't mean."

Watching him kneading her foot with a pensive expression on her face, Cassandra didn't retort with a snarky comment as he'd expected.

Perhaps she was too tired to come up with one.

"The guests are starting to leave. I need to go." He put the foot down. "Are you going to be okay?"

"Of course she is." Connor put a steaming cup of coffee in front of Cassandra. "I'm here to keep her company." He looked at her feet that were still nestled in Onegus's lap. "I see how it is. I'm not good enough for your toes." He cast her a mock reproachful look. "But he is?"

Lifting Cassandra's feet off his lap, Onegus got up and then laid them down gently on the chair. "I hope it's not going to take long."

"Off with you." Connor waved at him before leaning closer to Cassandra. "Let's gossip."

Walking toward the exit, Onegus scanned the room to estimate how many guests were still there. About half were gone, and only a few were lingering in the antechamber. The rest were either dancing or sitting at the tables. It was nearly three o'clock in the morning, and it wouldn't be long before the rest left. Especially since David and Sari had already retired, as had the rest of the royal family as he liked to refer to them.

Annani usually didn't stay long, probably because she knew that her presence was intimidating to many of the clan members, and that they would have more fun and be less inhibited with her gone. Amanda, who usually stayed until the very end, was pregnant and tired easily, and the same was even truer for Syssi. She could barely walk.

He found Yamanu in the hallway, leaning against the wall next to the ladies' room. "Just the guy I was looking for. Are you waiting for Mey?"

He nodded. "I'm not going to make her stay until the end. She's going home with Jin and Arwel."

"Good thinking. I'm going to check on Gerard's people and see when they are ready to leave."

"I spoke with him already. The kitchen is done, but they still need to collect all the serveware from the ballroom. He thinks it will take them another hour to clean, and then they need to load everything including themselves into the vans, which probably will take another half an hour."

After the staff left the building, Gerard was going to have them stop up front for an inspection, and that was when Yamanu would manipulate their memories, changing the event's location and blurring the faces they had seen.

Onegus groaned. "It seems like you and I are not leaving here before four-thirty in the morning."

There was no way Cassandra would last that long.

He could have Connor take her home, but that meant that he would have to thrall her first.

Since Kalugal and Jacki had left already, asking him to compel Cassandra's silence wasn't an option. Eleanor could do that as well, but it meant taking Cassandra to the dungeon.

That was actually not a bad idea. The converted cells were as nice as any hotel room, and Cassandra wouldn't mind spending the night in one. She didn't need to know that they used to be prison cells. He could tell her that they were underground apartments or safe rooms.

She was probably too tired for having *the talk* tonight, but they could sleep in each other's arms and save it for the morning.

Following Ingrid's advice, he would tell Cassandra the truth and ask for her consent to induction in writing.

After that was done, he would give her the option of either a thrall to forget what he'd revealed or compulsion that would force her to keep it a secret.

Cassandra

Sometime during Connor's endless prattle, Cassandra must have dozed off.

The next time she opened her eyes, she was sprawled over a row of chairs, and everyone except her and Connor was gone.

An older guy in a suit and a bow tie was vacuuming the floor, but she was too tired to ponder who he was or where he'd come from.

The noise he made with that infernal vacuum was probably what had woken her up.

Shifting up, she stifled a yawn. "How long have I been asleep?"

"A little over an hour," Connor said. "Onegus is almost done. He should be back any moment now."

"Thanks for staying with me." She picked up the cold cup of coffee and took a sip. "You didn't have to. I'm sure that I'm perfectly safe here."

"That's true, but I was afraid that you would roll off these chairs. My other option was to lay you out on the table, but I didn't think you would approve."

Cassandra chuckled. "No, I wouldn't. I can't believe that I didn't wake up when you laid me out on the chairs."

"You were out like a rock. People stopped by to say goodbye, and you snored right through it."

"I did no such thing. I don't snore."

"Yes, you do. Tiny little snores like a kitten."

She was about to answer when Onegus walked in, looking as fresh and as energetic as if it was the middle of the day.

"I'm sorry it took so long." He patted Connor on the back. "Thanks for guarding my lady."

"Anytime." Connor pushed to his feet. "I'll see myself out." He leaned down and kissed Cassandra's cheek. "Good night."

"Good night, Connor." She watched him walk away before turning to Onegus. "What now?"

He crouched next to her and picked up her shoes. "You have two options. I can put these shoes on your feet, and you can walk, or I can put them in my pockets and carry you."

"There is a third option. I can walk barefoot."

He shook his head. "I'm not letting you walk without shoes through that antechamber. Small glass shards might have remained after the servers cleaned the mess. They didn't do a thorough job."

Cassandra considered her options.

Just thinking about putting the shoes back on made her feet throb with pain, and other than the guy with the vacuum, there was no one else around. Besides, being carried in Onegus's strong arms sounded very appealing.

"Will they fit in your pockets? If not, I can hold them."

Given the satisfied grin on his face, that was the answer he'd hoped for.

"Let's see." He pushed up with a shoe in each hand, then spun them like a gunslinger before shoving them into his pockets, the spiky heels sticking out like gun handles.

"Show-off."

"You have no idea." Onegus bent at the waist and picked her up effortlessly.

She wrapped her arms around his neck. "I'll tell you a secret." She nuzzled his neck. "I like it when you carry me."

He chuckled. "I know."

Cassandra had never met a guy who could be so charming and full of himself at the same time. It was an art form.

"Where are you taking me?" she asked as he stopped in front of the elevators.

"A place not many get to see." He held her up with one hand while pressing his thumb to the button.

"Your secret lair?"

"Yes."

"Oh, wow. Is it like Batman's cave?" She laughed. "The guy who was vacuuming in a suit, is he your Pennyworth?"

"He's a butler, but he's not mine. He is Kian's." Onegus carried her into the elevator and pressed his thumb to one of the down buttons.

"So, if Kian is Batman, are you Robin?"

He gave her a scornful look. "I'm no one's sidekick."

"No, you are not." She kissed his neck. "You are Captain America."

"I like that much better."

As the elevator door opened, Onegus stepped out and turned into a wide corridor, which was lined with many doors. It looked like a dormitory or a school. There were no windows to the outside, and the ones on the doors were on the bottom instead of on the top.

Her arms tightened around his neck. "What is this place?"

"We have safe rooms down here."

"Safe from what?"

He stopped in front of one of the doors, hoisted her up with one arm, and punched a series of numbers on the keypad. "Safe from our enemies." He stepped back.

As the door started moving, its mechanism making a low buzzing sound, it became very apparent that it wasn't an ordinary door. The thing was a foot thick and made from some kind of alloy.

Was he taking her into a safe or a nuclear shelter?

"Put me down," she demanded.

"What's wrong?"

It was an instinctive response that hadn't been rooted in logic.

If Onegus wanted to imprison her inside that room, she would be helpless to do anything about it, and it wouldn't matter whether she was on her feet or in his arms. She couldn't outrun him, and even if she could run fast enough, she couldn't use the elevator.

"Hi, Chief," a woman behind them said. "What are you doing here?"

"What does it look like I'm doing?" He turned so Cassandra could see her.

"This is my girlfriend, Cassandra."

"Hi." The woman smiled. "I'm Eleanor. Nice to meet you, and good night." She ducked back into the room she came out of.

Eleanor had looked amused, not troubled or alarmed, and knowing that there was another woman around made Cassandra feel less apprehensive.

"Who is she?"

"A member of my team." He walked into the room, which was decorated like any upscale hotel room, but it didn't have a window. Maybe it was indeed a safe room.

"As promised," Onegus said. "A queen-sized bed with a comfortable mattress."

He didn't take her to the bed, though. He put her down on the small sofa.

Damn. It seemed like she was going to get the talk after all.

Onegus

Cassandra had had a nice long nap, and she seemed wide awake, which meant that they could have the talk tonight instead of waiting for the morning.

Except, now that Onegus had her where he wanted her, he didn't know how to broach the subject.

How had the other men done it? Four out of his six head Guardians had found love with Dormants, but each case was different. Brundar hadn't told Callie anything until she'd started transitioning because he hadn't believed she was a Dormant.

Arwel had had it easy because Jin had already learned the truth from her sister. And Kri also had had it easy because Michael already learned he was a Dormant from Kian and Amanda. Wonder was already an immortal when Anandur had met her, so the only one who'd had to jump through hoops had been Yamanu. How had he done it?

He'd asked Kian's permission to bring Mey into the village, but had he told her before or after?

Perhaps opening with Cassandra's power was the way to go.

Her denial had been a lie, and he knew that she was aware of the destructive power she possessed and feared it.

She might be more positively predisposed to what he was about to tell her if it offered an explanation and possibly even a solution for something that must have been giving her trouble for years.

"Can I offer you something to drink?" Onegus asked.

Hopefully, Okidu kept the small fridge stocked with fresh bottles of water and soft drinks. If not, he would have to go up to the lobby and get her something from the vending machines. Or better yet, he could send Eleanor or Alfie to get it.

"Coffee would be nice." Cassandra leaned sideways to look at the small bar he was blocking from her view. "I see a Nespresso coffee maker. They are easy to operate."

That's right. He'd forgotten about that. "Coffee coming up." He examined the pods. "I assume that you want a strong cup of java?"

"Yes, please. The strongest you have."

He filled the small container with water from the faucet, inserted a pod into the slot, put a mug under the spout, and turned the device on. It took moments to produce a decent cup of coffee, and he repeated the process to make the second one.

"Cream and sugar?"

"Yes, please."

He opened the cabinet and pulled out a container of sugar packets and another one of powdered creamer.

"I hope that's okay." He brought everything to the coffee table. "These rooms are not used very often, so everything in here is of the long-lasting variety."

Cassandra took a look around. "Someone must be keeping them clean. There is no dust."

"The butler you saw upstairs comes here twice a week."

He sat next to her on the couch, still not sure where to start.

She emptied two packets of sugar and one creamer packet into her coffee, stirred them with a spoon, and then took a long sip. "It's better than I expected."

"I'm glad."

After several long moments of silence, Cassandra put the cup down and leaned back. "Is it that bad that you can't bring yourself to get it out?"

He forced a smile. "Not at all. It's all good. I just don't know where to start, which is surprising. I'm rarely at a loss for words."

"Does it have anything to do with your mother? She doesn't seem to like me. Is that a problem?"

"In a way, it has to do with my mother, but not with her liking you or not. And just so you know, that was Martha trying her best to be nice. Usually, she's much worse, which leads me to believe that she likes you."

"Oh, my. I can't imagine what she's like at her worst."

He chuckled. "Imagine yourself when one of your snowflakes annoys you."

She arched a brow. "Are you saying that your mother and I are similar?"

"In more ways than you realize. You are both alphas, which is why you locked horns. Just like you, Martha is smart, capable, assertive, and doesn't take shit from anyone."

Cassandra grimaced. "It must be true that men seek out women who are like their mothers."

"It would seem so." He turned to face her. "There is one major difference, though. Not counting a sharp tongue, my mother doesn't have any special powers."

It wasn't entirely true. Martha could thrall to some extent, but nothing else.

Her back stiffening, Cassandra picked up her coffee cup. "What are you talking about?" She took a sip and kept looking at it, most likely to avoid his eyes.

"You know what I mean. When you get angry or overly excited, you emit energy that makes things explode. The glass at the rooftop bar, the vase at the apartment where we spent the night together, and now the punch bowl. Your power is dangerous, and you need to learn to control it."

Cassandra

That was what Sylvia had said.

Fear twisted Cassandra's gut.

Did they all know that the punch bowl incident had been her fault?

That didn't make sense. Onegus had covered for her, and Sylvia couldn't have learned it from him because he hadn't left Cassandra's side until they met Sylvia and his mother in front of the bathrooms.

She must have guessed it as well. But how? No one had ever suspected before because outside of movies and books, people weren't supposed to have such powers.

"Why do you think that I had anything to do with those incidents? Other than being a jinx, that is."

Smiling indulgently, he took her hand. "I can feel the power swirling inside of you. I know that it intensifies when you get angry or irritated, and I know that sex helps defuse it." He winked at her. "I volunteer to be your defuser."

Pursing her lips, she regarded him from under lowered eyelashes. "Let's assume for a moment that you are right. Doesn't it bother you? Most people would be scared, thinking that I'm a witch or a dangerous freak."

He chuckled. "You are a dangerous freak, but so am I, as well as most of the people you met at the wedding. I don't blame you for hiding what you can do and denying culpability. Humans are not known for their tolerance, especially when they fear you. My people and I hide our freakishness as well, but we do a better job of it than you."

She had no idea what Onegus was talking about, but he'd given her the opening to turn the tables on him.

"In what way are you and your people dangerous freaks? Your good looks? Your mother's freakishly young appearance?" She narrowed her eyes at him. "Or the exclusion of the older generation from taking part in your events so they don't spoil the family photos?"

She'd been mocking him, but to her surprise he nodded.

"We are immortal. We are stronger, faster, and we can manipulate human minds. That makes us dangerous."

Was he insane?

The oddities she'd noticed suddenly started making sense. The people at the wedding weren't really Onegus's family. They were a strange cult of people who believed they would live forever. The gorgeous glowing priestess was obviously their leader, using her beauty and charisma to lure her followers. Onegus had even said that she was the head of their clan, but what he'd meant was the head of their cult.

Cassandra should have gotten a clue then.

Onegus's relatives weren't really related to him. They'd been recruited into the cult, and they didn't just look about the same age, they were indeed in their early twenties and thirties. Those were the age groups that the glowing beauty recruited from. She only accepted the best-looking people, which also explained why Cassandra hadn't seen even one unattractive guest.

Furthermore, Martha wasn't Onegus's real mother, only his cult mother.

What a mess. Could she save Onegus from wasting his life by living a delusion?

The better question was how she was going to save herself.

What did they want with her? Was she a new recruit? Was the invitation to the wedding about getting the cult members' approval? She must have passed the scrutiny if he was telling her that nonsense.

"What's going through your head, Cassandra?"

"I assume that you are telling me this now because you want to recruit me into your cult. Was tonight a test? Did the other members approve of me?"

Tilting his head, he made a face that was part perplexed and part amused. "A cult? You think that my family is a cult? I'm curious to hear how you arrived at that leap of logic."

Cassandra knew all about plausible deniability, had been playing that game for years. Did Onegus think that his dumb act was going to work on her?

Crossing her arms over her chest, she looked down her nose at him. "It's quite obvious. A large group of twenty to thirty-something individuals, all attractive, led by a charismatic woman-child of unparalleled beauty, who think of themselves as family and believe that they will live forever. Was Martha your recruiter? Is that why she's considered your cult mother?"

Onegus's shoulders started shaking, and a moment later, he burst out laughing.

She glared at him. "There is nothing funny about it. You are brainwashed, and you're wasting your life living in delusion."

"It is funny." He wiped tears from his eyes. "I'm just stunned. If you ask me, vampires would have been a more logical suspension of disbelief than a cult."

He was mocking her, which was a great tactic for discrediting her observations. That's how they'd dealt with all those people who'd reported UFO sightings. The strategy was incredibly effective, convincing millions of people that those reports were made by loonies.

She'd been one of those who'd ate it up and thought those people were either crazy or prone to hallucinations. But then the former head of the French equivalent of NASA had come out with a statement that a small percentage of those sightings couldn't be explained as anything other than alien crafts, operating on alien technology. No aircraft made by humans could accelerate that fast or move in such a manner.

That had changed everything for her, and not only about UFO sightings. From that moment on, she doubted any statements made by people who had something to gain or lose by making them. The only ones she deemed credible were retired scientists and military personnel who were too old to care about what the government would do to them for spilling the beans, and who had nothing they could be blackmailed for.

"Making fun of my observations is not going to change my mind about what I saw and what I deduced. Save it for the weaklings who cave under social pressure."

Onegus

Stubborn, smart woman.

Cassandra's deduction wasn't crazy. In fact, it was the most logical explanation she could have come up with, given what she'd observed.

Onegus tugged on her arm, uncrossing it, and took her hand. "I'm not mocking you, and I'm not discrediting what you saw. I'm merely offering a different explanation. The glowing priestess, as you call her, is a goddess. One of the only two remaining from those you're familiar with from different mythologies. We are her descendants. When gods mated with humans, their children were born immortal, possessing some of the gods' powers, but to a lesser extent. But when immortals mated other immortals or humans, the children born to them were born human, but all was not lost. The immortal genes passed through the mothers, and the children born to immortal females possessed the genes in a dormant form. They found a way to activate them. Later, they discovered that those genes could pass in dormant form from mother to daughter throughout many generations and still could be activated."

He paused, waiting for Cassandra to ask questions or dispute what he'd told her, but she was looking at him wide-eyed, either thinking that his tale was incredible or that he was insane.

"Many of the dormant carriers possess supernatural abilities," he continued. "Which is why I believe that you are a Dormant, and so is your mother. Although in her case, I suspect that someone activated her a long time ago, and she's already immortal. You are too close to her to realize it, but Geraldine doesn't look any older than Martha, and you had a hard time believing that she was my mother."

Cassandra narrowed her eyes. "Why does that make sense to me?"

"Because you are smart, and you are already connecting the dots. Your mother's memory lapses could be real, or they could be her way to hide that she is much older. Just think about her manners. She acts like someone who grew up in the fifties."

Cassandra huffed. "She's definitely not a prude."

He smiled. "That's because immortals are inherently intensely sexual beings. She couldn't help it. Then there is the story about her losing her driver's license and not bothering to renew it. She might be avoiding doing that because it would give her away. Besides, she's probably using an alias."

"It can't be true."

"Which part? My story or your mother being immortal?"

"Everything."

"I'm not a hundred percent sure about your mother, and I can't prove that she's immortal without further investigation, but I can prove that what I told you about myself is true. I'm an immortal."

"How can you prove it?"

"One of the many benefits of being an immortal is our rapid healing. If I make a small cut on my arm, the wound will close in front of your eyes. The other way to prove it is to show you how different I am from a human male."

"Start with the last one, and I hope it doesn't involve your dick and some weird tentacles it can sprout during sex." She shuddered. "As much as I like you, that's a deal-breaker."

He laughed. "What the hell have you been reading?"

"One of my mother's sci-fi romances." She grimaced. "Talk about disturbing."

"Fortunately, I don't have tentacles, and I'm glad this is the only thing that you consider a deal-breaker." He lifted his finger and tapped her nose. "Remember that you said it when I show you my fangs."

"Fangs?" She shifted away from him. "What fangs? You don't have fangs."

"They elongate when I'm aroused or in response to aggression."

Her hand flew to her neck. "Are you a vampire? Did you suck my blood?"

"My fangs deliver venom. I don't consume blood."

Her face twisted in a horrified expression. "Venom? Like a snake's? Is it poisonous?"

"The venom acts as an aphrodisiac and euphoric when used during sex. In battle, it can be used to immobilize an opponent, and either put him in stasis or stop his heart, depending on the dose."

Cassandra shook her head. "I don't understand. How can it do one thing during sex and then another during a fight?"

"The venom glands react to stimulation, and the venom produced is different depending on the stimuli."

"What if you get aggressive during sex?"

"As long as I'm aroused, my glands will only produce the stuff that induces orgasms and euphoria." He leaned closer. "You've experienced it twice so far, and you loved every moment."

The good thing about the direction their conversation was taking was his rising arousal. Without forcing his body to stifle its reactions, his eyes were probably already glowing, and his fangs tingled, indicating that they were elongating. In a moment, he would have proof for Cassandra.

The bad thing about it was her reaction to finding out she'd been bitten twice already.

"How come I don't remember that?" She rubbed her neck at the exact spot he'd bitten her.

Her subconscious remembered it, and all he had to do was to release those memories and let them float to the surface. It would serve as additional proof.

"I thralled you to forget my two bites. But I can release those memories."

"What do you mean when you say you thralled me? Is it like hypnosis?"

"It is, and it's not. I don't need to speak to you to affect your mind, and I can also see your most recent memories. A hypnotist can't do either. When I entered your mind, I pushed the memory of my bite below the surface of consciousness. That's why your hand is rubbing the exact spot I bit. Your body remembers it. You might also have dreamt about it."

"I haven't. But I have a big problem with you entering my mind without my permission."

"I didn't look at anything other than the sex we shared. It would have been a violation."

"Weren't you tempted to take a look at how I feel about you?"

"I don't need to infiltrate your mind to know that." He leaned closer and sniffed. "There is one more thing immortals can do that I forgot to mention. Our sense of smell can discern strong emotions. I know when you are aroused, and I know what pleases you. That's one of the things that makes me such a great lover."

Her lips twitched with a stifled smile. "You are so full of yourself." She lifted her finger and pointed it at his face. "Your eyes are glowing."

He smiled, letting her see his partially elongated fangs. "That's what talking about sex with you does to me. I'm aroused."

Unafraid, she leaned closer to examine his fangs. "I know for a fact that you were aroused at other times, but your eyes didn't glow, and you didn't sprout fangs. How come it's happening now?"

"I'm not actively suppressing my reactions. I have very good control over my body."

She looked down at the erection pressing against his slacks. "You don't seem to be able to control that."

"I could if I wanted to. But since it's not strange for a male to get a hard-on, I don't bother. My only concern is hiding my immortality. The very existence of my people depends on no one discovering that we exist."

Cassandra

Cassandra didn't know what was more unbelievable, the story Onegus had told her, or the fact that she was inclined to believe him.

"Aren't you taking a risk by telling me?"

"I can make you forget."

"So why tell me in the first place?"

"Because I need your consent to induce you. I won't do it without getting it first."

"What are you talking about?"

"You are a dormant carrier of immortal genes, I'm willing to bet my right hand on it, which means that those genes can be activated, and you can turn immortal. But I won't do it unless you agree to it. There are some risks involved."

Shaking her head, she lifted a hand. "First, tell me how this induction is done. Because if it's anything like Bella had to go through when Edward was saving her life, I'm out."

Relying on a movie was the epitome of stupidity, but since what Onegus had told her was partially covered by myth and turned out to be true, maybe the author of *Twilight* had based her story on a myth that was actually a true account as well.

When Onegus looked like he had no clue what she was blabbering about, Cassandra rolled her eyes. "It's from a movie about vampires called *Twilight*. Don't tell me that you haven't heard of it." She snorted. "That could be used as proof that you're an alien."

"I've heard of *Twilight*, but I didn't read the books or watch the movies. Many of my female relatives did, though, and there was this whole silliness going on about team Edward versus team Jason."

"Jacob, not Jason. But to make a long story short, Bella was dying after giving birth to a half-vampire daughter, and Edward saved her by biting her all over and injecting her with his vampiric venom. She made it, but she suffered through hellish pain while her body transitioned from human to vampire."

"Really?" He cocked a brow, but his lips were twitching with a stifled smile. "You would give up immortality to avoid a little pain?"

"That's a lot of pain, mind you." She shifted away, creating some space between them. No way was she going through that.

Besides, he'd said the process was risky, just like in *Twilight*, which meant that she could die. She'd rather live out the remainder of her human life than submit to torture that might or might not result in her gaining immortality.

"Then you'll be glad to know that our induction process is much more pleasurable. All that's required is unprotected sex and venom bites, which you've enjoyed greatly. I can't contract or transmit diseases, so that's not a problem, and if you are worried about pregnancy, contraceptives other than condoms and spermicides don't interfere with the process."

"What about the risk?"

"Our doctor warns that older Dormants might not make it through the transition, but so far, we haven't lost even one, and some were much older than you and not in as good health."

She frowned. "Hold on a moment. You said that it's all fun and sex, although I will need my memories back to determine whether it was as fun for me as it was for you. So, what's the risky part?"

He took her hand in both of his. "The induction is the fun part. When the transition process actually begins, it's not as fun. It starts with symptoms of mild flu, fever, muscle aches, etc. and after that, most transitioning

Dormants lose consciousness, some for a few hours, others for days. Each case is different. The moment the transition starts, though, you will be admitted to our clinic and monitored by our doctor, who by now is very experienced with the process. Other than the flu-like pains, it doesn't hurt. Well, for females. Males have to grow fangs and venom, and that's painful as hell."

Judging by his grimace, he'd experienced that and remembered it vividly.

"Did you go through that? You said that children of immortals are not born immortal."

"Correct. I was induced at thirteen. That's when Dormant boys go through their transition. It's treated like a rite of passage, and there is a small ceremony."

"What about the girls?"

"They transition at a much earlier age. Usually as toddlers."

"How come?"

"That's how it was always done."

"That's not an answer, but I get it. Tradition doesn't always make sense. How many Dormants have your people discovered so far?"

"Not many, and all of them recently. The Fates have neglected us for a very long time, and then suddenly decided to smile upon us. Syssi, Kian's wife, was the first. Amanda discovered her about four years ago."

"How? Does Syssi have a paranormal talent?"

Onegus nodded. "Precognition. Amanda is a neuroscientist, and when Syssi volunteered for testing, she scored off the charts. Amanda hired her as a lab assistant and introduced her to Kian. The rest is history."

"I bet there is much more to it."

"There is, and the other Dormants' stories are no less fascinating, but now is not the time for them. I need an answer from you. Do you consent to induction or not?"

"I need to think about it. That's not an easy decision."

"It's not." He rubbed his hand over his jaw, looking vulnerable for the first time since he'd started his incredible tale. "There is another part to this. Usually, when the Dormant is a female, her inducer is her chosen mate." He lifted his glowing blue eyes to her. "Am I your chosen guy?"

Cassandra hesitated.

Her gut's answer was an unequivocal yes, but he'd just dropped on her a load the size of an aircraft carrier. It would take time to process it.

"We haven't been together long enough, and now with all that you've revealed, I need time to think."

"What does your gut tell you?"

"That you're the one for me, fangs and glowing eyes and all. But despite my short fuse, I'm not an impulsive person. I don't want to make promises that I would later have to break."

"Fair enough." He'd either taken her hesitation in his stride or had read through it, realizing that she was just stalling because she was scared. "Do you want your memories back? They might help you make up your mind."

"Aha, so that's the ace up your sleeve. Go ahead. I'm ready."

"Look into my eyes."

"Easy enough."

His eyes were gorgeous, even more so than usual, now that they were glowing.

Cassandra's only warning was a gentle squeeze of her hand, and then the memories flooded her mind in a rush, as if a dam had collapsed. At first, the pressure was too much, and she pulled her hand out of Onegus's grip to press the heels of both hands into her temples.

Thankfully, he hadn't suppressed a lot of memories, and the flood ended in a few seconds.

Closing her eyes, she let them wash over her, and the erotic images flashing before her eyes, as well as her body's recollection of the sensations she'd experienced, had her grow moist and needy in an instant.

"You weren't kidding," she breathed. "No wonder I can't get enough of you."

Onegus

As the scent of Cassandra's arousal flared, Onegus hissed, "You are killing me." He reached for her and lifted her into his lap. "All I want now is to make love to you, but I didn't secure your consent yet."

"It can wait for the morning." She wrapped her arms around his neck. "I want to experience that bite again, and this time, don't make me forget."

Closing the distance between their mouths, she licked at the seam between his lips. "Let me in."

He gripped her nape to hold her back. "Careful. You might get your tongue nicked by my fangs. They are very sharp."

"I want to touch them."

He'd never let a woman kiss him, penetrate his mouth with her tongue, and the idea of Cassandra being his first was like dousing a fire with gasoline.

"I've never had a woman's tongue anywhere near my fangs."

She smiled against his lips. "How exciting. I'm going to take your fangs' virginity."

As she licked into his mouth, Onegus groaned, and as she folded her tongue around his right fang, he nearly exploded in his pants. Then she licked the other one, and it took every ounce of self-control to stop himself from taking over, throwing her on the bed, and tearing her dress off.

Onegus lasted for about ten seconds before taking over the kiss, his tongue sweeping in and conquering Cassandra's mouth.

She moaned, and it was his undoing. Gripping her nape even tighter, he kept kissing her while his other hand pushed the one strap holding her dress up down her arm.

Except, the dress was too form-fitting for him to tug it off without ripping it. Some semblance of restraint had him search for the zipper and lower it slowly enough not to destroy it.

As the bodice finally fell away, he discovered that Cassandra wasn't wearing a bra, and the last of his self-control snapped.

Lifting with her in his arms, he crossed the two feet to the bed and put her down.

"Is it a yes?" he asked as he shrugged his jacket off and tossed it on the couch.

"Yes." She shimmied out of the dress and pushed back against the headboard in her panties.

He needed to know precisely what she was agreeing to. "Yes to sex, or yes to sex without a condom?"

"Condom. I need more time."

It was disappointing, but he wasn't in a position to argue. All he wanted was to bury himself in her heat, and if it had to be with a damn condom, he'd take it.

"Take off your panties," he commanded as he tore off his bow tie and attacked the buttons of his shirt.

Onegus would have torn that off too, but he had nothing to change into. After the first two buttons were open, he remembered the cufflinks and pulled them out before tugging the shirt over his head.

"You move so fast." Cassandra's eyes roved over his bare chest. "Have you been holding back before?"

"You still have those panties on."

Her long fingers traveled to the gusset, and she pulled it aside, just enough for him to take a peek at the glistening slickness. "I want you to take them off me."

"Of course you do." He toed his shoes off along with the socks and dropped his pants.

Cassandra sucked in a breath. "No wonder you look like a statue of a Greek god. You have their damn genes."

He was on her between one heartbeat and the next, his fingers replacing hers in the slick heat, sliding in and out of her.

She was soaked, ready for the taking, but even though she didn't need any preparation, he needed a taste of her.

Sliding down her body, he tugged the panties off and then pushed her legs apart and dove between them.

As he treated her to the first lick, Cassandra jerked up, her bottom lifting and opening her further for his tongue to plunge.

He fucked her with his tongue, savoring her taste and her moans and her undulations, but he was too close to climaxing to torment her for much longer. He needed her to come so he could bury himself in her to the hilt.

Replacing his tongue with two fingers, he sucked the bundle of nerves at the apex of her thighs into his mouth.

With a growl, Cassandra bowed off the bed, her climax tearing through her like an explosion. He kept on licking and sucking, wringing every last drop of pleasure out of her. At some point her fingers threaded in his hair, and she tugged on his curls hard enough that the slight pain penetrated his sex-addled brain, and he let go.

Cassandra

If not for the memory of that bite, Cassandra would have let herself drift off to sleep.

The orgasm Onegus had wrung out of her had left her sated and boneless, and given how tired she'd been before he'd carried her to bed, it was a wonder she wanted more.

He kissed her inner thigh, one side and then the next, and as she lifted her head and looked at him, he smiled and licked his lips.

"Come here." She tugged on his hair.

He didn't need to be asked twice.

Kissing up her belly, he reached her right breast and licked the nipple, then moved to the other one before settling in the cradle of her legs.

Poised above her, he was all muscles, fangs, and glowing eyes, and he was hers. Somehow, he didn't look alien to her, or scary. He was her Onegus, too gorgeous to be real, too charming, too much of everything, but he was hers, and she was not giving him up.

As the tip of his shaft nudged at her entrance, she debated whether to remind him to sheath himself in a condom or to pretend that she'd forgotten as well and just let it happen.

"I almost forgot." He leaned over the side of the bed and lifted his slacks. "We need this."

He pulled a condom packet out of his pocket, tore it open with his teeth, or rather fangs, and pulled the rubber on.

The whole maneuver had lasted only a couple of seconds, and then he was at her entrance again, pushing into her and kissing her at the same time.

Cassandra was so wet from her climax that he didn't need to go slow, but he did anyway, inching into her until he seated himself fully.

They both groaned.

Lifting his head, Onegus withdrew and then surged in, all the time watching her face with an intensity that made her feel like she was precious to him.

She wrapped her arms around his muscled back, her long legs around his powerful hips, and lifted to take him even deeper.

And still, that wasn't enough.

She wanted him wild and unrestrained, but despite all her bluster, she wasn't comfortable asking for what she wanted.

He'd said that he could read her needs, smell them, couldn't he tell that she needed him fast and hard?

Onegus smiled, his fangs gleaming white in the darkened room. "Tell me what you want, Cassy."

So, that was the game he was playing.

She could play as well. "Can't you guess?"

He pulled almost all the way out and then slammed back, propelling their bodies toward the headboard.

Stilling again, he looked into her eyes. "Is that what you want?"

"Yes. Don't stop."

He pulled out again, going to the very edge, and then slammed back in. Gripping her hips, he started pounding into her with abandon, and all she could do was to hiss, "Yes, yes!"

That kind of pounding would leave marks, and Cassandra knew she would be sore and bruised in the morning, but she didn't care.

This was Onegus unleashed, and he was magnificent. She wanted to take all he had, to give herself to him completely like she'd never given herself to any man before.

For tonight, he could be her master, and she relished the submission, so rare for her that she doubted she could do it again.

When his pounding became even stronger and faster, and his shaft swelled impossibly larger inside her, she knew it was time for what she'd been waiting for and turned her head, offering him her neck.

Except, he didn't bite her right away. Even though he was seconds away from climaxing, he licked the spot, preparing it for his bite, and when it came, the slight pain was just enough to hurtle her over the edge.

Cassandra climaxed, her sheath tightening around Onegus's impossibly thick shaft, and as the venom entered her system, she climaxed again, and again, until she must have passed out.

Soaring on a cloud of euphoria, she let herself drift away into the magical lands the venom had opened up for her.

Onegus

After Cassandra had drifted off to wonderland, Onegus had lain awake for a long time. Last night had been a turning point in their relationship, but he wasn't satisfied with where it was. He hadn't told her that he loved her yet, and she hadn't said the words to him either.

Did he love her?

Did he even know what love was?

Onegus was an old immortal, and the only real love of his life was his work. While others had pined for mates, lamented about their loneliness and the never-ending revolving door of lovers, he'd been happy with his life. The tight control he had over himself meant that he didn't have to spend much of his time and energy hunting for sex partners, and when he did, it was mostly enjoyable and quite satisfying.

He hadn't been looking for an emotional connection.

Perhaps Cassandra had been right when she'd accused him of being a player at heart.

The thing was, she'd changed all that, and he had no problem envisioning life with her as his partner. She had her own career, was her own woman, and she wouldn't put unreasonable demands on his time.

They could make it work.

But that wasn't what Cassandra was after. She wanted his heart, his soul, and he wasn't sure he had it in him to surrender them to her.

Even if he and Cassandra bonded, love was not really part of the equation. Contrary to what most clan members believed, the bond wasn't some mythical thing ordained by the Fates. It was a biological reaction, hormones, or pheromones, or some other chemical process that created that insufferable need for mates to be together.

Love was different. Love came from the soul, and he wasn't sure that he was wired for love. Falling in like, or rather in lust, was the best he could hope for, and for him, that was enough.

It wouldn't be for Cassandra, though, and she wasn't the type of woman who would compromise on anything less than everything.

She'd told him that she could easily fall in love with him and had asked if he would break her heart.

He'd promised Cassandra that her heart was safe with him.

He would never betray her, and if she transitioned and became his mate, he would stay with her forever. But he couldn't promise her love without it being at least partially a lie.

To make her happy, though, he would have to do it. Onegus hated liars, didn't want to be one, but the alternative was to let her go, and he couldn't do that either. If she didn't turn, he would be forced to, but if she transitioned, he wanted to keep her.

Perhaps love would come later. Or maybe it was already there, but he didn't recognize it.

Turning to look at Cassandra's beautiful face, Onegus knew that he would love waking up next to her each morning, love talking to her over breakfast, and then love meeting her again in the evening after their workday was done. The other kind of love would come later.

He pressed a soft kiss to her cheek and then got out of bed.

It was five o'clock in the morning, and the Guardians would be switching shifts in an hour. He had to go up to the apartment, change into his day clothes, and get breakfast for him and Cassandra.

After he washed up and got dressed, Onegus stopped by the bed and spent a long moment looking at Cassandra's beautiful face. Her expression was one of bliss, and he loved that he'd put it there.

He should leave her a note in case she woke up before he returned.

Taking a napkin from the minibar, he wrote her a short message and put it on the pillow next to her where she couldn't miss it.

As Onegus opened the door with his phone, the mechanical whizzing sound didn't wake Cassandra or even make her stir.

Taking one last look at her before stepping out, he smiled. He would be back before she woke up.

Cassandra was probably going to sleep until noon, but in case she didn't, he left the door open, just enough for her to squeeze through, but not enough for someone walking by to see her sleeping in the nude.

After all, she wasn't a prisoner, and if he closed her in, she might panic.

Heading toward the elevator, he dialed Bhathian's number. Onegus had left him in charge of the night shift, not expecting any trouble, and hopefully, there had been none.

"Good morning, Chief," the Guardian answered.

"Good morning. Anything to report?" Onegus entered the elevator.

"Nope. All the guests made it safely to their beds last night, although some later than others. Several of our buddies from Scotland stayed with us in the lobby to chat. They left less than an hour ago."

"No news, good news."

"You got it, Chief."

When he reached the apartment, Onegus entered it as quietly as he could, trying not to wake the Guardians sleeping there. Six of them were crammed into the two-bedroom apartment, but it was a temporary situation, and no one was complaining.

After a quick shower and a change of clothes, he walked into the kitchen and started making breakfast, which inevitably woke nearly everyone up, but it was fine. Their shift was starting at six o'clock, and it was time for them to get ready.

Cassandra

Cassandra was cold, which was what had woken her up. Onegus was gone, and with him his warmth.

He'd left her a note written on a napkin, saying that he went to check on things and would be back with breakfast.

Shifting to her back, Cassandra pulled the blanket up to her chin and tucked it around her. She was still bone-tired, and if not for the jumble of thoughts swirling in her head, she would have gone back to sleep. But too much was going on for her to let it go.

Onegus was an immortal, and he suspected that her mother was as well. Not only that, but her dormant immortal genes could also be activated as soon as she consented.

Seemed like a no-brainer, especially since Onegus downplayed the risks, saying that his clan hadn't lost a transitioning Dormant yet. They even had their own clinic and an experienced doctor to supervise the transition.

So why was she still hesitating?

Not enough information, that's why.

It all seemed too good to be true, and there must be a downside. Like the mysterious enemies that necessitated all that cloak-and-dagger secrecy and security around the wedding. How dangerous were they? And what beef did they have with Onegus's clan?

Would she have to disappear and live in hiding?

If Geraldine was immortal as Onegus suspected, then she'd done a very good job hiding in plain sight. There was no reason for them to go into hiding.

And then there was the process itself.

Onegus had said that her inducer needed to be her chosen mate, and he'd asked her if he was the guy for her. He hadn't asked her if she loved him, hadn't told her that he loved her, and yet he expected her to marry him? Or mate him?

What if after she transitioned, they came to the conclusion that it wasn't working out? What would her options be?

Cassandra needed answers before she could give Onegus her consent. She'd promised him an answer by morning, but she would have to ask for an extension until she had all the facts and could make an informed decision.

As the door started moving, she pushed up on the pillows and tugged the blanket with her.

What if it wasn't Onegus?

Other people were staying down there. She'd met Eleanor, one of Onegus's security team members. There were probably more of them on this level.

He walked in, wearing a fresh outfit and holding a large tray in his hands. "Good morning, beautiful. I didn't expect you to be up." He put the tray down on the coffee table. "I thought that I would have to wake you up."

"I was cold. This place is freezing."

"I'm sorry." He pulled out his phone. "I'll turn the heat up."

She eyed the tray from the bed. "I don't have a change of clothes, and I don't want to eat breakfast in my evening gown."

Without a moment's hesitation, he pulled his dress shirt over his head and handed it to her.

"Thanks." Her eyes roamed over his muscled chest. "That's a nice view to have over breakfast." She pulled the shirt on and swung her legs over the side of the bed.

"Same here." His eyes blazed with an inner light. "It looks much better on you than it does on me."

"Give me a moment to freshen up." She ducked into the bathroom.

After using the facilities, she washed her hands, and then opened the first vanity drawer to see if there was anything she could use to clean up her smeared makeup.

She found a pack of makeup removal towelettes, a new toothbrush still in its store wrapping, a tube of toothpaste, and even a selection of lotions. Whoever equipped the little suite was definitely a woman, and she had Cassandra's thanks for thinking of all the essentials.

When she was done and walked over to the couch, Onegus pulled her onto his lap. "I need one kiss before I let you eat."

"Just one?" She cupped his freshly shaved cheek.

"For now." He took her lips in a gentle kiss, his hands roving over her back, her exposed outer thighs, and up her ribs, brushing the sides of her breasts.

Breakfast forgotten, she kissed him back, expecting to find sharp fangs, but even though he was very obviously aroused, Onegus kept them from elongating.

"Did I dream about you having fangs?"

He smiled, showing her a row of perfect pearly whites with canines that were just a little on the pointy side. "Unlike many immortal males, I have excellent control over my fangs and the glow in my eyes." Lifting her off his lap, he set her down next to him. "Coffee?"

"Yes, please."

He poured them both a cup from the thermos and then added cream and sugar to hers. "Just as you like it." He handed her the cup.

She took a sip. "Perfect."

"Yes, you are."

Onegus

Onegus bided his time, waiting for the right moment to ask Cassandra for her consent again, and to explain why she couldn't leave without him either thralling away the memory of everything he'd told her or forcing her silence with compulsion.

She was a smart lady, so she'd probably figured that out already, but she seemed in no hurry to finish her breakfast and have the talk she knew was coming.

When there was nothing more she could nibble on, and the coffee thermos was empty, she leaned back, crossed her arms over her chest, and cast him a wry smile. "Okay, let's hear it."

"That should be my line. Do I have your consent or not?"

"Not yet. I need to get to know you better, I need to learn much more about what I'm getting myself into, and I have to find out whether my mother is immortal."

It was a sensible approach.

Onegus couldn't fault Cassandra for being careful and not jumping headfirst into the deep before finding out precisely what was in the water.

Still, he couldn't help the pang of disappointment. "I understand." He sighed. "I'll have to either erase the memory of everything I've told you or compel you to keep it a secret."

She frowned. "Making me forget doesn't make sense. How am I going to think it through if I don't know what I'm supposed to do? And why bother getting my consent if I won't remember it?"

"I thought that I would get your consent in writing, then suppress your memories, and when you started transitioning, I would show you the written agreement so you wouldn't get mad. The other option was for you to come with me to the cabin, and we would have stayed there until you started to transition. That's why I suggested it. Not because I didn't want to be seen with you, but because I needed to take you somewhere secluded where you couldn't tell anyone what you've learned."

She smiled sheepishly. "I'm sorry for accusing you of being a player. I had no way of knowing."

He nodded. "Apology accepted."

"What if I don't transition?"

That was the hard part to admit, but there was no way around it. "It pains me to say it, but immortals and humans can't have long-term relationships, Cassy. It's just too complicated. First of all, because of the need for secrecy, and secondly, because it's just too painful."

"I get it." She looked away, and he suspected that it was to hide tears. "I don't like it, but I get it. Still, even if I don't transition, and we have to go our separate ways, I don't want to forget any of it. I'd take compulsion over memory wipe any day."

"If you don't transition, forgetting the entire thing will be easier for you. You could go on with your life without being aware that the promise of immortality was dangled in front of you and then taken away. It could mess you up." He shook his head. "But why are we even considering the possibility? I know in my gut that you are a Dormant. You have an incredible paranormal ability that's very rare. In fact, I know only one other immortal who has a similar power."

"Let me guess. Sylvia?"

"You guessed right. How did you know?"

Cassandra shrugged. "She made comments about my inability to control my energy. It wasn't hard to figure out that she knew what I was dealing with."

"Sylvia can't blow things up, but she can make electronics malfunction."

"Can she teach me how to control my energy better? It's a major pain," Cassandra admitted. "When I feel it rising, I panic, which makes it worse, and I have to find a receptacle. I can hold on for a little bit, but eventually I need to release it or it becomes uncontrollable."

"Sylvia can teach you how to channel it, but I don't think she can teach you how to discharge it." Smirking, he took her hand, lifted it to his lips, and kissed her wrist. "That's my job."

She chuckled. "With sex?"

"You are much calmer after orgasming a couple of times."

"True." She cast him a suggestive smile. "But that also means that you can't tease me for long. Then the energy builds up, and I become dangerous."

He nodded. "Duly noted. Also, don't forget about your mother. If she is an immortal, then there is no question that you are a Dormant."

"Speaking of my mother." She leaned to lift her purse off the table. "I need to text her. With all the excitement, I forgot to let her know that I'm spending the night with you." She pulled her phone out and typed up a short message. "Do you want to see the text before I send it?"

"Why would I?"

"Oh, I don't know," she mocked. "Maybe I texted her your secrets."

"Who's going to believe Geraldine? It would be just another fantastic story she added to her repertoire. Besides, I trust you."

"Really? Then why thrall my memories or compel me to silence? I can just promise to keep quiet."

"It's done to ensure that you don't blurt it out unintentionally, and that you can't reveal the information even under duress."

"Right. You need to tell me about those enemies of yours. That's also something I need to consider before I give you my consent."

Was she implying that he couldn't protect her?

"You have nothing to fear from them. I'll never let anything happen to you."

"Nevertheless, I need to know what I'm getting myself into."

"Does it have to be now?"

"No. There is no rush."

As Cassandra sent the text, he leaned over the phone. "I'm not reading your text. I just wanted to see Geraldine's picture, but there are none."

"My mother hates having her picture taken. In the few I managed to snap, she either looks away or turns her back to the camera."

"Didn't you find that suspicious?"

She shrugged. "Some people are camera shy."

"Immortals more than anyone else."

"Why?"

"Just think about it. We don't change. A picture taken fifty years ago would look exactly like a picture taken today. It's a dead giveaway."

"I just had a thought. What if my mother is a Dormant like me and just looks young? Can she go through transition?"

"I don't know. She might be too old even though she doesn't look it."

"Who makes that call?"

"Our doctor."

"Right. You told me that you have one who specializes in transitioning Dormants."

"Among other things."

"How can we find out whether my mother is an immortal?"

Cassandra

Onegus let go of her hand and got to his feet. "If we can get a good picture of her face, our in-house hacker can run it through DMV records using a facial recognition program." He pulled two bottles of water from the fridge. "If a driver's license with her picture pops out more than once, decades apart, that would prove it." He handed her a bottle.

"Thanks." She unscrewed the top and took a long swig. "You assume that she changed her name."

"She would have had to. That's what we do."

"We might have to corner her and take it when she doesn't expect it."

Onegus sat back on the couch, braced his elbows on his knees, and leaned forward. "There is also the cut or scratch test I told you about. If she heals rapidly, that's even better proof than the driver's license. Does she get sick? Flu? Colds?"

Staring at his bunching biceps, she had a hard time concentrating. Perhaps she should give him his shirt back and put on the dress.

Taking another sip from the water, she tried to focus on his face and not ogle his chest and arms. "Frankly, I don't remember her ever getting sick, but that's not a proof either. She might just have a good immune system. And as for your other suggestion, I can't just go up to my mother with a knife in hand and cut her or scratch her. What about the super hearing? We can go up to my room and talk about immortals. If my mother can hear us, she would get anxious."

Onegus winced. "Provided that she knows and remembers that she's not aging."

Yeah, with her memory issues, she might have come up with a fantastic story to explain her youthful appearance.

"Could the memory loss be the result of the transition?"

Onegus rubbed his jaw. "Not likely, but stasis can."

"What's that?"

"Immortals can go into stasis and stay in that state for thousands of years. We have a clan member who was buried alive in an earthquake. She woke up over five thousand years later, when they built an apartment complex over the place she was buried in, and a pipe burst. Emerging from her stasis, she didn't know who she was or where she came from. Somehow, the Fates guided her to us, and with time she regained her memories."

Cassandra shook her head. "My mother can't be that ancient. Could a short stasis have done that?"

"Maybe. I don't know."

"How did she turn immortal in the first place? Did she hook up with some random immortal male who didn't use protection?"

He nodded. "It's possible. We have a clan member who was induced by a random hookup. Many immortal males don't use condoms because we can't get or transmit diseases, and our fertility rate is so low that pregnancy is not an issue either. I'm just more cautious than others."

"Right." She rubbed her temple. "I'm getting a headache from all this speculating. I need to go home, take a shower, and sleep until noon."

"I also need to get back to work." He looked at her with those intense blue eyes of his. "So, what will it be? Thralling, compulsion, or staying here until you transition?"

She looked around the small room. "Definitely compulsion. I would go nuts in here, and I need to be at work on Monday."

"Very well." He pushed to his feet. "I'll call Eleanor."

"What for?"

"She's a compeller, and she happens to be down the corridor."

"Can't you do it?"

"Compulsion is a very rare talent, which I don't possess. I can only thrall. Do you still want to be compelled?"

"Yes. I want to own my memories, good and bad. After watching my mother suffering from memory issues all my life, I can't tolerate the thought of losing my memory. It terrifies me."

"Oh, Cassy." He crouched next to her and took her hands. "I should have realized that memory is precious to you."

"That's okay. Just call Eleanor in here, and let's get it over with. Compulsion is scary too, but not as scary as the alternative."

"The cabin is still on the table."

"Yeah, well. You can't leave until after your boss's birthday, and I can't wait in this room until you can. Besides, I can't take a vacation that long."

He nodded. "I'll get Eleanor."

"Hold on." She pulled his shirt over her head and handed it to him. "I don't want her ogling my guy."

His eyes riveted to her bare breasts, he swallowed. "Now, I can't move."

Laughing, she gave him a slight shove. "Go. I need to get dressed."

Onegus

Onegus found Eleanor in Arwel's suite, alone.

"Where is Alfie?"

She looked up from the monitor she'd been staring at. "He went upstairs to shower and change."

"He shouldn't leave you alone here."

She rolled her eyes, which he found disrespectful. It was okay when Cassandra did that, but not from an underling.

"I know not to open the door to Emmett's cell without backup. Alfie is going to get his breakfast, and I'm going to bring it to him."

"Has Emmett been behaving?"

"Yep. He hasn't given me any trouble at all."

Onegus glanced at the screen. Emmett was up, sitting on the couch with a book in his hands. "What's he reading?"

She shrugged. "I don't know. Arwel brought him a bunch of books. He likes to read."

"Good for him." Onegus rubbed a hand over the back of his neck. "I need your help. I need you to compel Cassandra not to reveal anything about us."

A smile bloomed on Eleanor's thin face. "Sure thing, boss. Is she your one?" She rose to her feet.

"I don't know yet. Cassandra is great. She's everything I ever wanted in a woman, a mate, but love is a foreign concept to me. At least romantic love. And she's not going to settle for anything less than everything."

He had no clue why he was sharing his inner struggle with Eleanor. Perhaps because he still viewed her as an outsider, an objective observer who would not interject her own feelings into the situation.

"Cassandra shouldn't settle for anything less than your love and devotion, and neither should you. Take your time. That's the only advice I can give you." She smiled sadly. "My romantic track record doesn't qualify me as an expert."

"Yeah, mine neither."

"What's Cassandra's talent?"

He chuckled. "She blows things up when she gets mad."

Eleanor grinned. "My kind of girl."

When they walked into the room, Cassandra rose to her feet and offered Eleanor her hand. "Good morning." She smiled. "I hope Onegus didn't drag you out of bed."

She was dressed in her evening gown and the stilettos with the red soles, looking like a magazine cover model, even without any makeup and her hair in a messy bun.

"I was already up." Eleanor shook her hand. "Let's get comfortable." She motioned to the couch.

As the two women sat down, Eleanor lifted her eyes to Onegus. "Compulsion needs to be very precise. Do you want me to exclude you from the compulsion not to mention immortals, Dormants, and this place?"

"Good idea. Also include fangs and venom. And an override clause. Cassandra can talk about everything when I'm around and approve."

"Okay. That's going to be a bit tricky. I need a moment to formulate it precisely."

"Take as long as you need," Cassandra said. "I don't want you to compel me to do or not do anything other than what's absolutely necessary."

Eleanor nodded. "Look into my eyes and listen carefully. Until I release you, you are not allowed to say, write, type, whisper, or mime the following words: immortal, Dormant, fangs, and venom. You are not allowed to tell anyone the location of this building. If anyone asks, you were driven here, and you didn't pay attention to where you were taken. You are allowed to say that it was somewhere downtown. Also, don't repeat any of the names you've heard while attending the wedding. However, if you are with Onegus and he allows it, you can talk about all those things that you are not allowed to mention when he's not around."

"Is that all?" Cassandra asked.

Eleanor turned to Onegus. "I think I covered everything. Anything you want me to add?"

"We forgot gods and goddesses, but that's fine. It's meaningless without the rest."

"Let's test it." Eleanor smiled at Cassandra. "Tell me what's special about Onegus."

"He's handsome, charming, smart, bossy, and he has teeth that elongate and eyes that glow." Cassandra smirked. "You didn't think of everything."

"Oops." Eleanor looked at Onegus. "Should I include that?"

He shook his head. "That's fine. Who's going to believe it, right?"

"I'm not going to tell anyone." Cassandra pushed to her stiletto-clad feet. "If we are done, I would like to get home before my neighbors wake up and see me arriving in the morning wearing an evening dress."

Cassandra

"You know what I'm thankful for?" Cassandra opened the passenger side window to let the fresh morning air in.

Onegus turned to look at her and smiled. "Letting Kevin persuade you to attend the gala so that you could meet me?"

"That too." He was so full of himself, but in a charming and disarming way that she had to admit she adored. "Contrary to what you believe, not everything revolves around you. This one is about me. I'm glad to finally understand where my strange power comes from, and that I'm not a witch."

He arched a brow. "Is that what you thought it was?"

"What else could I think? It terrified me. I could hurt people." And she had, but she wasn't ready to share that with him yet. "I was desperate to get rid of it, or at least learn to control it. I tried meditation, I even tried relaxants. But I didn't have the patience for meditating, and relaxants made me sleepy. I even read books on magic, but they were either a bunch of nonsense or impossible to understand."

"You should talk to Sylvia. Perhaps she can train you."

"I would like that."

His expression turned serious. "There is still so much I need to tell you. I wish we could go away for a few days."

"I would like that too." Cassandra sighed. "I feel like a slave to my work."

"You said that you often take work home."

"What about it?"

"We could go away together someplace nice, and you could dedicate a few hours a day to work, but we can have fun the rest of the time."

"That's a great idea, except I can't do everything that needs to be done in a few hours a day. It's not going to be fun for you to wait for me to finish my work."

"True." He turned to look at her again. "Then maybe you can stay with me for a few days? You'll do your work, and I'll do mine, but at least we will be together."

It was on the tip of her tongue to say that she would try to make it work, but then her mother's face flashed in front of her, and she knew she couldn't do that.

"I can't leave my mother alone."

"Not even for a few days?"

"Two or three, but no longer than that." She pushed a loose strand of hair behind her ear. "That's another thing you should consider. My mother and I are a package deal."

He grimaced. "Does that mean that she would have to live with us?"

"Either that or next door. She needs me."

"I'm okay with next door."

Cassandra shook her head. "Look at us. We are planning the rest of our lives as if everything is settled when, in fact, nothing is."

He reached over the center console and took her hand. "One step at a time, Cassy. First, you need to decide when you want to start working on your transition."

It wasn't only about the when, but also about the who. Was Onegus the one?

He squeezed her hand. "A penny for your thoughts."

"You said that my inducer should be the man, or immortal, who I chose to spend the rest of my life with. What if things don't work out between us?"

For a brief moment, Onegus looked as if she'd slapped him, but he recuperated quickly, and when he spoke, he sounded as calm and collected as usual. "We are great together, and I don't foresee that changing, but if, Fates forbid, something happens, and we part ways, you can choose someone else. Eleanor wasn't romantically involved with the guy who induced her. He was just a hookup, but later they gave a relationship a try. It didn't work out, and now she's on the prowl, looking for her one and only."

Cassandra blew out a breath. "I hope our relationship will keep on growing stronger, but knowing that agreeing to the induction doesn't mean a life-long commitment is a relief."

When he stopped at the gate to her community, she waved at the guard who recognized her and let them through without asking to see Onegus's driver's license.

A couple of moments later, Onegus pulled up in front of her house and turned the engine off.

A muscle ticked in his jaw when he turned to look at her. "Other than Eleanor, there was only one other female Dormant who didn't mate her inducer. Neither of them had known that she was a Dormant, and when she started transitioning, he was long gone. All the other transitioned Dormants are happily mated to their inducers."

He hadn't told her he loved her yet, but he was upset because she needed an exit clause?

Sometimes it was difficult to understand the way men thought, and apparently, that included immortals who'd been around long enough to think with their brains and not their male hormones.

"I hope we will be one of those happy couples, but we are not there yet." She pinned him with a hard stare. "Do you love me, Onegus?"

When he swallowed, she shook her head. "That's what I thought." Leaning toward him, she put her hand on his arm. "It's okay. I don't believe in love at first sight, and I don't expect you to fall in love with me in one week. By the same token, you can't expect me to commit to you after such a short time."

He nodded. "I've never been in love, so I don't know whether what I feel for you is love. What I know, however, is that I've never enjoyed being with a woman as much as I enjoy being with you, and that when I'm not with you, I can't wait until we meet again."

"I feel the same." Leaning over, she kissed his cheek. "For now, that will do, and it's a good start."

CASSANDRA & ONEGUS'S CULMINATES
The Children of the Gods Book 52
Dark Power Convergence

Turn the page to read the excerpt—>

Join the VIP Club
To find out what's included in your free membership, flip to the last page.

Dark Power Convergence

The threads of fate converge, mysteries unfold, and the clan's future is forever altered in the least expected way.

Kian

In a rare moment of peace and contentment, Kian flipped through the wedding pictures posted on the clan's website that morning. The photographer had captured beautifully the heart-warming slices of life.

So far, Kian's favorites were Syssi dancing with Andrew and Phoenix, the girl riding on her father's shoulders and beaming with happiness, David and Sari gazing into each other's eyes as they stood in front of Annani on the podium, Wonder laughing at Anandur's goofy dance moves, and Kalugal toasting the happy couple with a glass of whiskey.

First thing Monday morning, Kian was going to ask Shai to add these to the compilation on his screensaver.

Putting the highlights from past clan celebrations on Kian's computer had been one of his assistant's better attempts at helping him to reduce his stress levels.

As he found himself gazing at the compilation throughout his workdays, it never failed to bring a smile to his face. The pictures he loved the most were of Syssi, some from their own wedding, others from Andrew and Nathalie's and other celebrations. Their trips to Hawaii and to Scotland provided many more.

He could spend all day looking at pictures of her beautiful face and lush body, but it would be even better to get up from his chair and go find her.

They were hosting a family Sunday brunch, and although Syssi was supposed to leave all the work to Okidu, Kian had no doubt that he would find her in the back yard, fussing over the final details, and making sure everything had been done according to her instructions.

As he entered the living room, he spotted her standing on the back porch, her fists pressed into the small of her back, a pose she assumed a lot lately because her muscles strained with carrying her very pregnant belly.

Kian walked up behind Syssi, leaned over her back, and kissed her neck. "Why are you out here?"

"I wanted to make sure that everything is ready."

He wrapped his arms under her huge belly and hoisted it up. "You were supposed to let Okidu handle everything."

"He has his limits. If I let him handle the music, Fates only know what he would choose. I still remember the polka compilation he put on the last time."

The soft instrumental piece playing through the outdoor loudspeakers was definitely a better choice. It added to the festive mood but wouldn't overwhelm the conversation.

"I concede in regards to the music. What else does he need help with?"

"Nothing. I just wanted to make sure that it wasn't too hot out here. The day has turned out to be perfect, though. The breeze is enough to cool down the air but not strong enough to blow away the decorations."

Kian looked up at the stuff Okidu had salvaged from the wedding and hung from tree branches and bushes around their backyard.

Had that been his own idea?

Probably not.

Someone must have suggested it to him because Okidu couldn't make decisions like that on his own.

That wasn't how his programming was supposed to work.

Or at least that was what Kian used to believe. Reading about the latest developments in artificial intelligence had made him reevaluate his opinion.

He wasn't a computer expert like William, but from what he'd read, he had garnered that the latest artificial intelligence design was based on neural networks that mimicked the multi-dimensional connections in the brain. When the network was presented with a tremendous amount of data and given an objective, it could learn and make decisions.

That made intuitive sense to him.

What Kian found strange was that the inner workings of the artificially made system were just as mysterious as the inner workings of the living brain, and the

researchers didn't actually know how the A.I. arrived at its decisions.

Over the millennia of Okidu's existence, he'd accumulated an enormous amount of data, and his neural networks were probably incalculably more advanced than those found in even the most robust present-day artificial intelligence systems. Could he have reached some level of sentience?

What exactly constituted sentience?

Kian shook his head.

Philosophy wasn't his forte, and he should leave it to those much smarter than he was.

Turning her head to look up at him, Syssi smiled. "Did you come out here just to hoist up my belly? Or did you have something that you needed to tell me and forgot?"

He chuckled. "I might be two thousand years old, but I'm not senile. You were standing with your fists pressing into the small of your back. I figured you needed help carrying our daughter around."

She kissed the underside of his jaw. "Can you do this all day long? I feel so much lighter."

"Two and a half weeks to go, love." He kissed her cheek. "You should take it easy."

She snorted. "If I take it any easier, I won't get out of bed in the morning. I need something to do other than worry."

Thankfully, his stubborn wife had listened to the doctor, who'd advised her to take a leave of absence from work for the last four weeks of her pregnancy. Bridget's argument was that labor might start unexpectedly, and if it happened while Syssi was en route to work or at the university, it might complicate things.

The argument had been convincing, but it had added another layer of anxiety that Syssi could have done without.

As Phoenix's happy squeal announced their first guests' arrival, Kian kissed Syssi's neck and let go of her belly.

A moment later, the toddler bounced into the backyard and unceremoniously flung herself into his arms.

"Uncle Kian." She cupped his cheeks. "Can we play horsey?"

Plucking the girl off his chest, he lifted her behind his back and deposited her over his shoulders. "Hold on tight."

"Yes!" She wrapped her little arms around his neck, choking him with a surprisingly strong grip. "Horsey, jump!"

Leaping over a lounge chair, Kian elicited an excited squeal from her, and when he leaped over the next one, Phoenix shouted, "Jump higher, horsey!"

"I can't watch this." Nathalie covered her eyes with her hands.

"Don't worry." Andrew wrapped his arm around his wife's waist. "Kian would never let anything happen to her."

"Damn right." Kian lifted the protesting Phoenix and handed her to Andrew. "That's enough horsey for today." He ruffled her hair.

"I want a pony," Phoenix said. "I want to teach him to jump over stuff like Uncle Kian does."

"When you're older." Andrew patted her back.

If her parents wanted her to train with horses, they would have to take her to a human equestrian center. Personally, Kian had nothing against the animals, but Amanda would lose her shit if they brought one to the village, especially now that she was about to have another child. Ever since she'd lost her son, she couldn't stand seeing kids anywhere near horses.

"Hello, everyone." Annani floated into the backyard, followed by Alena, Sari, David, and Ogidu.

"Good morning, Mother." Kian leaned down and kissed her cheek, then turned to his newlywed sister. "How does it feel to be a married woman?" He kissed Sari's cheek as well.

"Nothing's changed in the way I feel, except for being relieved that the wedding is behind me, and I can go back to my routine."

When he arched a brow, his sister cast him an apologetic glance. "That sounded ungrateful. The event and the ceremony were beautiful. David and I truly appreciate all that went into making it happen, and for enabling nearly the entire clan to attend."

"I get it." Syssi patted Sari's arm. "For me, it's draining to be the center of attention, but I thought that you were more extroverted."

"I am. I love being surrounded by people, but I'm also a creature of habit. Routine calms me down."

David took Sari's hand. "I want to thank you for hosting our wedding and for inviting us to your home today."

"You're welcome," Kian said. "It's our pleasure, and that's not a platitude. As far as I'm concerned, life doesn't get better than when celebrating happy occasions with my family."

Cassandra

Cassandra's bed felt as hot as an oven, but she wasn't ready to get up yet. Instead, she flung off the duvet, flipped her pillow around, and turned to her side. Given the sweltering heat of her bedroom, it was probably around noon, but since she'd gotten home in the early hours of the morning, she was in no rush to start her day.

The slight headache was a reminder of how much she'd had to drink last night. Could she have dreamt up the bizarre events that had taken place after all that drinking?

A part of Cassandra wished that she had, and another part wished that all of it was true. Like the revelation about Onegus's fangs and what they could do.

They were a little scary but also exciting, especially after he'd released her memories of his previous bites and the orgasms that had followed and then given her a live demonstration. Those mean babies delivered the kind of ecstasy poems could be written about.

Regrettably, Cassandra couldn't write hymns in their honor or even tell anyone about them because she was under compulsion not to reveal anything she'd learned last night.

Onegus was immortal, and so was his entire family. Not only that, but he also suspected that her mother was immortal as well.

If not for a lifetime of living with a strange power capable of blowing things up, Cassandra would have had a much harder time believing Onegus's story despite the proof he'd presented her with.

And as if all of that wasn't enough to send her head spinning, he'd told her that she was most likely a dormant carrier of the immortal genes, and he wanted to induce her transition into immortality.

Cassandra was in no rush to give her consent.

It wasn't that she didn't want to be immortal, but she would be a fool to jump in the deep end without checking all the facts first. To make a well-informed decision, she had to find out precisely what she was getting into and what she would be giving up.

According to Onegus, no blood drinking was involved, and the transition was difficult but not painful. It sounded a little too good to be true.

Her overly creative imagination provided her with a slew of potential pitfalls that Onegus had deliberately omitted. Some of them were relatively benign, although significant, like the low fertility he'd mentioned. Others were nastier and too fantastic to take seriously, but she couldn't help where her mind was going.

If keeping her immortality involved human sacrifices or devil worship, she was out.

Snorting, Cassandra got out of bed and padded to the bathroom.

That was probably taking it too far, but his comment about fertility could mean that she wouldn't be able to have children, and that was a big deal.

Would that be a deal-breaker for her?

Maybe. Did immortals adopt children?

Probably not.

She needed to call Onegus and ask him a gazillion questions. She also needed to figure out a way to find out whether her mother was immortal, and if she was, how it had happened.

Given what Onegus had told her, the only way Geraldine could have turned immortal was if she'd had unprotected sex with an immortal male. Her mother could have hooked up with a random guy, neither of them realizing who the other was, and transitioned without knowing what was happening to her.

That was enough to mess with anyone's head. Could that be the reason for her mother's memory issues?

So many questions. So few answers.

Once Cassandra was done in the bathroom, she changed into a pair of yoga pants and a cami and headed downstairs to the kitchen.

"Good morning." Her mother beamed at her. "The coffee just finished brewing."

"Thanks." Cassandra poured herself a cup and took it to the dining table.

"How was your date?" Geraldine pulled a carton of eggs and a tub of butter from the fridge.

"Great."

"I heard you opening the front door this morning, but I figured you would tell me all about it after you'd gotten some sleep."

Sipping on her coffee, Cassandra considered what she could tell her mother. The event was over, so security was no longer an issue. She could tell her about attending the wedding. Besides, she needed to tell Geraldine about

Onegus's mother because the four of them were supposed to have lunch together.

"It was a wedding." She smiled apologetically. "I'm sorry I couldn't tell you before, but Onegus made me promise to keep it a secret. His family has enemies, and it was important that no one found out about the event."

Cracking another egg into the pan, her mother turned to look at her. "What kind of enemies?"

"I don't know. He didn't say. Anyway, I met his mother."

As she'd expected, that got Geraldine more excited than the cloak and dagger secrecy around the wedding.

"Did you like her?" her mother asked. "What's she like?"

How to answer that?

"She's beautiful, like in a runway model beautiful, and she looks way too young to be Onegus's mom." Cassandra smiled. "Kind of like you." She observed Geraldine's expression closely, looking for any sign that the comment made her uncomfortable.

But there was none. "That's nice. Onegus is a very handsome man. I'm not surprised that his mother is a beautiful woman." Geraldine scooped the scrambled eggs onto a plate, added some toast, and brought it to the table. "Here you go, sweetie." She smiled. "You must be hungry after partying all night."

"Thanks." Cassandra took a bite out of the buttered toast. "Aren't you going to eat too?"

"I've already had breakfast." Geraldine refilled her cup with fresh coffee and joined Cassandra at the table. "Tell me more about Onegus's mother."

Aha. So her curiosity had been piqued.

"She's blond, like Onegus, and her hair is also curly, but she keeps it long. She's tall like me and has a killer figure. She's also a snotty Brit, or rather Scot, who thinks that Americans are loud and obnoxious. I told her that you and I will change her mind about that."

Geraldine arched a brow. "Me?"

"Yeah, you. You can give Martha a run for her money." Cassandra waved a hand. "You know all about being prim and proper. I suggested that we meet for lunch, and she liked the idea."

Hopefully, that wasn't a mistake, and her mother wouldn't slip into story-telling mode. Cassandra had no doubt that she'd do that eloquently, adding charm and humor to her stories, but the effect would be the same. Martha would think that Geraldine was nuts.

"When?"

"Soon. Onegus's mother is going back home next Sunday."

Onegus

As the door to Onegus's office opened, he lifted his head ready to scold whoever it was for not knocking before entering.

Seeing who it was, he said, "Good morning, Ingrid."

After working together over the past couple of weeks and him sharing things with her he normally didn't share with anyone, they'd become buddies. That didn't entitle her to just walk in whenever she pleased, but he would let it slide this time. He owed her for all the good advice she'd given him.

"How did it go last night?" Ingrid pulled a chair out and sat down. "You didn't introduce me to your lady friend."

"You were busy with one of Kalugal's guys." Ingrid had been expecting an introduction, and Onegus had promised her that he would, but it had slipped his mind. Luckily, he'd noticed her locking lips with the former Doomer and could use that as an excuse. "What's his name? Dandor?"

A sly smile bloomed on Ingrid's face. "Yeah, that's the one." She crossed her legs. "Nevertheless, I wasn't busy with him the entire evening, but whatever. Just don't forget to introduce us during Kian's birthday celebrations."

"I haven't invited her yet. Should I?"

She shrugged. "Ask Kian if that's okay with him." The sly smile was back. "Just make sure that Gerard doesn't plan on bringing another punch bowl to the party."

Onegus shouldn't be surprised that Ingrid had figured out the punch bowl incident had been Cassandra's doing. She'd known about her energy and about the vase that had fallen victim to her temper. It wasn't difficult to connect the dots.

"Did you tell anyone?"

Ingrid affected an affronted expression. "What do you take me for? A snitch? I heard that you covered up for her. I wouldn't betray you." She leaned forward. "But it doesn't take a genius to figure out that it was Cassandra's fault. If you've told Kian about her energy, he probably suspected that she had something to do with it."

"Kian knows, and so does Sylvia, and probably Roni. I just don't want it to become the next item on the gossip-grapevine express. Kian and I talked about it briefly last night, and he wants Sylvia to train Cassandra to control her power."

Ingrid arched a brow. "Did you finally tell her who you really are?"

He nodded. "I told Cassandra the gist of the story last night, and I gave her the option to choose between written consent and thralling away her memories as you suggested, or compulsion to keep quiet. Cassandra chose compulsion, and I asked Eleanor to do it."

"Good." Ingrid pulled out her phone to check an incoming message. "It seems that my break is over." She pushed to her feet. "Another group of guests wants to visit the village, and they need me to arrange a ride."

"Do you want me to check if any of the Guardians are available?"

"No need. I was planning on going back shortly, so I might as well take them with me." She cast him a smile. "I wish you and Cassandra the best of luck." Tucking her purse under her arm, she headed for the door.

"Cassandra didn't consent to the induction yet."

Ingrid paused mid-step and turned around. "Why not?"

"She's cautious. I only told her the bare minimum last night, and she feels that she needs more information before making her decision."

"Makes sense." Ingrid pursed her lips. "Well, as I said before, best of luck."

When the door closed behind her, Onegus leaned back in his chair and crossed his arms behind his head.

Cassandra wasn't in a rush to commit to anything, which normally would have suited him just fine, but not this time. Seemingly, there was no urgency, but letting things drag on while her head was full of clan secrets was not a good idea.

He needed to speed up the process, and the best way to do that was to show Cassandra the wonderful community she and her mother could join as soon as she transitioned. Also, she needed training, and the only one who could help her with that was Sylvia, who had a similar talent.

With Annani currently visiting the village, security at the keep and the building hosting the guests could be easily handled by Bhathian, freeing Onegus to take Cassandra on a tour.

Perhaps he could also arrange a meeting with Sylvia if she wasn't busy.

When his phone rang, he knew it was Cassandra even before looking at the screen. He figured she would probably sleep late, but as soon as she woke up, she would remember last night and want more answers from him.

"Good morning, beautiful."

"Good afternoon is more like it. Did you get any sleep at all?"

"I don't need as much."

"Is that part of being..." She stopped, probably because she wanted to say immortal but couldn't before asking his permission. "Long-lived?"

Clever lady.

She'd found a synonym that Eleanor hadn't included in the list of forbidden words.

"It is, but that's not something we should discuss over the phone. Your line is not secure."

"Really? You told me about the wedding over the same unsecured line."

"That was different." The words wedding and enemies were not trigger words for the echelon system. Immortal and compulsion were. "I hope you don't have any plans for later today."

"Why? What do you have in mind?"

"It's a surprise. Can you be ready in an hour?"

"Ready for what?"

"I want to take you somewhere special."

"You need to tell me more so I'll know how to dress. If it's lunch with your mother, I'm putting on one of my power outfits."

He chuckled. "We are not meeting my mother. You can dress casually."

"Can you be more specific?"

He smiled. "Dress as you would for visiting good friends on the weekend."

She was quiet for a moment. "Are you taking me to your place? The one you share with Connor?"

Smart lady.

"You figured it out."

"Awesome. I'm looking forward to that. I like Connor a lot."

"Good. I'll see you in an hour." He ended the call and placed another one to his roommate.

"What's up?" Connor sounded sleepy.

"Are you still in bed?"

"What's it to you?"

"I wanted to give you a heads up that I'm bringing Cassandra over in about an hour and a half."

"To the village?"

"Where else? I told her part of our story last night, and Eleanor compelled her to keep silent about it. I need Cassandra to start training with Sylvia, so I'm inviting her and Roni over as well. Do you want me to get takeout, or do you want to whip something up?"

"I'll make lunch."

"Thanks, Connor. You're the best."

His roommate sighed dramatically. "You're saying that now, but in a week or two, I'll be looking for a new place to live."

"Why?"

"Because Cassandra will move in with you."

"Even if she does, you don't have to move out. We can share the place."

Connor chuckled. "For an old guy, you are incredibly naive. Cassandra wouldn't want to share you with anyone."

"Why wouldn't she? She likes you."

"Whatever, dude. I just woke up, and I need to tidy up the place and start cooking. We will talk later."

Kian

"It's getting hot out here." Syssi fanned herself with her hand. "I vote for having coffee and dessert inside the house."

"Of course, love." Kian pushed to his feet and offered her a hand up.

Their living room was spacious, enough to fit the fifteen adults, but he doubted it was big enough to contain Phoenix. Thankfully, Ethan was a quiet little guy. At eighteen months, he could be running around like his overactive older niece, but he was content observing her or playing with his toys and didn't like leaving Eva's side.

Across the table, Kalugal helped Jacki up as well. She wasn't even showing yet, but his cousin liked to act gallantly.

He stopped next to Kian. "If everyone is going inside, we can enjoy a cigar out here."

Jacki lifted one brow. "Isn't it too early for that?"

Kalugal shrugged. "I don't enjoy cigars by myself, and I doubt Kian will invite me again this evening. So it's now or some other time."

Kian didn't contradict him because Kalugal was right. He loved his family, but he could take them only in small doses.

"Fine." Jacki patted Kalugal's arm. "But no whiskey."

"Can I join?" Eva surprised him.

"Of course. I didn't know you smoked."

"I don't. But I like the smell."

"I'll take Ethan inside," Nathalie offered. "Come on, sweetie, give your older sister your hand."

Ethan regarded her with his too-smart eyes and then looked at Eva. "Mommy."

She leaned and kissed his chubby cheek. "Go with Nathalie, baby. I'll come in a few minutes."

When Ethan gave Nathalie his hand, and the two stepped inside, Eva let out a breath. "He's a sweet child, really, but sometimes I need a little breather, and with Bhathian helping Onegus at the keep, I don't have a moment to myself."

"You don't have to apologize," Alena said. "It's perfectly understandable."

"I used to love the smell of cigars," Syssi said. "But now that I'm pregnant, I can't stand it. My body is telling me that it's not healthy for the baby."

"You are both weird." Amanda wrapped her arm around Syssi's shoulders. "I've always hated it."

"Are you coming, Mom?" Lisa asked Ronja.

"I'll stay out here for a little while longer." She looked at Annani. "Are you going inside?"

"I will stay with you." His mother motioned for Ronja to sit next to her.

Perhaps Annani would manage to cheer the woman up.

Throughout brunch, Ronja had seemed subdued. Her smiles, which usually came easily, had been forced, and she hadn't participated in the conversations unless someone asked her a direct question.

Kian had a good idea of what was troubling her.

Ronja had probably seen Bowen fussing over Margaret during the wedding and had figured out that they were a couple. Apparently, she'd had feelings for the Guardian despite Bowen insisting that there had been nothing between them.

Once everyone who was either too hot or didn't want to smell cigar smoke had gone inside, Kian opened the box of cigars Okidu had rushed to bring from the humidor.

"Help yourself, ladies and gentlemen."

Ronja opened her purse and pulled out a pack of cigarettes. "Would it bother you if I smoked?" she asked Annani.

"Not at all, dear. But you should not smoke. You are not immortal, and your body can not heal the damage these things cause. It is unhealthy for you."

"I know." Ronja sighed. "I don't indulge often, but sometimes I just have to have one."

David, who'd decided to partake in the cigar fest, leaned over his mother's shoulder and kissed her cheek. "Can I get you anything to drink?"

"Thank you, but I'll wait for Okidu to bring out coffee."

"Coming right up, mistress." The Odu rushed inside the house.

Kian could have sworn that Okidu seemed excited to serve Ronja.

It was becoming more and more difficult to dismiss all the little oddities in his behavior. Something was up with him, and Kian wanted to find out what.

"I heard that the punch bowl incident wasn't caused by faulty glass," David said.

"Who told you?" Kian pulled a cigar out of the box and handed it to his newest brother-in-law.

"Sari talked with Amanda this morning. Is it supposed to be a secret?"

Kian glanced at Ronja.

He didn't mind the family knowing about Cassandra's power, but he didn't want the rumor spreading to the entire clan before her dormancy was confirmed.

"It's not a secret, but the lady in question is not part of the clan yet, so I'd rather any information about her stayed contained for now."

"I understand." David used the cutter to snap the cap off his cigar.

The sliding door opened, and Andrew stepped outside. "Is there a cigar left for me?"

"Of course." Kian offered him the box.

"How are things progressing with the China expedition?" Andrew pulled one out.

Kian handed him the cutter. "Jin and Mey are studying Chinese with Morris, and they are about to start Kra-ell lessons with Emmett."

"You can't expect them to learn anything in such a short time." Andrew cut the tip off. "Are you considering postponing the trip?"

Kian let out a sigh. "I don't know. On the one hand, I don't want the trail to get even colder, but on the other hand, it might be a fool's errand to send the two best sleuths for the job without providing them with the proper tools first. It would have been fantastic if we had a telepath who understood Chinese. He or she could enter Mey and Jin's minds to translate what they hear."

"I can enter their minds," Annani said. "But I don't speak Chinese."

Kian huffed. "Even if you did, I would never allow you to go."

As Annani's expression hardened, Kian regretted his choice of words. He'd been disrespectful.

She arched a brow. "Allow? I assume that you meant advise against or discourage me from going?"

He dipped his head. "Precisely. I've misspoken."

ORDER DARK POWER CONVERGENCE TODAY!

JOIN THE VIP CLUB
To find out what's included in your free membership, flip to the last page.

The Children of the Gods Series
Reading Order

THE CHILDREN OF THE GODS ORIGINS

1: Goddess's Choice

When gods and immortals still ruled the ancient world, one young goddess risked everything for love.

2: Goddess's Hope

Hungry for power and infatuated with the beautiful Areana, Navuh plots his father's demise. After all, by getting rid of the insane god he would be doing the world a favor. Except, when gods and immortals conspire against each other, humanity pays the price.

But things are not what they seem, and prophecies should not to be trusted...

THE CHILDREN OF THE GODS

Dark Stranger

1: Dark Stranger The Dream

2: Dark Stranger Revealed

3: Dark Stranger Immortal

Dark Enemy

4: Dark Enemy Taken

5: Dark Enemy Captive

6: Dark Enemy Redeemed

Kri & Michael's Story
6.5: My Dark Amazon

Dark Warrior
7: Dark Warrior Mine
8: Dark Warrior's Promise
9: Dark Warrior's Destiny
10: Dark Warrior's Legacy

Dark Guardian
11: Dark Guardian Found
12: Dark Guardian Craved
13: Dark Guardian's Mate

Dark Angel
14: Dark Angel's Obsession
15: Dark Angel's Seduction
16: Dark Angel's Surrender

Dark Operative
17: Dark Operative: A Shadow of Death
18: Dark Operative: A Glimmer of Hope
19: Dark Operative: The Dawn of Love

Dark Survivor
20: Dark Survivor Awakened
21: Dark Survivor Echoes of Love
22: Dark Survivor Reunited

Dark Widow

23: Dark Widow's Secret
24: Dark Widow's Curse
25: Dark Widow's Blessing

Dark Dream

26: Dark Dream's Temptation
27: Dark Dream's Unraveling
28: Dark Dream's Trap

Dark Prince

29: Dark Prince's Enigma
30: Dark Prince's Dilemma
31: Dark Prince's Agenda

Dark Queen

32: Dark Queen's Quest
33: Dark Queen's Knight
34: Dark Queen's Army

Dark Spy

35: Dark Spy Conscripted
36: Dark Spy's Mission
37: Dark Spy's Resolution

Dark Overlord

38: Dark Overlord New Horizon
39: Dark Overlord's Wife

40: Dark Overlord's Clan

Dark Choices

41: Dark Choices The Quandary
42: Dark Choices Paradigm Shift
43: Dark Choices The Accord

Dark Secrets

44: Dark Secrets Resurgence
45: Dark Secrets Unveiled
46: Dark Secrets Absolved

Dark Haven

47: Dark Haven Illusion
48: Dark Haven Unmasked
49: Dark Haven Found

Dark Power

50: Dark Power Untamed
51: Dark Power Unleashed
52: Dark Power Convergence

Dark Memories

53: Dark Memories Submerged

Geraldine's memories are spotty at best, and many of them are pure fiction. While her family attempts to solve the puzzle with far too many pieces missing, she's forced to confront a past life that she can't remember, a present that's more fantastic than her wildest made-up stories, and a future that might be better than her most heartfelt fantasies. But as more clues are uncovered, the picture starting to emerge is beyond anything she or her family could have ever imagined.

54: Dark Memories Emerge

The more clues emerge about Geraldine's past, the more questions arise.

Did she really have a twin sister who drowned?

Who is the mysterious benefactor in her hazy recollections?

Did he have anything to do with her becoming immortal?

Thankfully, she doesn't have to find the answers alone.

Cassandra and Onegus are there for her, and so is Shai, the immortal who sets her body on fire.

As they work together to solve the mystery, the four of them stumble upon a millennia-old secret that could tip the balance of power between the clan and its enemies.

55: Dark Memories Restored

As the past collides with the present, a new future emerges.

Dark Hunter

56: Dark Hunter's Query

For most of his five centuries of existence, Orion has walked the earth alone, searching for answers.

Why is he immortal?

Where did his powers come from?

Is he the only one of his kind?

When fate puts Orion face to face with the god who sired him, he learns the secret behind his immortality and that he might not be the only one.

As the goddess's eldest daughter and a mother of thirteen, Alena deserves the title of Clan Mother just as much as Annani, but she's not interested in honorifics. Being her mother's companion and keeping the mischievous goddess out of trouble is a rewarding, full-time job. Lately, though, Alena's love for her mother and the clan's gratitude is not enough.

She craves adventure, excitement, and perhaps a true-love mate of her own.

When Alena and Orion meet, sparks fly, but they both resist the pull. Alena could never bring herself to trust the powerful compeller, and Orion could never allow himself to fall in love again.

57: Dark Hunter's Prey

When Alena and Orion join Kalugal and Jacki on a romantic vacation to the enchanting Lake Lugu in China, they anticipate a couple of visits to Kalugal's archeological dig, some sightseeing, and a lot of lovemaking.

Their excursion takes an unexpected turn when Jacki's vision sends them on a perilous hunt for the elusive Kra-ell.

As things progress from bad to worse, Alena beseeches the Fates to keep everyone in their group alive. She can't fathom losing any of them, but most of all, Orion.

For over two thousand years, she walked the earth alone, but after mere days with him at her side, she can't imagine life without him.

58: Dark Hunter's Boon

As Orion and Alena's relationship blooms and solidifies, the two investigative teams combine their recent discoveries to piece together more of the Kra-ell mystery.

Attacking the puzzle from another angle, Eleanor works on gaining access to Echelon's powerful AI spy network.

Together, they are getting dangerously close to finding the elusive Kra-ell.

Dark God

59: Dark God's Avatar

Unaware of the time bomb ticking inside her, Mia had lived the perfect life until it all came to a screeching halt, but despite the difficulties she faces, she doggedly pursues her dreams.

Once known as the god of knowledge and wisdom, Toven has grown cold and indifferent. Disillusioned with humanity, he travels the world and pens novels about the love he can no longer feel.

Seeking to escape his ever-present ennui, Toven gives a cutting-edge virtual experience a try. When his avatar meets Mia's, their sizzling virtual romance unexpectedly turns into something deeper and more meaningful.

Will it endure in the real world?

60: Dark God's Reviviscence

Toven might have failed in his attempts to improve humanity's condition, but he isn't going to fail to improve Mia's life, making it the best it can be despite her fragile health, and he can do that not as a god, but as a man who possesses the means, the smarts, and the determination to do it.

No effort is enough to repay Mia for reviving his deadened heart and making him excited for the next day, but the flip side of his reviviscence is the fear of losing its catalyst.

Given Mia's condition, Toven doesn't dare to over excite her. His venom is a powerful aphrodisiac, euphoric, and an all-around health booster, but it's also extremely potent. It might kill her instead of making her better.

61: Dark God Destinies Converge

Destinies converge, and secrets are revealed in part three of Mia and Toven's story.

Dark Whispers

62: Dark Whispers From The Past

A brilliant scientist and programmer, William lives for his work, but when he recruits a young bioinformatician to help him decipher the gods' genetic blueprints, he find himself smitten with more than just her brain.

A Ph.d at nineteen, Kaia is considered a prodigy and expects a bright future in academia. But when William invites her to join his secret research team, she accepts for reasons that have nothing to do with her career objectives. Wiliam's promise to look into her best friend's disappearance is an offer she just can't refuse.

63: Dark Whispers From Afar

William knows that his budding relationship with the nineteen-year-old Kaia will be frowned upon, but he's unprepared for her family's vehement opposition.

Family means everything to Kaia, so when she finds herself in the impossible position of having to choose between them and William, she resorts to unconventional means to resolve the conflict.

64: Dark Whispers From Beyond

The sacrifices Kaia and her family have to make for a chance of gaining immortality might tear them apart, and success is not guaranteed.

Is the dubious promise of eternal life worth the risk of losing everything?

Dark Gambit

65: Dark Gambit The Pawn

66: Dark Gambit The Play

67: Dark Gambit Reliance

Dark Alliance

68: Dark Alliance Kindred Souls

69: Dark Alliance Turbulent Waters

70: Dark Alliance Perfect Storm

Dark Healing

71: Dark Healing Blind Justice

72: Dark Healing Blind Trust

73: Dark healing Blind Curve

Dark Encounters

74: Dark Encounters of the Close Kind

75: Dark Encounters of the Unexpected Kind

76: Dark Encounters of the Fated Kind

The Children of the Gods Series Sets

Books 1-3: Dark Stranger trilogy—Includes a bonus short story: **The Fates take a Vacation**

<u>Books 4-6: Dark Enemy Trilogy</u> —Includes a bonus short story—**The Fates' Post-Wedding Celebration**

Books 7-10: Dark Warrior Tetralogy

Books 11-13: Dark Guardian Trilogy

Books 14-16: Dark Angel Trilogy

Books 17-19: Dark Operative Trilogy

Books 20-22: Dark Survivor Trilogy

Books 23-25: Dark Widow Trilogy

Books 26-28: Dark Dream Trilogy

Books 29-31: Dark Prince Trilogy

Books 32-34: Dark Queen Trilogy

Books 35-37: Dark Spy Trilogy

Books 38-40: Dark Overlord Trilogy

Books 41-43: Dark Choices Trilogy

Books 44-46: Dark Secrets Trilogy

Books 47-49: Dark Haven Trilogy

Books 50-52: Dark Power Trilogy

Books 53-55: Dark Memories Trilogy

Books 56-58: Dark Hunter Trilogy

Books 59-61: Dark God Trilogy

Books 62-64: Dark Whispers Trilogy

Books 65-67: Dark Gambit Trilogy

Books 68-70: Dark Alliance Trilogy

Books 71-73: Dark healing Trilogy

MEGA SETS

INCLUDE CHARACTER LISTS

The Children of the Gods: Books 1-6
The Children of the Gods: Books 6.5-10

TRY THE SERIES ON

AUDIBLE

2 FREE audiobooks with your new Audible subscription!

PERFECT MATCH SERIES

Vampire's Consort

When Gabriel's company is ready to start beta testing, he invites his old crush to inspect its medical safety protocol.

Curious about the revolutionary technology of the *Perfect Match Virtual Fantasy-Fulfillment studios*, Brenna agrees.

Neither expects to end up partnering for its first fully immersive test run.

King's Chosen

When Lisa's nutty friends get her a gift certificate to *Perfect Match Virtual Fantasy Studios*, she has no intentions of using it. But since the only way to get a refund is if no partner can be found for her, she makes sure to request a fantasy so girly and over the top that no sane guy will pick it up.

Except, someone does.

> **Warning:** This fantasy contains a hot, domineering crown prince, sweet insta-love, steamy love scenes painted with light shades of gray, a wedding, and a HEA in both the virtual and real worlds.
>
> Intended for mature audience.

Captain's Conquest

Working as a Starbucks barista, Alicia fends off flirting all day long, but none of the guys are as charming and sexy as Gregg. His frequent visits are the highlight of her day, but since he's never asked her out, she assumes he's taken. Besides, between a day job and a budding music career, she has no time to start a new relationship.

That is until Gregg makes her an offer she can't refuse—a gift certificate to the virtual fantasy fulfillment service everyone is talking about. As a huge Star Trek fan, Alicia has a perfect match in mind—the captain of the Starship Enterprise.

The Thief Who Loved Me

When Marian splurges on a Perfect Match Virtual adventure as a world infamous jewel thief, she expects high-wire fun with a hot partner who she will never have to see again in real life.

A virtual encounter seems like the perfect answer to Marcus's string of dating disasters. No strings attached, no drama, and definitely no love. As a die-hard James Bond fan, he chooses as his avatar a dashing MI6 operative, and to complement his adventure, a dangerously seductive partner.

Neither expects to find their forever Perfect Match.

My Merman Prince

The beautiful architect working late on the twelfth floor of my building thinks that I'm just the maintenance guy. She's also under the impression that I'm not interested.

Nothing could be further from the truth.

I want her like I've never wanted a woman before, but I don't play where I work.

I don't need the complications.

When she tells me about living out her mermaid fantasy with a stranger in a Perfect Match virtual adventure, I decide to do everything possible to ensure that the stranger is me.

The Dragon King

To save his beloved kingdom from a devastating war, the Crown Prince of Trieste makes a deal with a witch that costs him half of his humanity and dooms him to an eternity of loneliness.

Now king, he's a fearsome cobalt-winged dragon by day and a short-tempered monarch by night. Not many are brave enough to serve in the palace of the brooding and volatile ruler, but Charlotte ignores the rumors and accepts a scribe position in court.

As the young scribe reawakens Bruce's frozen heart, all that stands in the way of their happiness is the witch's bargain. Outsmarting the evil hag will take cunning and courage, and Charlotte is just the right woman for the job.

My Werewolf Romeo

The father of my star student is a big-shot screenwriter and the patron of the drama department who thinks he can dictate what production I should put on. The principal makes it very clear that I need to cooperate with the opinionated asshat or walk away from my dream job at the exclusive private high school.

It doesn't help matters that the guy is single, hot, charming, creative, and seems to like me despite my thinly-veiled hostility.

When he invites me to a custom-tailored Perfect Match virtual adventure to prove that his screenplay is perfect for my production, I accept, intending to have fun while proving that messing with the classics is a foolish idea.

I don't expect to be wowed by his werewolf adaptation of Red Riding Hood mesh-up with Romeo and Juliet, and I certainly don't expect to fall in love with the virtual fantasy's leading man.

The Channeler's Companion

A treat for fans of *The Wheel of Time*.

When Erika hires Rand to assist in her pediatric clinic, she does so despite his good looks and irresistible charm, not because of them.

He's empathic, adores children, and has the patience of a saint.

He's also all she can think about, but he's off limits.

What's a doctor to do to scratch that irresistible itch without risking workplace complications?

A shared adventure in the Perfect Match Virtual Studios seems like the solution, but instead of letting the algorithm choose a partner for her, Erika can try to influence it to select the one she wants. Awarding Rand a gift certificate to the service will get him into their database, but unless Erika can tip the odds in her favor, getting paired with him is a long shot.

Hopefully, a virtual adventure based on her and Rand's favorite series will do the trick.

Note

Dear reader,

I hope my stories have added a little joy to your day. If you have a moment to add some to mine, you can help spread the word about the Children Of The Gods series by telling your friends and penning a review. Your recommendations are the most powerful way to inspire new readers to explore the series.

Thank you,

Isabell

FOR EXCLUSIVE PEEKS AT UPCOMING RELEASES & A FREE COMPANION BOOK

Join my *VIP Club* and gain access to the VIP portal at itlucas.com
To Join, go to:
http://eepurl.com/blMTpD

INCLUDED IN YOUR FREE MEMBERSHIP:

YOUR VIP PORTAL

- Read preview chapters of upcoming releases.
- Listen to Goddess's Choice narration by Charles Lawrence
- Exclusive content offered only to my VIPs.

FREE I.T. LUCAS COMPANION INCLUDES:

- Goddess's Choice Part 1
- Perfect Match: Vampire's Consort (A standalone Novella)
- Interview Q & A
- Character Charts

If you're already a subscriber, and you are not getting my emails, your provider is sending them to your junk folder, and you are missing out on **IMPORTANT UPDATES, SIDE CHARACTERS' PORTRAITS, ADDITIONAL CONTENT, AND OTHER GOODIES.** To fix that, add isabell@itlucas.com to your email contacts or your email VIP list.

**Check out the specials at
https://www.itlucas.com/specials**

Printed in Great Britain
by Amazon

54798460R00255